DRY GULCH TRAIL

*Also by William MacLeod Raine
in Thorndike Large Print®*

Arizona Guns
Bucky Follows a Cold Trail
Fighting Edge
Glory Hole
Gunsight Pass
High Grass Valley
Under Northern Stars

This Large Print Book carries the
Seal of Approval of N.A.V.H.

DRY GULCH TRAIL

William MacLeod Raine

Thorndike Press • Thorndike, Maine

Library of Congress Cataloging in Publication Data:

93B621

Raine, William MacLeod, 1871-1954.
   Dry gulch trail / William MacLeod Raine.
     p.   cm.
   ISBN 1-56054-569-0 (alk. paper : lg. print)
   1. Large type books. I. Title.
[PS3535.A385D79   1992]   92-2473
813'.52—dc20   CIP

17.95

Thorndike Large Print® Western Series edition published
in 1992 by arrangement with Patricia R. Barker.

Cover design by James B. Murray.

The tree indicium is a trademark of Thorndike Press.

This book is printed on acid-free, high opacity paper. ∞

DRY GULCH TRAIL

1. His Tail in a Crack

Clay Sanger leaned indolently against the adobe wall of Bowker's New York Emporium, one leg crossed in front of the other with the toe of the dusty boot resting on the wooden sidewalk. He was in high heels, levis, a checked cotton shirt, and a wide-brimmed hat faded by a thousand summer suns. His attitude was easy, almost negligent, but the gray eyes took vigilant note of the details that went to make up a scene which might be set for tragedy. The Diamond K held trapped in the courthouse a man it intended to rub out within the hour.

The courthouse square, drowsing in the warm spring heat, looked peaceful as old age. On the streets fronting the quadrangle there was little activity. A few horses hung their heads sleepily in front of saloons and gambling-houses. In the dusty road a hound lay and hunted for fleas. Occasionally a pedestrian moved rather hurriedly to his destination. Half a dozen cowboys were to be seen, two at Riddle's livery stable, one on each side of the courthouse, another sitting on the steps of the Cowboys' Rest Hotel. Clay observed that all of them held patiently to their posts.

One looking for it could have found evidence of the turbulent night life which made Powder Horn one of the wildest cow towns in the state. Cards littered the sidewalks. In a window of the Emporium which Clay could have reached out and touched were two bullet holes. A whiskey bottle lay in the road where somebody had tossed it. On the courthouse porch a cowboy was snoring in sodden drunken slumber.

Sanger needed no proof of Powder Horn's lawlessness. There was a tension in the atmosphere almost tangible. At any moment the quietness might be shattered by exploding guns. The lounging cowpunchers had been stationed at strategic points. When the signal came they would waken to violent action.

Out of the Cowboys' Rest Hotel a girl came. She wore a white dress with a wide blue sash and she carried a parasol. Clay observed her with interest. He did not see much of her these days, though he heard plenty. He could remember when Effie Collins had been a freckled tousle-haired hoyden tagging after her brother Stan and Clay whenever they would let her. That had been in the days when the two boys had been inseparable buddies knit together in a comradeship so close that their teacher dubbed them Jonathan and David.

Years ago they had come to the parting of the ways, the friendship ended, and Effie had gone with Stan. Since then the wild long-legged little colt had grown into the prettiest girl in a day's ride.

The man on the hotel porch was Stanley Collins. Sanger watched him and his sister. He could tell that they were arguing. Evidently she had dressed to go down to the stores to shop and her brother was objecting. The argument grew heated. She stamped her small foot in protest and tried to pass. Stan blocked the way. Effie lifted her parasol to strike, thought better of it, and turned back abruptly into the hotel. Clay grinned. He knew her capacity for quick anger. She probably did not know what trouble was brewing, but by now she must have guessed that some mischief was afoot and Stan in it.

Ray Terrill came round the corner toward the Emporium. He was the town marshal, and Clay had known him for twenty-five years. He had been a rider for Sanger's father, had gone up the trail with him more than once. Terrill had never been important in the community. He was rather a small man, not at all impressive in appearance, friendly, and often a little bewildered.

"How's everything?" he asked of Sanger.

"Fine as the wheat. All right with you?"

"Sure," the marshal answered quickly — a little too quickly.

Clay knew that he was troubled, and with good reason. He represented the law in Powder Horn, and a group of men were in town who intended to defy the law. The fears of the marshal were written on his tanned wrinkled face.

They talked, casually, of cows and crops and the prospects of rain. What they said was not significant, but what they omitted to say held a deeper meaning. Both of them knew that soon — probably within the hour — Terrill would have to meet an acid test of the mettle that was in him. Clay wondered what the little man meant to do. Would he vanish into the suburbs of the town until the crisis had passed? That would be the easiest out for him. Or would he stand up and go through to a fighting finish? As peace officer of Powder Horn he had been able to handle the drunken jamborees of young cow hands well enough, but this was going to be something quite different. The Diamond K outfit was ruthless and would not brook opposition.

Terrill broke through the commonplaces they were exchanging.

"Boy, I've got my tail in a crack sure enough," he said. "Right soon there will be war in Georgia. Clint Black is in the courthouse hiding."

"Does Savage know he is there for sure?"

"I dunno. His men have got the place surrounded."

"Why don't you raise a posse?"

"Don't reckon I could. Black is a bad egg, and good citizens don't want to get shot defending him. Why should they? I wouldn't ask it of them. No, sir. This is my own personal jag of grief."

Clay did not ask him what he meant to do about it. This was strictly none of his business. Why mix himself up in it? In any case he would not have found time to get an answer, for three men came out of the hardware store on the corner and moved toward them. One of the cowboys on the street lifted a hand slightly in greeting. None of the three gave any sign of seeing it.

The one in the middle was a neatly dressed man of middle height wearing what was known in the cow country as store clothes. He was Bert Savage, owner of the Diamond K. On the right of him strode his foreman, Niles Benton, a big rangy fellow with broad shoulders, deep chest, and bulldog face. Rock Holloway held the other flank. His size was not impressive, but he moved with a certain stealthy fluency that caught the attention and held it. The deep-set eyes were a peculiarly

11

icy gray, very steady and very cold. Rock was the Diamond K killer.

At sight of the marshal the Diamond K men drew up. Without waiting for any word of greeting Benton flung out at the officer a blunt challenge.

"Are you trying to hide Clint Black?"

Terrill was a slow thinker. He rasped the palm of a hand across a stubbly chin while he searched for the best answer.

"Why, no, Niles. Nothing like that. If I knew where he was at I would arrest him."

The foreman laughed, an unpleasant jeering note in his voice. "Don't worry about that. We know where he is. But I don't reckon we'll trouble you."

"That's what I'm paid for," Terrill said hesitantly. "Folks in this town feel there has been too much killing here. They want a peaceable place for their women and children. Course that's what we all want. I'll arrest Black —"

"No," interrupted Savage. "We know all about that. He'd break jail and be out of the country inside of a week. The Diamond K will attend to Black. He killed one of my boys yesterday. He has come to the end of his crooked trail."

The marshal protested, mildly and ineffectively. Savage was the most important man in the district, dominant and unscrupulous.

The little officer would have felt unhappy at having to oppose him even if there had been no danger in it.

He said deferentially, "I got to enforce the law, Mr. Savage, and I can't have any rookus in town."

"Can't you?" the ranchman said curtly. "Then don't go hunting for it. I won't stand for any interference, Terrill. Don't crowd me. Men have tried it before, and —" He finished the sentence with a sweep of the hand that left its deadly meaning to be inferred.

The owner of the Diamond K had hitherto ignored Sanger. Now abruptly he turned on him. "Do you know where this killer spent the night?"

The cool eyes of the young man drifted to Rock Holloway and back again to Savage. "What killer?" he asked blandly, with a faint edge of insolence.

"Don't bandy words with me," Savage warned. "He was seen near your ranch. I think you took him in." His searching gaze, arrogant and cruel, fastened on Sanger. In that lean inscrutable face, as expressionless as a brick wall, he found no answer. "I've had about enough of you. Take a lesson from what is going to happen to your friend Black."

"Is he my friend?" Clay inquired negligently.

Angrily Benton broke into the talk. "You can't tell me you haven't seen Clint Black since he shot Fleagle," he charged.

"Then there wouldn't be any use trying," Sanger answered evenly.

"I think he spent the night at your place," the foreman continued. "Or else you hustled him into town after dark. We shot his horse from under him. He came in on one of yours, I'd bet my boots."

There was a faint satiric smile on Sanger's face. In the twenty-odd years he had lived his reckless feet had carried him on many dangerous trails. A tough hard man, he was one not easily bullied. Few of those who challenged him found any profit in the encounter.

"Make up yore mind," he drawled. "Which was it?"

"When did you see him last?" demanded Savage.

"Lemme see." Clay considered the question, his brow knitted in thought. "Lemme see. I saw him day before yesterday — or was it Monday? — riding a fleabitten roan, on Skunk Creek, about a mile above the junction. He stopped me to borrow a smoke. But I don't reckon he is still there."

"Smart, ain't you?" Benton snarled. "Think you can play horse with us, do you? For two hits I'd score yore back with my quirt."

14

"That would be interesting," Clay said, with deceptive gentleness. "But painful — for somebody."

"Not now, Niles," the Diamond K boss ordered. "It will be his turn soon, but today we've got other fish to fry. We know where he stands. Birds of a feather. When a man runs with rustlers watch his branding iron, I say."

"But be right careful not to mention his name, Savage," Clay suggested, "if his initials happen to be C. S."

The owner of the big ranch did not care to provoke an immediate collision with Sanger. He knew better ways than that to win his victories. Though no coward, it was his settled custom to hire other men to do his fighting for him. This young fool's punishment could be deferred till later.

"A man is known by the company he keeps," Savage remarked stiffly. "I'm older than you, Sanger. I advise you to mend your taste in friends."

"I'm some bull-headed," Clay retorted carelessly. "My friends suit me."

Benton said over his shoulder as they left, "Stick around, fellow, and watch us smoke one of 'em out from where he's holed up in the courthouse."

"You might make it, since you are about

a dozen to one," Sanger called after him derisively.

The Diamond K men did not answer. They turned in at the Trail's End, bellied up to the bar, and ordered whiskey.

"My idea would be to finish the job and celebrate afterward," Holloway said. "Serve us right if this guy broke through and made a getaway while we're foolin' around."

"No chance," Benton boasted. "I'm wagon boss of this job. The courthouse is covered from every angle. Not a door or a window that isn't being watched. Let Black sweat awhile. He knows his clock has run down."

Holloway let his narrowed eyes rest on the foreman. He did not like Benton and he had little confidence in him as a leader. "I've heard of a guy's friends busting in and helping him. But of course since you are running the roundup everything will be jake," he said derisively.

A bowlegged man in chaps came into the Trail's End and reported to the foreman. "Black is sure enough in the courthouse," he confirmed. "Shorty seen him lookin' out of an upstairs window."

"We'll make the gather now," Savage said. "Tell the boys there is to be no shooting unless necessary. I want to hang this fellow as a warning to his rustler friends. When I give the signal we'll close in on him."

The Diamond K men walked out of the Trail's End and separated, two of them following the west side of the square and the others the north. They met again at the northwest corner of the quadrangle. In the course of that short walk all the sentries had been instructed that the fireworks were about to begin.

2. Effie Takes a Hand

The marshal's unhappy eyes watched the Diamond K men vanish into the Trail's End. He turned a haggard face on Clay.

"They've got every exit from the courthouse plugged," he said. "Black hasn't got a dead man's chance."

"Just about," agreed Sanger. "He had to see his girl. I told him to light a shuck *pronto*, but you never could tell Clint anything."

"He's not the only one in a jam," Terrill mentioned. "I can't do a thing for him — not a thing. The Diamond K will go through hell for leather. Savage won't be satisfied till he has collected him."

"No." Clay observed that the oldtimer was swallowing down a lump in his throat. The color had washed out of his lips. Something close to panic was gripping him. The young man offered no word of false encouragement. Terrill must fight out the battle with his fear alone. He must find in himself, if at all, the courage to carry on.

The marshal moistened his lips. "He acts like he's czar of Roossia. That's no way to do. This is a free country, ain't it?"

The oldtimer had no need to mention more definitely the man to whom he was referring. Everybody in the Powder Horn country knew how arbitrary and dominating Savage was. Nesters and homesteaders got short shrift from his tough riders.

"Since when has this neck of the woods been free?" Clay asked sardonically.

"He comes rampaging to town with a bunch of his warriors the same as if there was no law in the land."

"Except the law he makes," the young man added.

"He's got us all scared to stand up to him."

"In this district he is sure cock-a-doodle-do," Sanger agreed, his voice carefully non-committal.

"Dad burn it, I'm marshal," Terrill went on. "He knows I'm expected to protect Clint. He hadn't ought to ask me to lie down. And I won't either. I've sent for my deputies. They live in a shack the other side of the river."

Clay glanced up and down the street. "They had better hurry."

"That's right. I didn't get on to this in time — not till Savage rode in with his bunch." The officer finished the conversation on a note of timorous bravado. "Well, be seeing you at Sunday School some time. So long."

He turned his back on Sanger and walked

19

across the dusty road to the courthouse lawn. Without once looking back he waded through the dogfennel to the steps. Doggedly he went up them and disappeared.

Into Sanger's cold eyes crept a warmth born of admiration and sympathy. "The darned little cuss is scared stiff, but I believe he's going to do his job," he murmured. "Or else he's going to make a bluff and save face."

It would be soon now, Clay decided. More of the Diamond K riders were in evidence on the streets than there had been. He saw Savage and his companions come out of the Trail's End and separate, the foreman to go along the west side of the square and the other two to head in his direction.

The boss of the big ranch did not stop this time to talk with Sanger. Just before he reached the Emporium there came to them the popping of guns not very close. The sound drifted to them from the direction of the section of the town across the tracks known as Hell's Half Acre. Clay was a little surprised. In the course of twenty-four hours there might be a good deal of gunpowder burned in Powder Horn, but most of it was in the night or late afternoon. Some of the shooting was due to the harmless exuberance of cowboys on a spree. The rest of it to more sinister reasons. But at this time of day the town was usually as quiet as a church.

The grim hard smile on the face of Savage enlightened Clay. The fireworks in Hell's Half Acre were designed to draw Terrill away from the serious battle front. He was being given a reasonable excuse to set out for the sporting end of the town to stop the trouble there.

As the two men passed Sanger he heard Rock Holloway say to his employer, in a cold flat monotone, "Funny how often innocent bystanders get plugged when they stick around." The chill eyes of the killer were resting on the face of the young man.

Clay found evidence that the town was looking for trouble in the fact that there had not been a woman on any street of the square for half an hour. They had been warned by their menfolk to keep away from the downtown district. Now one walked down the sidewalk toward the New York Emporium. She moved with the grace of movement that comes from youth and the buoyancy of perfect health.

Bert Savage stopped her. "Miss Effie, if I were you I would go back to the hotel. There's going to be trouble. Let me take you there."

"What trouble?" the girl asked directly, her dark eyes unwaveringly on him.

"A fellow who killed one of my men has taken refuge in the courthouse. We're going

21

to have to dig him out. This is no place for you."

"Is Stan in this?" she demanded.

"All of us who believe in preserving order are in it. I think we had better go."

The girl frowned at him, uncertain what to do. He was a good-looking man, still young, a power in the land, and one who meant soon to ask her to marry him, unless she read the signs wrong. She was flattered at his attentions and interested in the prospect. Moreover, it was fascinating to feel that she was important to a man who had such an influence in the country which was her little world. There were times when he stirred queer emotions in her. But she did not trust him. He was not one she understood. His reactions were cold and considered, not warm and passionate as hers were.

"I don't like it," she said.

He answered suavely, "None of us like it, but it has to be done."

"I don't think so," she protested. "There's law in the land. Why can't you wait for it?"

"Because the man wouldn't be here when the law wanted him," he explained. "The time has come to put fear into the hearts of these bad men."

"Clint Black isn't so bad. I've danced with him."

22

He said, with the kindly condescension one shows a willful child: "I don't think a young lady like you can judge a case like this. It's a rough business, and it has to be handled by men."

"You don't have to drag my brother into it!" she cried. "This last year he has changed. He didn't used to be so . . . hard."

"Stan is growing from a boy to a man. This is a tough country, and no man of any account can be soft. Don't worry about Stan. He's all right. I suggest we walk back to the hotel now. Stan ought not to have let you come."

"He tried to stop me, but I slipped out the back way." Effie pushed past him to speak to Clay. She was surprised to see him here, for she knew he was not friendly with the big ranch outfit. During the past year she had seen very little of him, after a violent quarrel provoked by her, but some impulse drove her forward now.

"Are you in this too?" she asked, sharp criticism in her voice.

Clay thought she had grown into a lovely young woman. She was tall and slender, of a rounded fullness of breast and limb. The smoldering fire in her eyes suggested a high and sometimes too impatient spirit.

"Oh, no," he corrected. "I'm just an innocent bystander. Just sticking around to see the elephant. Mr. Holloway will certify to that."

"Aren't you going to do anything about it?" she wanted to know scornfully. "Are you going to stand by with your hands in your pockets and let them kill Clint?"

Clay left his hands in his trouser-pockets. There was a flicker of a sardonic smile on his brown face. "What do you advise me to do?" he inquired.

"Why — stop it — get somebody to help you. This is dreadful. Clint is your friend, isn't he?"

"Not exactly," he corrected. "I've eaten chuck with him at the roundup, and I've played in the same game of poker. But I haven't branded other men's calves with him."

"Anyway, you know him. Surely you don't want to see him — murdered."

"He'll live a long time if he doesn't die till I murder him." Sanger passed the buck with a wave of his hand to the owner of the Diamond K. "Why don't you speak to your friend here about it? He seems to be master of ceremonies."

The mouth of Savage was a thin straight slit, the eyes flinty and bleak. "I don't like the word you use when you refer to me — murder," he said. "Justice is what I call it."

"Yes," agreed Clay dryly. "You would."

Effie spoke up hurriedly. "I used the word, not Mr. Sanger." Beneath her eyes the cheeks flamed red. "What word ought I to use? Twenty men against one. It doesn't matter what he has done. He ought to have a chance to speak for his life. But I don't want to call names. Please let us not quarrel. You can stop this awful thing, Mr. Savage. Won't you do it — for me? I'll always be grateful." Her low throaty voice promised more than the words.

If they had been alone Savage would have given way, first making sure that he was going to get value received as a reward. He would have let young Black go — until he had a chance to rub him out without witnesses. But he could not do it now before his men without losing face, not after he had brought them to town to destroy the fellow. He would lose ground immensely if he weakened because a woman asked it.

"No," he barked. "It's too late. I can't help him. Black brought this on himself by killing Fleagle." Savage caught sight of Clay's mocking grin and flashed out a challenge. "Have you anything to say about it?"

"Not a thing," Sanger murmured softly. "Clint ought to have known better than to have defended himself from a Diamond K man in a fair fight."

"That's a lie!" the big ranchman cried.

"Perhaps you were there. I wasn't. I'm taking Clint's word for it. But likely he was prejudiced."

"Then you did hide him at your place."

Clay looked at him coolly. "No information on that point, Mr. Savage."

"You're headed for trouble, looks like," Holloway said to Sanger out of the corner of his mouth.

"What, me! An innocent bystander, without a chip in the game!"

"I've known more than one guy who talked himself into a wooden box," the killer threatened, an ugly rasp to his low voice.

The girl had started to speak to Savage, but she caught the words of the gunman and turned quickly to Clay. She had no mind to let another deadly quarrel flare up. "Will you see me back to the hotel, Mr. Sanger?" she asked.

"All right," he said indifferently. "Let's go."

The Diamond K boss flushed angrily. He was a man who expected to get what he asked for, and he resented it that the young woman had chosen another escort. He drew back, a red-hot devil of malice in his eyes. Clay Sanger was one of the few men who did not kowtow to his power. Always he had disliked the young

26

man's mocking irony, pointed casually to deflate his arrogance. He had additional reason for hating him now. It flashed across his mind that some day he would have to destroy the fellow.

Effie did not speak until they were close to the hotel. She wanted Clay to understand that the estrangement between them still existed, that he need not presume on this to attempt the old footing.

She said stiffly, "I asked you to come with me, Mr. Sanger, because I don't want trouble to start for fear my brother might get into it."

One of his eyebrows twitched whimsically as he slanted a look at her. "And I thought you asked me on account of my fatal charm," he told her.

Angry color beat into her face. "You didn't think anything of the sort. I was afraid I had started something between you and Mr. Savage, and I didn't want to be responsible for what might happen."

"That was nice of you — to be concerned for the safety of a stranger like me."

"I'm not in the least concerned about your safety. You know that very well. It's just —"

She stopped, to find words that would sting him. He was the most exasperating man she had ever met. Somehow she had been led into shifting ground from the original reason she had given to one that implied she was interested in protecting him.

"Just your sweet Christian charity," he finished for her. "Nothing personal at all. A Good Samaritan act. No doubt you'll get your reward in heaven."

The mocking light dancing in his eyes made her furious. Even as a boy he had possessed the knack of getting under her skin with his drawling thrusts at her occasional girlish poses.

"I think you are the most hateful man I ever met," she flung at him, and turned to walk into the hotel, her chin in the air.

Clay chuckled. She was the same hot-tempered little pot of pepper she had always been. "Nice to have had this pleasant stroll with you," he called after her.

Stanley Collins came out of the hotel and stopped at sight of his sister. "Where have you been?" he demanded. "I told you to stay here."

"And I told you I would do as I pleased," she countered.

Her brother caught sight of Sanger and stiffened. "What are you doing here?" he asked sharply.

Effie was annoyed at both of them. "I asked Mr. Sanger to see me back to the hotel," she said.

"Why?" Stanley snapped.

"Because I wanted to talk with him. That's my business, not yours."

"You have nothing to talk with him about," Stanley said harshly.

"The days of auld lang syne, you know," Clay mentioned. "The happy memories when I dipped her pigtail in the inkwell and stole the apples from her lunch basket."

"You go your way and we'll go ours," Collins flung out. He was a dark handsome black-haired youth with a brittle and uncertain temper.

"What is your way?" the girl wanted to know of her brother. "Are you going to help Mr. Savage kill Clint Black?"

"Who told you they were going to kill Clint?"

"I'm not a complete fool. Everybody in town knows it. I want to know what you have to do with it?"

Clay smiled pleasantly. "This seems to be a family matter. If you'll excuse me I'll be going."

He went down the street whistling "Auld Lang Syne."

3. The Law Functions

When Terrill left Clay Sanger standing in front of Bowker's store he walked into the courthouse and up the stairway to the second floor. Turning to the right, he opened a door upon which was printed the words COUNTY CLERK.

A man with a forty-five in his hand faced him. He was a long lean man with bitter eyes of washed-out blue set deep in a brown leathery face. As soon as he knew it was the marshal he lowered the point of the revolver.

"Thought it might be the Diamond K come to stop my clock," he told the officer. "What's eating them? Why don't they come and rub me out?"

Clint Black had the reputation of a hardy man. He had trodden forbidden trails boldly enough, but he had now the drawn look of one harried by anxiety. It was one thing to risk life in the open, another to wait helplessly for death to close in on him.

In Terrill's homely puckered face the outlaw could read no hope for himself. The marshal gave no answer in words to the questions flung at him.

"Well, speak yore piece," Black went on irritably. "I know where I'm at."

"I had a talk with Savage and Benton," the officer told him. "No use trying to fool you. They're hell bent on getting you for killing Fleagle."

"Sure, because he was a Diamond K rider," Black flung out. "He was shooting at me, wasn't he? I had to let him have it or be killed."

Terrill sidestepped the merits of the quarrel. There might be something to be said on both sides. The big ranch was overbearing and had no regards for the rights of others. Clint was suspected, with some evidence, of being a rustler. The marshal had no doubt it was true.

"I told Savage I would arrest you and the law could decide on the case, but he told me he wouldn't stand for that."

The harassed rustler moved to the window and looked out. "They are out there waiting to get me," he said. "I can see Jerry Ault and Shorty Pierce. What did I ever do to them that they have to hunt me down as if I was a wolf?" he asked bitterly.

Terrill could not answer that one. There were a lot of things in life hard to understand.

Black swung back from the window. "You're the law in this town, Ray. What you aim to do about this? Are you gonna let them wipe me out without a chance for my white alley?"

"No, sir. Like you say, I'm marshal." The little man rubbed with a hand his unshaven chin. "They can't take you without a fight, seeing that you are my prisoner."

"You've got a posse," Clint said eagerly.

The marshal shook his head. "No. I've sent for Bud Miller and Frenchy, the boys who have the other shifts. Maybe they will be along in time."

"And if they are not?"

"Why, I reckon I'll have to try to stand them off alone."

"Don't be crazy," Black replied. "You can't do it — not for a minute."

"You don't need to tell me that. I know it doggoned well. They will make me look like a plugged nickel."

The hunted man stared at him in surprise. He desperately needed help, but this would be a useless sacrifice. "Why, you darned old buzzard-head, there's no sense in you butting in on this alone. You wouldn't last as long as a snowball in hell. If yore deputies will fight with us, that will be fine. If not, you had better skedaddle. I'll send one or two of 'em to Kingdom Come before I go."

"I'm staying right here," Terrill answered doggedly. "I draw wages to uphold the law, and by God! I'm gonna do it."

"They'll wind up yore ball of yarn for sure, you spunky old horned toad," the cow thief responded. "That wouldn't buy me a thing. Four of us just might make it too hot for them, if luck was sitting right on our shoulders every minute. But you and me alone — not a chance. I'm in this jam, not you. If yore men don't show up in time, you light a shuck outa here."

"I aim to do my job," the marshal blurted out. "They can't take you from me long as I'm able to pull a trigger. I got to play the cards the way they are dealt me. 'Course I know I won't be one-two-three with them. I wish Bud and Frenchy would get here. They're good boys. They wouldn't throw me down. But I ain't dead sure my message got to them."

Someone in the street below raised his voice in a shout. "Come outa there before we drag you out with a rope around yore neck, Clint Black."

The hunted man walked back to the window. "They are moving in closer," he announced. "You'd better burn the wind, oldtimer. Too late to do anything for me."

Terrill said, "I'm gonna talk to them from the upstairs porch."

"You can't talk that damned sidewinder Savage outa killing me. But go ahead. It costs nothing Mex to make oration."

The officer passed down the corridor to the porch. From the doors and windows of stores and saloons men were watching. He called down to a Diamond K cowboy.

"I want to talk with Mr. Savage, Jerry."

The owner of the big ranch came out of a store. His foreman and Rock Holloway were with him. "What do you want?" he demanded.

Terrill cleared his throat. "I've got Clint under arrest, Mr. Savage. I don't aim to turn him over to anybody. He's my prisoner."

"That's fine," Benton jeered, his voice heavy and raucous. "You've spoken yore say-so. Now you can make yore bluff while we come in and get Black."

"I'm not going to bluff," the marshal told him. "I hate to do this, Niles. You-all are my neighbors in a way of speaking. But I got to do my duty. If necessary, I'll shoot to kill."

There was a quaver in his high thin voice. As Clay Sanger came down the street he heard the little man's challenge and knew he meant to stand off the attack as long as he could. *The little cuss is scared stiff,* he thought, *but he is going to game it out.*

"Don't get any fool idea that you are anything but a white chip in this game, Terrill," the foreman shouted. "Start smoking with that

34

gun of yours and you'll be a goner."

A yell lifted from the throats of several Diamond K men. Clint Black had joined the marshal on the porch. That cry for vengeance from his enemies appalled the rustler. He knew that a circle of death surrounded him. But he lived by the code of the outdoor frontier West. A man had to go through without weakening. He crushed back the shocking despair, the wild fear, so that men would say later he died game. From the breast-pocket of his shirt he fished a sack of smoking tobacco and a book of cigarette papers. Jiggling tobacco into a paper, he drew the mouth of the sack tight with his teeth and rolled the cigarette. A match flared and smoke came from his lips.

"How many warriors did you bring to get me, Benton?" he scoffed hardily. "Does it take a dozen Diamond K heroes to bump off one guy?"

"Come down with yore hands in the air," ordered the foreman.

"You'll have to come and collect me if you want me," Black retorted. "And get this right. I'll not be the only one buried in Boot Hill tomorrow. If I'm lucky I'll take you to hell with me, Benton."

"I warn you, Mr. Savage, not to go on with this," the marshal interposed. "I'm the law.

Like I told you, Black is my prisoner. I mean to keep him."

One of the cowboys, Jerry Ault, laughed harshly. "Yeah, he looks like a prisoner, sitting on that railing smoking a cigarette and wearing his guns big as Cuffey."

"Get away from Black," Benton snapped at Terrill. "We don't want you but him. Yet if you stomp around talking big you'll sure enough get hurt."

"No," the marshal flung down at him. "I can't do that, Niles."

"All right. If you've got hell in the neck don't blame us when you get shot up."

The scared old rooster has guts, Clay thought. *He was my father's friend. Blamed if I don't take a hand.*

Sanger walked swiftly across the grass toward the courthouse entrance. The big body of Benton barred the way.

"Where you going?" the foreman asked.

"I am going to attend to some business I have."

"You can't do that now. Nearly everybody has vamosed from there right at this time. You'll have to wait."

"My business won't wait."

The two faced each other, neither ready to yield an inch. Beside Benton, Clay looked slight. The other man's great frame dwarfed

36

him. But the size of Sanger was deceptive. Hard smooth muscles packed the bones. He was lithe and springy as a wildcat.

"You're not going in," the Diamond K man told him.

Clay did not argue the point. He lashed out at the salient jaw of the foreman, all the driving power of shoulders and body back of the blow. Taken by surprise, Benton went over backward to the ground.

The young man darted forward, racing for the doorway. For a moment the Diamond K men did not make a move to stop him. He ran like a deer, and was halfway to the porch before Rock Holloway's pistol barked at him. The steps he took three at a time. Roaring guns sounded as he plunged into the building and charged up the stairs.

"Dog my cats!" Jerry Ault cried. "He went through us like blue blazes."

The words were used of Sanger a hundred times in the troublous days that were to follow. In his actions there were at times a sudden violence, a reckless swiftness, that made those watching him adopt Ault's phrase as a nickname. Before a month had passed half of Powder Horn knew him as Blue Blazes.

Clay's dash was the signal for the attack. Before he reached the second floor bullets were spattering against the wall back of the two men on the upper porch. Both of them had their revolvers out and were answering the fire. Sanger joined them.

"We can't stay here," he said. "They'll come in the back way and up the stairs to take us from behind."

"How about where I was — in the county clerk's room?" Black asked.

"No. They would pour in and have us cornered. We had better try to hold the stairs."

"Whatever you say, Clay," the marshal agreed. He had instantly accepted Sanger as leader, though he was the youngest of the three.

"Right," Black said. "If they crowd us we can fall back into the clerk's room. It opens into a hall and a back stairway. Maybe if they all attack from the front we can slip out down it and make a break for a getaway."

They took their stand at the top of the stairs, which had a bend to the right halfway down. Until they reached that point the attackers could not get at them, unless some of the Diamond K men remembered the back stairs and came at them from the rear.

The cowboys crowded up and reached the bend. Clay fired over their heads.

"Get back, boys!" he cried. "We can kill you fast as you come."

Benton was in front. Gun in hand, he glared

up at Sanger. "Damn you, I said you were in this neck deep," he shouted. "One cow thief helping another."

His pistol blazed. Terrill staggered and caught hold of the banister. Before the roar in the stair well had died down the answering shot of Sanger struck the foreman in the thigh. Benton stumbled against his men and they fell back out of sight.

"Hit hard, Terrill?" Clay asked.

There was a bewildered look on the officer's face. "Why, I reckon not so bad," he said. "In the shoulder. I can make out."

Sanger gave orders to Black. "Take him back into the room, Clint, and fix him up well as you can. Keep an eye on the back stairs. About now they may be remembering them. I'll hold this end."

4. Guns Roar

The Diamond K men gathered on the front porch of the courthouse around Benton. He cursed savagely, while Ault took a look at the wound.

"That jugheaded fool Sanger shot me," he snarled. "I'll hang his hide up to dry for this."

"What did you expect, Niles?" asked Holloway dryly. "You took a crack at him and hit Terrill. Were you lookin' for love and kisses?"

"Better get him to the drugstore and send for Doc White," the boss of the Diamond K said. "Ault, you and Shorty help him across the square."

Benton departed, complaining bitterly, supported by the two cowboys.

"Where do we go from here?" Holloway inquired of his employer.

"We get hold of those two scalawags and send them to hell in smoke," Savage answered harshly.

"Suits me fine," Rock said with sly malice. "How do we get them? Are you aiming to lead a charge up the stairs?"

His employer had a plan. "We'll get ladders and break in through windows on the east and west sides. Two or three of us will sneak up the back stairs and be ready for a rush. When the time comes I'll call Black and Sanger to the front stairs for a peace talk. While we're discussing terms you will pour in on them from all directions and they won't have a chance."

"Sounds reasonable," Holloway agreed. "I'll lead the back-stairs party if you like."

"The thing is to time the attack just right. The fellows with the ladders will cut across the grass as soon as I draw them into a talk. Don't fool with these birds. They are dangerous. Shoot to kill first chance you get."

"Not Terrill?" a rider asked.

"No, let that old buzzard go. It's the other two I want."

Sanger tiptoed down to the bend in the stairway and peered out. He saw the enemy forces gathered round their leader and guessed that there would be no immediate action. It would be a risk to leave his post on the landing but probably not a great one. If he knew Savage there would be finesse in the next attack. He would not attempt to storm the place by a frontal charge.

Clay joined his allies in the clerk's room. The marshal was leaning back in a chair looking worn and white while Black was washing the wound. At Sanger's entrance the rustler jumped up and reached for his revolver from the table where he had put it close at hand in case of need.

"How is Ray?" asked Sanger.

"He'll make the grade," Clint said. "Of course he feels right mean. A fellow does when he has had lead pumped into him."

Terrill opened his eyes. "I'll be all right soon as I can see a doctor," he mentioned, not too cheerfully. "What are those fellows doing?"

"Having a gab-fest. Savage is laying out his campaign to them, I reckon. He was talking too low for me to hear when I slipped halfway down the stairs. From what I heard one fellow say I reckon they have sent Benton to see Doc White. I've got to go back to my post. Better lie down on a bench and try to take it easy, Ray. Soon as this is over we'll turn the doc loose on you. He'll fix you up fine."

Clay kept his voice light and cheerful, but he was not as confident as he pretended to be. Savage would not give up with one repulse. He was a hard and stubborn man, and he could not afford to accept defeat with odds so greatly in his favor. He would be a joke for fifty miles around Powder Horn. His own men would lose faith in him. One of his great assets was that he always won.

Ten minutes dragged out without a sign from the besiegers. Occasionally a voice drifted to Clay, but it told him nothing of what they were doing. Again he soft-footed part way down the stairs to look and to listen. A snatch of a sentence drifted to him.

". . . gettin' a ladder from Bowker."

"Don't talk so loud, you fool," Savage snapped.

On his way back up to the second floor Clay guessed what was to take place. They would come through a window and probably charge up both stairs simultaneously. He saw at once that this would succeed. There would be no chance of stopping them, since the besieged men could not defend the building in which they were forted from an attack made at the same time by sorties at different points.

Clay consulted with his companions.

"They have got us," Black said. "Well, I'll say *Adios,* boys. You did yore best for me. Sorry you got shot up, Terrill." Gun in hand, he moved toward the door.

"Wait a minute," Clay demurred. "Where you going?"

"No use in you fellows getting killed on my account. I'll slip down the back stairs and make a run for it. Maybe I'll reach a horse."

"No," Clay vetoed. "You wouldn't get ten yards, and you know it. And don't get the idea that Savage would be content to get you and let me go. I'm in this as deep as you are now."

"They'll come in through a window in the courtroom," Terrill said. "A chimney runs up the wall outside, and the ladder is less likely to be seen there."

"Good. Maybe I can fire down on them and stop that little game," Clay suggested. "We'll have to leave you alone for a little while, Ray. This door into the back hall is bolted. After we go lock the other one. When they bust in don't offer any resistance. They are not crazy enough to shoot you. We are the ones they want."

"All right," Terrill said, no hope in his voice. "Be seeing you later, boys."

As the two men stepped into the corridor a voice shouted up the stairway. "I want to make peace talk, Sanger. I'll come partway up the stairs. Don't fire at me."

"Savage talking," Black commented. "Maybe he'll make a deal to let you and Terrill out of here."

"No. It's a trick. But I'll talk with him while you take a look at the windows. Don't shoot to kill, Clint. It will do just as well to hit them in the legs unless they crowd you too much."

Sanger called down to the leader of the cowboys. "What have you got to say, Savage? Spit it out sudden. You're not fooling me any. I know you are trying to distract my attention while you pull off some Diamond K treachery."

"Don't talk like that to me," Savage retorted angrily, appearing on the midway landing. "I'm offering you and Terrill a chance to leave."

"And Clint?"

"He's through. Try to help him, and you'll get killed too."

"I would anyhow," Clay told him with grim contempt. "If I surrendered now you would have me shot before I got out of your hands. The only peace talk you can make that goes with me is to take your men away and get out."

"I always said you were a fool!" Savage cried. "Now I know it."

"But not fool enough to believe you. Listen, Mr. Big. If your men show up with ladders they'll be shot down. Don't think they won't."

"Who said anything about ladders? I'm giving you and Terrill a last chance. Surrender now and —"

The crack of a revolver interrupted the owner of the Diamond K. Before the sound of it had died away there came a spatter of shots, and almost at the same instant the crash of rifles.

Savage raised his arm and fired at the man above. Immediately Clay answered the challenge. His bullet struck the ranchman in the hand. It knocked the .45 to the landing. With a yelp of pain and anger Savage turned and ran down to the porch.

A man with a Mexican hat came running round the corner of the house. "Shorty is down," he panted. "Black got him as he started up the ladder. And some guys are shooting at us with rifles from Doan's saloon."

At once Savage made up his mind. He had not come to town to fight a battle but to destroy one man. His plans had miscarried, and if he tried to bull them through now the cost would be too much.

"Call the men off," he ordered. "I've been hit too. Pick up Shorty and bring him to Doc White's office. Tell the boys to gather there with the horses. We'll get Black later — and this damned interfering fool Sanger too."

Holloway waved a white handkerchief and the firing stopped.

5. Clay Advises the Study of Shakespeare

Clay met Black in the corridor at the entrance to the courtroom.

"They are pullin' out," the rustler said, amazed relief on his face. "Someone has been plugging at them from across the street."

"Likely Terrill's deputies. I heard firing from the courtroom. Hit anyone?"

"I got Shorty in the leg as he started up the ladder. You don't reckon this is a trick to get us out into the open, do you?"

"No. I hit Savage in the hand. He has had a bellyful of fight. When the rifles began to cough at his men he threw up the sponge. Of course there will be an open season on you and me from now on."

"I don't get it," Black said, a puzzled frown on his face. "Why did you butt in? I understand about Terrill. He wasn't going to run out on his job. But you weren't in this."

"Ray worked for my father. He was his friend."

"Hmp! You sure went the whole hog for him. And you saved my life too. I'll not forget

47

you hid me last night and pulled me out of a bad hole this morning. I reckon you think I'm a bad egg. But if ever a chance comes to help you I won't run out on it."

"Forget it. Let's go see if we can do anything for Terrill."

When he was sure who they were the marshal opened the door for them. He looked very white and worn.

"The battle is all over, Ray," Sanger told him. "Your boys crashed in with rifles and sent the Diamond K scooting for cover. Lie down and let me look at your wound. We'll get the doctor soon as it is safe."

"There's a bucket of water in the court-room," Black mentioned.

"Get it. And then keep guard while I fix Ray up."

Five minutes later somebody tapped on the door leading to the back hall.

"Who is it?" Black demanded, a hand on his gun.

"Bud Miller and Frenchy."

Terrill nodded. "That's Bud, all right. Let him in."

Miller stared at the marshal. "You been shot, Ray?" he asked.

"In the shoulder," Clay replied. "You got here in the nick of time."

"When the message came we slapped saddles on our horses and burned the wind getting to town." Miller explained. "All the kid told us was that trouble was brewing. We figured some bunch of cowboys had gone haywire."

Bud Miller was a slender straight-backed man with high cheekbones and long straight hair. There was a considerable strain of Cherokee Indian blood in him. His companion, Frenchy, was a swarthy heavy-set silent man noted for his great physical strength. Bud usually talked for them both.

"Where did you get the rifles?"

"Borrowed one from Doan's and the other from Bowker. With so many Diamond K warriors maverickin' around we couldn't come out in the open. At that distance six-guns weren't any good."

"Hit any of them?" Clay asked.

"We didn't try. Figured that when we butted in Savage would lay off, and that's what he did. Soon as it was safe we slipped across the square to join you."

"They might start in on us again after they have talked it over," Black surmised.

"No." Clay spoke with crisp decision. "They ran into difficulties they didn't expect. For the present they have had enough. Savage is no bull-headed fool."

Sanger turned out to be right. Within the hour the Diamond K men left town in a body,

Shorty and Benton in a wagon, the bed of which was filled with hay. As soon as they were gone Doctor White dressed the wound of the marshal, after which he was carried to the hotel and put to bed.

The town buzzed with excitement. Since the first sod houses had been built it had been the paradise of wild and reckless men. They came to Powder Horn to spend the money earned by buffalo hunting and railroad building, and there were always plenty of gamblers, saloonkeepers, and dancehall girls to help the visitors empty their pockets. After the earliest frontier days had passed the cowboy and the rustler took the place of the buffalo hunter and the railroad builder. Line riders saved their wages for months to spend them in two or three days of swift debauchery. The town had a reputation for depravity all over the country. Newspaper correspondents from Eastern cities wrote articles about its wickedness and its rowdyism, its lack of respect for law and decency. The local residents did not accept that interpretation of Powder Horn's morals, though they admitted that it was "a little wild." Privately the best people were anxious to improve conditions and get rid of the parasites who preyed on those who earned an honest living, though some of the business men found their desires a little mixed, since an open town meant lavish spending.

But even Powder Horn was not used to an invasion of a score of armed men intent on inflicting punishment in open disregard of law. This was quite different from the frequent shooting affrays between men excited by liquor and jealousy. Moreover, the Diamond K was unpopular in the community. Savage was too arrogant and overbearing. He treated homesteaders and nesters as if they were trash to be got rid of without consideration of their rights.

There was a good deal of muttered resentment at so flagrant an outrage. Ray Terrill won whole-hearted approval for his game stand to enforce the law. Even for Clint Black there were apologists. No doubt he was a rustler, but Savage had made him one by burning the house he had built on his homestead claim. If he had killed Fleagle it had been in self-defense. Much to his disgust Clay was voted the hero of the battle. He had jumped in to aid the marshal, with no obligation to involve himself in trouble that would very likely prove fatal to him. A good many onlookers had seen his dash to the courthouse. The mayor said openly that he deserved a medal for having wounded Savage and his foreman.

Effie Collins met him in a store a few hours after the fight. She was greatly pleased at the result of the Diamond K attempt to wipe out Black. Her brother had not joined in the attack, and like many others she was delighted to see Savage come a cropper. There was a question about the owner of the big ranch she had not answered yet in her mind, but she was quite sure that in the meantime it would do him good to be taken down a peg. Secretly she was glad that Clay had played so great a part in the humiliation. As a child she had silently idolized him in a small girl's fashion. At the time of the break between him and her brother, though she had sided with Stan out of loyalty, there had been grave misgivings in her heart. Both of the young men were small cattle-owners. With other ranchers and homesteaders they were tacitly banded against the encroachments of the Diamond K and two other big stock outfits. For reasons of his own Savage had weaned young Collins away from this alliance by favoring and flattering him. Though Effie found herself excited and interested in meeting a new social group, wealthier and more sophisticated than those among whom she had been brought up, there were hours when she was swept by waves of nostalgia for the more simple life of her early years. She told herself that she hated Clay Sanger for the unspoken cool contempt of his judgment. He thought that she and Stan were deserters. Indignantly she resented this. Yet hidden deep in her breast there was admiration for his inflexible consistency.

"I see you took your hands out of your pockets," she said by way of greeting.

"So I did," he nodded, a flicker of mirth in his eyes. "Proving that a young lady I know was right when she told me I never could mind my own business."

"A man can't be wrong every time. Maybe it was your business to save Clint Black."

Clay was quite fed up with praise for what he had done. Everybody he met had some word of approval. Three ladies had surrounded him in a store filled with people and gushed over his heroism until he had broken through and fled. As he looked at it, he had given way to a crazy impulse and through luck had got out of it alive. It embarrassed him acutely to have so much made of it. Now he sidestepped discussion of the subject by introducing another one.

"There seemed to be a little breeze in your neighborhood when I saw you last," he said. "I hope all is harmony now in the Collins family."

Effie flushed. "Still not minding your own business," she began, and pulled herself up with the assurance that she had a better line of attack. "But I must forgive that in our new hero."

Usually Clay had had the upper hand in their sparring, but she had found a weapon that got under his hide. He was unreasonably annoyed.

"You stop that darn foolishness right now," he warned.

"Why, I'm only telling you what all the town is saying," she replied sweetly. "Blue Blazes they call you, because you are so brave and went through Mr. Savage's men like lightning. It must be nice to know that you are a hero."

Clay looked at her darkly, for once shaken out of his sardonic derision. "I always knew you needed spanking. Your folks ought to have put you across their knees frequently when you were growing up instead of letting you develop into a pest. I don't know that it's too late now."

The girl lost the advantage she had gained. "Maybe you would like to try it," she flamed.

He shook his head. "I reckon not. I've topped outlaw broncs aplenty, but I wouldn't want to tackle that. You would probably bite and claw, like that Katherine Shakespeare writes about in a play. She sure was a caution — stepped as high as a blind dog in stubble." He concluded on a hopeful note, "But her husband certainly knew how to handle her."

"I suppose he whipped her," she said contemptuously.

"I'll send back to Kansas City for a copy of the book. You would enjoy reading it. She was one spoiled vixen. But, gentlemen, hush! When this Petruchio got through with her she was a right nice gentle lady. Ate out of his hand. No, ma'am, he didn't whip her. He wouldn't let her sleep or eat. Roared and scolded, not at her but at everybody who tried to make things easy for her. He played it was all for love of her, claiming the food wasn't cooked right and the fine clothes he ordered did not fit, until she was worn to a frazzle. Pete was a champ woman-tamer. I'll make a note not to forget to send for the book to-morrow. It's educational."

"I would like to see a man treat me that way," Effie said angrily.

"Exactly what I was thinking," he murmured softly.

"I never met another man as poison mean as you," she told him hotly, and turned on her heel.

Clay chuckled. "There's more than one way to skin a cat," he said to himself. "I stopped that darned hero talk pronto. Lucky I went to that Petruchio play when I was in Denver. It came in mighty handy."

He ran into Bud Miller cruising over his beat. The deputy marshal had a message for him.

"Cap Winters wants to see you before you go back to the ranch," he said, grinning at the young man. "I'll be dadgummed if I know why you're so important. All you did was bust into the Diamond K show, slam Benton in the beezer, and shoot up him and Savage. My rifle made twice as much noise as yore popgun, and the mayor ain't sending for me."

"No justice," agreed Clay. "You and Frenchy used your heads, ended the battle, and saved the three of us. I'm much obliged for that noise you made."

Winters was a big stout man, red-faced and bald-headed. He had been a captain in the Civil War and had drifted west at its conclusion. In turn a buffalo hunter, a railroad grade contractor, and a storekeeper, he had become mayor of Powder Horn by reason of natural fitness. A rough and ready frontiersman, hammered to toughness by the dangers and hardship of pioneer life, he was one of many thousands on the high plains who fought sturdily for law and order during the formative years.

He took Clay into the boarded-up corner of the store he called his office and motioned him to a chair.

"Smoke?" he asked, offering his visitor a cigar.

When Sanger declined, he lit up, puffed out a cloud of smoke, and relaxed into a seat. "Well, young fellow, you sure cut the mustard today," he said at last after a long scrutiny of Sanger. "Don't you know that Savage is lord of the high justice and that it is treason to butt in and interfere with any shindig he starts?"

"I've known Ray Terrill ever since I was a kid knee-high to a duck. He went up the trail with my father and for years rode the line for him. They were good friends."

"You've known Savage quite some time too, haven't you?"

"Yes."

The dry answer, confined to a monosyllable, told as much as a long oration. The captain stroked his long thick gray mustache, his eyes studying this self-contained young man. Until today he had never given him more than casual consideration, though he had known from hearsay that he was no friend of the big ranch.

"Out on your ranch it's liable not to be too safe after this, don't you reckon?" he suggested.

"And so?" Clay asked quietly.

"Might be a good idea for you to stick around town for a spell."

"Meaning that Savage and his outfit will be on the prod."

"Looks reasonable. He's shy one finger, kindness of Clay Sanger, and that nice gentle foreman of his, Benton, totes a bullet in his leg, compliments of the aforesaid Sanger. Both of them are vindictive birds and they are going to try to even the score."

"Yes," agreed Clay.

"You'll be safer in Powder Horn."

"Have you a nice hole I can crawl into and draw it in after me?" Clay wanted to know.

"Now son, don't go off half-cocked," the older man admonished. "The thing to do is to size up the situation. Savage has an outfit of twenty-odd men, say. How many have you?"

Clay grinned. "Two. One of them is a Mexican, who admits he is gun-shy. The other is a kid from the East, nineteen years old, sent out for his health."

"You see."

That the mayor had some proposition to make Clay knew. He was curious to find out what it was, but he could wait until Winters came to it.

"Yes, I see. The Diamond K has run off several homesteaders, and two small cattle outfits sold out to Savage for half what they were worth because of his outrages. But I

58

reckon I'll stick, Captain."

"That's all right. I don't blame you." Winters hitched his chair a little closer and took the cigar from his mouth. "Terrill won't be over this wound for several months. Anyhow, he is getting too old for the job. He wants to resign and run that little place he has in the bottoms where he raises vegetables. I'm offering you his job."

Clay laughed outright. "And I thought you had in mind some nice safe berth for me. How many have been buried in Boot Hill during the past two years?"

"I wouldn't know exactly," the mayor evaded. "Powder Horn is right lively."

"Would twenty be a pretty good guess of those who died from lead poisoning?"

"Well — not quite that many, maybe."

"Two of them were marshals. Correct me if I'm wrong."

"Two is right. But one of them asked for it."

Sanger shook his head. "No, thank you, Captain. I'm a quiet peaceable rancher. All the excitement I want is roping cows out of swamps when they get bogged down. This town life is too fast for me. I'm going to ride back to the Circle S and listen to Juan play his guitar."

"Hmp!" snorted Winters. "You're going to

listen to the angels playing their harps if you go back there and make yoreself a mark for the Diamond K gun-toters. Listen, son. You know how this is as well as I do. There's a shift going on in this country. The big ranchers have always had the say-so here. They see settlers moving in on their range and they don't like it. You can't blame them for wanting to stay top dog. But they might as well try to sweep back the tide. The creeks are going to be homesteaded by the little fellows with the covered wagons. The Bar B Bar and the K L and the other big outfits aren't so bad. Of course they don't like their range being taken from them, but they wouldn't buck the law if Savage didn't egg them on. This thing simmers down to a fight between the Diamond K and those of us supporting the new order."

"I won't quarrel with you about that," Clay said. "Where do we go from there? If the settlers all moved into town like you want me to do on account of being scared of Savage and his warriors, that would suit him fine."

"It would suit him a lot better for you to stay in the hills and get dry gulched. Here's the layout in this county." The captain leaned forward and beat a thick forefinger into the palm of his other hand. "Right now Savage controls the commissioners and the sheriff's office. Jack Ballard is his man. He made him sheriff and Jack eats out of his hand. I want a marshal who will stand up for our side, one who won't let the Diamond K push him around. What I am asking myself is, have you the sand in yore craw to hold down a job like that?"

The white teeth of the rancher showed in a cheerful grin against the background of a brown tanned face. "Too bad you'll never find out," Clay murmured. He added, a moment later: "I'd kinda like to know myself what kind of a Wild Bill Hickok I'd make, but I'd rather speculate about it than try it."

"All right," the mayor said, and shrugged his heavy shoulders. "There's a fellow in Lampasas wrote me for the job in case there was a vacancy. I reckon I'll give him a try. Have you got any relatives you want messages sent to in case anything happens?"

"Nary a relative. I'll be drifting along, Captain. Thanks for your offer to me to join the Suicide Club."

Clay went back to the Circle S that afternoon. He noticed that Stan and his sister were on the road ahead of him. But he lost sight of them soon because he deflected from the road to take to the hills. For he knew that henceforth the price of life would be continual vigilance. He had flung down the gauntlet to Savage and his following. They would not forget that he had frustrated their vengeance and humiliated their outfit.

6. Clay Drops in on a Neighbor

Arrogant though he was, Savage had judgment enough to know when it was not wise to affront public opinion. Clay had stepped in to help the marshal uphold the law, and to rub him out now would be to inflame a sentiment already incensed against the high-handedness of the Diamond K. It would be better to make life miserable for Sanger during the next few weeks and then to destroy him quietly when there were no witnesses present.

The foreman of the ranch brought an El Paso paper to him a few days after the fiasco in Powder Horn. Benton flung it down on the table angrily.

"There's nearly a column in it about our little party," he yelped. "Read it. The fellow calls it the courthouse battle, and he writes it so we look like a bunch of jug-headed quitters. I say the thing to do is to snuff out both Sanger and Black soon as we can round them up. This whole county is sniggering at us."

Savage read the story. It filled him with rage, but he took care not to show it. "When

I get through with those two scoundrels there will not be anybody sniggering. But I'm going to take my time. Did you set fire to that haystack this morning?"

"Ault took care of that before daybreak. But hell's hinges! What does that buy us? I'm still limping from that pill he flung into me. Bump him off, I say. Right damn now."

"You'll do as I tell you," Savage told him coldly. "I'm running this campaign my way. Don't forget that for a moment."

To Sanger it was an extremely annoying way. His fences were torn down and his stock run off. He found one morning a Circle S cow with a bullet in its forehead. Visiting a mountain corral back of the ranch, he came on half a dozen of his horses penned up in it. They were so gaunt and exhausted that he knew they had been there two or three days without food or drink. Nobody had to tell him that some of the riders of the Diamond K had done this.

Jim Dall, a neighboring ranchman, was with him at the time.

"They are thin as gutted snowbirds," Dall said. "You wouldn't think a white man would treat horses thataway."

"Are Savage and Benton white men?" Clay asked. His mouth set like a steel trap and his eyes grew frosty. "I'm going to ride over to the Diamond K and tell them a thing or two."

Dall turned incredulous eyes on him. "Have you gone crazy?"

"No. You can see how this shapes, Jim. Savage must have given orders to his men to lay off me for the present. I'm not fooling myself. My name is on the black list, right at the top. He means to get me, but not in a way to make trouble for himself by stirring up public sentiment. That little matter has to be deferred for a month or two. Meanwhile he intends to bust me up in business."

"Looks like," Dall agreed.

"Well, I'm going over to read the riot act to him. He's such a big mogul that I reckon nobody ever has told him what a lowdown skunk he is. I'm electing myself to do it today."

"You might as well walk unarmed into a pack of hungry wolves."

"I don't think so. There may be some itching fingers, but Savage is too smart to let his men gun me there. He can find a better way than that."

"So you figure it. But you may be wrong. In which case you won't get a chance for second thinking."

But Clay had made up his mind to go and could not be talked out of it. Rather reluctantly Dall offered to ride with him. Sanger vetoed the suggestion. He was going alone. The boldness of the move would make for safety.

Dall was that rare product of the cow country, a fat ranchman. He was an oldtime settler. Crisscross wrinkles made diamond-shaped patterns on the back of his leathery neck. He opened his mouth to protest further — and changed his mind. Reckless imps of deviltry danced in Sanger's eyes. He was set on doing this foolish thing and no warning would stop him.

Clay knew that the most dangerous adventures were sometimes the safest, if one set about them with wary efficiency. He had no intention of being foolhardy, though he was willing that his visit should have that appearance. Therefore he did not take the valley road but followed a high ridge from which he could look down upon the folds of the hills below. More than once he caught sight of Diamond K riders working cattle. After a time the ridge dropped down to a cut, to the right of which were the buildings of the home ranch. The blades of the windmill in the corral heliographed sun flashes to him, and as he drew closer he could see men shoeing horses at the outdoor blacksmith shop. Leaning back in the saddle, he let his mount pick its way through the rubble of a stiff descent to the valley.

The house was a large rambling one with a comfortable wide porch sweeping around three sides of it. A saddle hung by a stirrup from a peg in the wall. On the floor of the porch a rifle lay, some dirty rags and a ramrod beside it. Apparently somebody had started to clean it and had been interrupted.

Out of the house came a Chinese man wearing a white apron above his wide flapping trousers. He took one startled look at the approaching rider and hurried back into the hallway. Sanger knew that his arrival was about to be announced. He noticed that the two men at the blacksmith shop had stopped work and were looking at him.

Savage came from the house to the porch. He wore a bandage on one hand. "Why did you come here?" he demanded, anger sharp in his voice.

"I came to tell you what a yellow coyote I think you are," Clay answered, his voice not loud but very clear and ringing.

A man and a woman had followed the owner of the ranch to the porch. They were Stan and Effie Collins. Evidently they had been at dinner, for the girl carried a napkin in her hand. Sanger was glad to see her. He felt that her presence increased his margin of safety.

The audience was growing. A man in chaps had come out of the stable and moved forward to a cottonwood halfway between it and the house. Another appeared in the doorway of the men's bunkhouse and stood there. He carried a rifle, the butt of it grounded. The two who had been shoeing a horse had drawn nearer. Probably all of them were armed, Clay thought. They were ready for action, waiting for any signal that might be given them.

"When you burn my haystacks and tear down my fences in the night that's only what I would expect from you, the cowardly tactics the Diamond K has always used to defeat those with nerve enough to tell it to go to hell," Clay continued, the anger in his voice cold and biting and steel-hard. "But when you fasten helpless animals in a corral without feed or water and leave them to die you are threating them as even an Apache would not have done. Savage, you and your hired assassins can give points in cruelty to the lowest Indian tribe of them all."

"You fool — you besotted lunkhead — do you think you can come here and talk that way to me?" Savage flung back, his mouth a thin and cruel line. "Do you think — ?"

He stopped, his rage surging up too fast to find words.

"You have an idea you are God in the Powder Horn country," Clay went on. "Better forget it. You are just a bully who gets away with murder because you have a paid army of scoundrels at your back. You rule by fear. Honest men can't say how contemptible they think you are lest you burn them out of house and home and put their families in the road. Beside you a horse thief and a rustler stand out honest and clean."

The gaze of Effie Collins did not shift from him, except once to look at the dark set fury in the face of Savage. He must have been mad to come here to the stronghold of his enemy, she thought, and fear of the consequences flowed over her. The ranchman had only to give the signal and bullets would riddle that strong lithe body. But back of the fear was a high deep pride in this supple horseman who could ride unafraid into such desperate peril. He had taken off his wide-rimmed hat, and the sun shone on the brindle hair above the lean brown face. Clay was not handsome like her brother. He could never be that. But he was intensely masculine. The lift of the head, the fine shoulders packed with smooth muscles, the strong indomitable force in him, moved her tremendously. There came to her a swift conviction that no other man could ever mean to her as much as he did now. The knowledge staggered her. She had thought she detested him — his mockery and insolence, as well as his blunt and reckless disregard of her opinion — and all the time she must have loved him without knowing it. The rush of emotion that swept over Effie frightened her. It was shocking to learn that the feeling for this man could so utterly possess her.

"Don't, Clay, please. Don't talk so . . . so hard." The words, low and pleading, came from the girl's lips as by some inner compulsion.

Sanger gave no heed to them. He did not look at her, but finished what he had come to say. Scabrous epithets dripped from his lips slowly, each one a deliberate insult to the man from whose face his eyes never wandered. All the pent-up contempt of years found expression.

Though he gave his mind to telling off Savage and his outfit, an undercurrent of thought watched warily the effect. He did not miss the malignity in his enemy's tight face. The man was looking past him at somebody Clay could not see without turning. To right and left and back of Sanger were the Diamond K warriors. If their leader spoke the word, if he lifted a hand as a signal . . .

Savage said, his mouth a thin straight slit: "I've taken a lot from you — a lot — but you've gone too far this time. You're fixing to kill me. I can see that, and I'm going to protect myself."

70

A man moved forward slowly into the orbit of Clay's vision. It was Rock Holloway. He stood seven or eight yards from the Circle S man, the icy gray eyes fixed on him. A thumb was hitched in his belt close to the butt of a revolver. He said nothing. His gaze did not shift. He waited. In that tense moment one could almost hear the ticking of eternity.

"Stop it," Effie cried to her host in an anguished voice.

Her brother stepped forward, ran down the porch steps, and placed himself between Holloway and Sanger. "Nothing doing!" he cried. "Don't let your men go crazy, Bert, just because this fellow has blown off steam. It's only talk. You know he isn't aiming to kill you. He's a fool for coming here, but that is no reason for shooting him."

Savage drew a long deep breath. For a moment his eyes had been glassy and the lust to kill imperative. But the caution that was a dominating factor of his policy was reasserting itself. He must not destroy the man here, at this time, before protesting witnesses.

"Get out of here," he ordered hoarsely. "If you ever show your face on my ranch again I'll blot you out. Hit the trail, you fool, before I change my mind."

Clay nodded to Stan Collins. "Much obliged," he said. "You're right. It wasn't smart to come, but I had to get it out of my system."

He turned and rode out of the yard. As he swung up the slope toward the ridge a momentary weakness ran through his supple body, a reaction of the strain through which he had passed. He knew that he had grazed death. If Stan and his sister had not been visiting at the ranch Savage would have destroyed him. The visit had been a mistake. He must not yield to any more impulses of that sort. He had misjudged the psychology of his foe. The man was generally wary, but there was in him too an urgent hate impelling him to immediate action.

Out of the adventure he found one satisfaction. Though Stan and Effie were no longer friends of his they had not been willing to stand back and let him be killed. No doubt they thought his appearance at the Diamond K a bit of theatrical bravado. Perhaps it was. But he had seen a look on the girl's face that told him there was still in her some wistful memory of the old days when they had been one for all and all for one.

He had the same feeling. Though he had often told himself their past companionship was a closed chapter, he found his mind reverting to it sadly.

7. Two Visitors

Clay did not play any more tricks with Fate. In deciding to visit the Diamond K Ranch he had thought the risk not too great. But he had been given a bad five minutes during which his heart had died under the ribs. Having had his lesson, he did not mean to take any more unnecessary chances. At night he stayed indoors with blinds drawn and doors bolted. Usually he played cribbage with Hal Lander, the tubercular lad who was regaining his health in the light dry air of the high plains. Since Hal was young and impressionable he thought his bronzed impassive employer the most daring man he had ever met.

In the morning Clay did not leave the house until he had taken a long and careful look out of the windows. When he walked even as far as the corral he carried a rifle with him.

Juan had cut out some calves for branding, and though Sanger helped at the job he took care to have the Winchester within reach as he did so. The Mexican did the roping and the owner of the brand stamped the Ⓢ on the sizzling hide of the calf. After the hot iron had been applied the calf was released and freed to join its mother. Usually it stood for a moment blatting unhappily and then ran to join the cow for comfort and to have the wound licked. Within two minutes it had forgotten all about the pain.

The sound of a cantering horse came to the working men. Clay picked up his rifle and turned to see who his visitor was. Effie Collins pulled up outside the corral fence.

Clay strolled forward to meet her. She asked him in Spanish how he was.

"Dios, y gracias,"[1] he answered.

"But not to your own good sense," she chided.

"I'll plead guilty to that," he admitted.

"Why did you go to the Diamond K?" she asked.

"I don't exactly know. Maybe because I thought it was time somebody told Mr. Big where to get off. Maybe it was just dumb bravado."

"Did you have to tell him at his own ranch with five or six of his fighting men around him?"

"That wasn't so clever," Clay admitted. "I overplayed my hand. If you and Stan hadn't been there it would not have been so good for me."

---

[1]"Well, thanks to God and you."

"You'll have to be careful. Both Mr. Savage and his foreman are furious at you."

"I gathered as much."

She looked across at the hills before she spoke again. There was a wave of pink in her cheeks. "I happened to be coming this way, so I thought I would stop and warn you."

"That's very good of you, since I am the most hateful man you ever knew."

"You can be very aggravating when you choose," she told him, defending herself. "It must be a gift. Do you suppose Mr. Savage enjoyed having you lay him out before his men? Was there any sense in infuriating him after you had wounded him and his foreman not ten days before?"

"No. If I hadn't got a break I might have been playing on a golden harp by now."

"Don't make a joke of it, please. I want you to look after yourself — all the time, every minute."

He replied seriously: "I'm doing just that, Effie. You'll notice I have a tried and true friend beside me." With his left hand he patted the barrel of the Winchester.

"Yes, but —"

She stopped, looking down with a troubled frown at his lean whipcord strength and into the eyes so audacious and so reckless. The combination did not reassure her. He was tough and hard and enduring, but none of these qualities would help him against an unexpected shot from the brush. What she had seen the other day at the Diamond K had frightened her. A picture jumped to her mind — a bareheaded man pelting Savage with bitter words while the ranch gunmen drew closer waiting silently for a sign.

"I think you are in terrible danger," she went on. "I didn't understand until the other day. You ought not to stay here on the ranch."

What she said was not news to him. But he could not run away and leave his holdings with no excuse except that he was afraid. He must keep his own self-respect.

"Where should I stay?" he asked, with a thin grim smile.

"I don't know. Not here, so close to your enemies."

He shook his head. "I can't let myself be driven out just because I have enemies. You know that. But don't worry. I'll not throw down on myself. I'm watching every minute."

"Well," she answered, unsatisfied but aware that nothing she could say would move him to leave. "Only, do be careful." She gathered up the reins to leave.

He laid a hand on the bridle, looking up at her with a whimsical grin on his brown face. "You can't pretend this time that you're trying to help Stan. The truth is that the old days are tugging at you, just as they do at me sometimes. You're holding out an olive branch."

"Yes," she admitted. "I think we have been foolish. We were all too hot-headed. I'd like to be friends again." The words came hard for her, and the dark shy eyes fell away from his.

They shook hands on the pact.

"What about Stan?" he asked.

"Stan is stubborn. He won't admit he feels as I do. But he does. If nothing happens to drive you two apart still further you may be friends again some day."

She turned and went down the road, holding her mount to a walk. He watched her, a warm glow in his heart. He was a man who valued friendship, and it was good to know that this fine lovely girl had come to brush away the misunderstanding between them.

All morning he carried her in his thoughts. He knew that she would try to bridge the gap between him and her brother. Though Clay felt that Stan had done wrong in allying himself with Savage and his friends, he knew the young man had good stuff in him. He was hot-tempered and willful, but there was in his character a base of integrity. If and when his eyes were opened to another viewpoint there would be a chance yet to renew the old comradeship.

Later in the day Clay had another visitor, Captain Winters. He came in a buckboard and at the invitation of his host stayed for supper. Not till they were alone did he come to the reason for his call, and even then his approach was gradual.

The big red-faced man came from talk about the need of rain to personal matters.

"I been hearing more about you, Sanger," he said. "Opinion is divided as to whether you are a plain lunkhead or just temporarily crazy with the heat."

"Let me know when you find out," Clay said amiably. The mayor rolled the cigar between his lips and took his time to answer. "There's no denying one thing," he went on, his appraising eyes watching the ranchman. "You have the luck of the Irish. The betting ought to have been about a golden eagle to a dollar Mex that those sons-of-guns at the Diamond K would never let you leave the ranch alive after the way you rough-tongued Savage. And you ride away clean as a whistle."

"Yes, I had luck," Clay admitted.

Winters leaned forward and tapped him on the knee with a forefinger. "It won't last, not if you stick around the hills here. Savage is as vindictive as an elephant and as ruthless as a wolf. You can't make him look like a fool and get away with it. He is proud as all get out. What do you suppose he keeps that killer Holloway around him for, except to take care of fellows of your stripe — guys who are too stiff to knock under to him?"

"I am not taking any chances."

"You're taking chances every time you walk out of this house, every time you go into the pasture to rope a horse, every time you ride down the road. Don't load yoreself, young man. He's waiting for the right time to strike — and when he does it will be good night."

There was a flicker of amusement in Clay's eyes. "And you drove all the way out here to tell me that I'm crazy and Savage is mean," he murmured.

"No, sir. I had a better reason for coming."

"Now you're talking turkey, Captain. I take it that the gent from Lampasas did not make good as marshal."

The mayor laughed. "All right. I'm putting in a lick for you and one for myself. No, sir, the fellow was a false alarm. He wore his hair down to his shoulders all right and carried two big guns strapped to his sides, but he wasn't there when the rub came. A bunch of boys from the Pitchfork outfit rode into town and cut loose night before last. The marshal grabbed their cook and tossed him into the calaboose. Those hellions busted open the jail and freed the cook. When the long-haired bird tried to interfere they cut his hair off and flung him into one of the horse troughs on the square. They soused him plenty and gave him orders to light out. He took down the road, the boys shooting at his heels as he went. When last seen he was running like the heel flies were after him. I don't reckon he quit traveling till he reached Lampasas."

"So Powder Horn is shy one marshal. Why don't you promote Bud Miller? He is a good man, game and reliable."

"Too slow on the uptake. Bud is fine for a deputy, but he has no initiative. He can take orders fine, but he doesn't know how to give them. He knows it and doesn't want the job."

"Hmp! Someone with initiative, a game guy who will go through. Why, I know the very man for you." The face of Clay was completely sober, except for a mocking gleam in the eyes. "Rock Holloway. Half of these wild towns pick a bad man for marshal so as to overawe the other killers. Rock ought to be tough enough for you."

"Now look here, young fellow," Winters reproved. "This is serious business. You know doggoned well I don't aim to turn the town over to Bert Savage. His outfit is one of the reasons why we need the right kind of a man."

80

"I see. You want a fellow who is either a plain lunkhead or crazy with the heat."

"I want *you*. The way I figure it you are tough enough and not too tough. Stick around here, and you are a dead duck. You can come to town as marshal and still save face, because it is sure enough a man-sized job. Turn yore stock over to some neighbor to run it on shares. We'll pay you a top salary, a hundred twenty-five a month. You'll have two deputies. It isn't a safe spot, I'll grant you that. But it isn't certain death as it would be for you to stay up here. And you'll have the satisfaction of helping to bring law and order into the country."

The points made by the mayor were cogent. Clay saw the force of them. No matter how vigilant he was, the warriors of the Diamond K would in all likelihood get him if he stayed. He could get Dall to look after his ranch interests on shares. Nor could anybody accuse him of running away from Savage, since he was going to Powder Horn to take a job at which two men had been killed, another wounded, and several run out. The salary alone would not have tempted him, but he needed money to develop his ranch, and one hundred and twenty-five a month was a lot of money when one considered that a top waddy got only thirty.

"You've hired a marshal," Clay said, coming to swift decision.

"Good. When can you start?"

"Tomorrow, if you like."

"The sooner the better."

"You'll have to put up with short hair for a while," Clay grinned. "It will be several months till I can have a crop reaching to my shoulders like the Lampasas gent."

"I wouldn't care if you were as bald as I am," Winters told him. "There's just one thing, young fellow. You'll have to learn to shut yore eyes once in a while. We want a quiet town, but not too quiet. I wish there weren't so many guys toting guns in town."

"There won't be," Clay said.

The mayor gave him a quick look. "What do you mean?"

"I mean that whiskey and guns together aren't a good combination. We'll have the boys cache their guns at your store when they come to town."

"That will certainly be nice," the mayor said. "Just one little question: How do you expect to get them to do it? We've got an ordinance against gun-toting, but nobody pays any attention to it. When we put up posters calling attention to it, drunks rode up and down the streets shooting holes in them."

"Maybe I can talk the boys out of their bad

habits," Sanger said mildly.

Winters looked at him suspiciously. He recalled that Clay had not tried to talk Savage out of lynching Black. He had gone into direct action.

"You've got no such notion," the merchant charged. "I'll back up any play you make in reason, but of course you can't gun cowboys just because they are on a tear making some fireworks."

"No," agreed the ranchman. "Maybe I can't make the no-guns-worn-in-town idea stick, but I would like to try it out. It won't do any harm for me to kinda reason with them."

"Play the hand any way you like. All I ask of you is to clean up the town without massacré-ing nice boys trying to have a little fun. You can bump off all the honest-to-God bad men you like."

"If they don't bump me off first," Clay said. "Well, here's hoping."

Next day he made arrangements with Dall to take charge of his ranch and cattle. In the afternoon he rode over the hills to town, taking very good care not to expose himself to a shot from the brush.

8. Clay Strolls Down the Street

When Clay had talked of getting the cowboys to discard their weapons while in town he had not been speaking entirely at random. He had known of a marshal who had issued such an order and had made it stick in the wildest trail-end town of the West. Tom Smith of Abilene had been the man. By means of the strength and the courage that were in him he had tamed that wild corner of hell to outward decency and respect for law. But Tom had been the greatest peace officer ever seen on the frontier, and at the end of six months he had been killed in the line of duty.

Clay had heard his father speak of Smith. In talk one time the marshal had suggested the rule he followed. Anybody could bring in a dead man, he had said, but the good officer brought his prisoners in alive. It was Sanger's intention to be a good officer if possible. He had never killed a man. He wanted never to have to do that. But he was a man who faced facts, and without positing the question he knew that in self-defense he must not hesitate to shoot down a ruffian.

Here as in many parts of the West the pioneer had pushed ahead of the law. In the earliest days each settler had to be his own law. When an emergency arose he could find protection only in the revolver strapped to his hip. But those border days were passing. Little red schoolhouses and churches began to dot the land. The ruffling gunman was out of step with the new order, and citizens looked to their peace officers for defense against such bullies.

After Captain Winters had pinned a star on him the first official acts of Sanger were to have printed and posted in conspicuous places a notice to gun-carriers. It read:

This is to call attention to a city ordinance against the carrying of weapons in town. Residents are asked to leave side arms at their homes or places of business. Visitors will please check them immediately upon arrival at the New York Emporium, the Powder Horn Hardware Co., or Winters' Dry Goods Store. Failure to comply with this law will subject the violator to arrest and fine.

CLAY SANGER, *Marshal*

Those who read this notice had sharply different reactions to it. Peaceable citizens wished the new marshal luck but remembered that other officers had issued similar orders and been unable to enforce them. Professional gamblers, bummers, and law-breakers scoffed at the notice. Sanger would either back down or get shot, they said. Either alternative suited their cynical interests, though they preferred the former since they had no ill-will to Sanger personally. All they wanted was a wide-open town where everything would be in order from rolling a drunk to shooting up Front Street.

Bud Miller walked in to the Cowboys' Rest and asked the proprietor, Peter Maloney, if he could tack a poster on the wall.

"Sure," Peter told him, and put a bottle with two glasses in front of a pair of ranch hands. "Anything you like, Bud." A moment later he revoked his consent. "You'll have to take that down. I don't want bullet holes in my walls."

The two punchers with their feet on the rail were Jerry Ault of the Diamond K and Red McClintock of the Bar B Bar.

"So they've appointed Blue Blazes," Jerry commented. "And he aims to ride herd on us. Well, I'll say this: If anybody could do it, I would say it would be that guy."

"He won't get any part of the way," Red

predicted. "In this town right now a hundred men have guns buckled to their hips. Think they are going to take them off because Clay says so? Not on yore tintype. He has bit off a lot more than he can chew."

"I reckon," the Diamond K rider agreed. "At that, I'd bet my boots he collects some guns from the boys before they puncture him."

"He's got you buffaloed, Jerry. I've ridden circle with Sanger, and I'll grant you he is no loud-mouthed blow-off. A quiet fellow, game enough, but no world beater. I'll take him on myself if he gets in my way. It's a cinch I'm not going to let him lift my six-gun from me."

"Nor I," Jerry agreed. "Still, I won't go outa my way to run into him."

"Hmp! If I meet up with him and he gets gay there will be trouble," McClintock said flatly.

Bud Miller had rolled up the placard and was leaving the room. At the door he turned. "Not the way to look at this, Red," he said amiably. "Like Clay says, liquor and guns don't go well together. We all ought to support him in this."

"I can hold my liquor," the cowboy replied. "I don't have to get any shorthorn marshal to tell me when to go heeled and when not.

You support him if you like, Bud. I reckon that is what you are paid for. Me, I'm a free citizen without any strings on me."

The deputy marshal said, with a not unfriendly grin, "Watch out you're not soon an unfree citizen with handcuffs on you."

McClintock did not like that, but Miller was gone before he had found a convincing retort. The more he drank the less he liked it. Once or twice he referred to it, irritably. "Where does Bud get off with the claim that Clay Sanger is a better man than I am? I'm good as he is any day of the week. By golly, I'll show him if I get a chance."

As it happened, he got the chance inside of fifteen minutes. When he stepped out of the Cowboys' Rest Clay was strolling along the sidewalk toward him.

The Bar B Bar man gave a shout. "Here he is! The guy who aims to make a Sunday School out of Powder Horn. I reckon we'll have to show him."

Red dragged out a revolver and took a swift shot at one of the new posters pasted to a telegraph pole.

Sanger moved forward steadily. He did not hasten his pace, nor did he reach for a weapon.

"That's against a city ordinance, Red," he said quietly.

"Yeah, and what are you gonna do about

it?" the cowboy jeered, waving his gun. "Maybe you'd like to make something of it."

As he approached, Clay held out his left hand. "Have to ask you for your gun."

"You don't get it, fellow." McClintock backed away, to have room for firing if necessary.

"Don't point that hogleg[1] at me," Clay said easily, without stopping. "It might go off accidentally."

The Bar B Bar rider had reached the adobe wall and could retreat no farther. He tilted the revolver at Sanger and yelped out an order.

"Keep back, or I'll plug you sure." He was disconcerted by the fact that the officer made no attempt to draw a weapon. "I'm not foolin', Clay. Sure as you're a foot high I'll —"

The cowboy did not finish the sentence. By this time Clay was within striking range. His right fist lashed out, the weight of the body back of it, and caught the vulnerable point of the chin. Taken by surprise, McClintock could make no defense. His head slapped hard against the wall. Ineffectively he tried to raise the barrel of the revolver. At the same moment Sanger's left fist buried itself in the other's stomach. The Bar B Bar man was through.

[1]A revolver was often called a hogleg in the seventies and eighties.

His knees sagged and he went down to the sidewalk.

Clay did not stoop to pick up the forty-five of the prone man. Swiftly he turned to Red's companion. "I'll take your pistol, Jerry," he said, hand extended, voice low and even, as he moved forward.

"Where's yore gun?" Ault demanded, stepping back a pace.

"I didn't bring one," the marshal told him coolly. "No need of one, is there?"

He was still walking toward the other, not hurriedly nor hesitantly. Jerry flung an uncertain glance around. A dozen men were watching, but he got no help from their interested faces. None of them were taking a hand. It was not their rumpus. Ault backed into some of them.

"Don't crowd me, you doggoned fool!" he cried. "Go get a gun and come back."

"I don't want any gun — except yours," Clay answered. He was close now, and Ault read in his face that he was ready to strike. Jerry could not kill an unarmed man. Powder Horn would not like that. Nor had the Diamond K man time to get rid of his gun and prepare for a rough and tumble. Clay was too near for that. The cowboy flung up his left hand in a sign of surrender.

"All right. You win. Take it." He thrust

the sixshooter at the marshal.

Clay took it. He stooped down and gathered in the one belonging to McClintock, after which he spoke to the others present.

"Now, boys, we'll adjourn to the New York Emporium and check all weapons with Bowker, if nobody has any objections," he said crisply. "Please lead the way, Mr. Foley."

Foley owned and ran the leading corral and wagon yard of the town. He was a good citizen and backed the officer at once.

"He's right, boys. Guns are out and little kids going to school are in. We'll cache our cutters[1] as Sanger tells us to do. The only way to stop a marshal as game as he is would be to kill him. Jerry could have done it but he had too much sense. He did right to hand over his gun. I say, let's stand by the law."

One or two grumbled dissent, but the chorus of approval beat down the negative votes. The steadfast daring of the new marshal had won their liking. Most of those who carried weapons did so only because they felt it necessary to be prepared against bad men and drunken cowboys. They were glad to get rid of them if the rule was going to be applied impartially to all.

From the doorway of the Cowboys' Rest

[1]Another local name for a revolver.

Pete Maloney backed up Foley. He followed into Bowker's store the owner of the Texas Corral.

"I never did like to pack a gun," he explained. "Always was scared the darned thing would get me into trouble somehow. If Sanger goes on the way he has started I won't need one."

The others present trooped in after him.

Clay gave instructions to Bowker. "Have each gun tagged with the owner's name. We'll have a rack made later where visitors can check their pistols. In a day or two those of you who live here can get your weapons back to take home and leave there. All I'm asking is that you obey the law and don't wear them in town."

The marshal helped the dizzy cowboy to his feet. "Sorry I had to knock you out, Red," he told the man, "but you asked for it. I won't have men waving guns here."

"Who do you think you are?" Red asked belligerently, in an attempt to save face.

"I'm the law, and what I say goes in this town," Clay answered curtly. "Better understand that right now."

"Some folks get mighty biggity with a little authority," the puncher grumbled. "The Bar B Bar won't like this. You're just laying up trouble for yoreself."

"It will be my trouble, and I'll take care of it. Don't worry about that any more than I'll worry about whether the Bar B Bar likes what I do or not. I'll not arrest you this time, since this is a first offense. Fork your bronc and get out of town *prontito*."

"You better not arrest me," Red blustered. "And you can't drive me outa town either. Yore authority doesn't cover that. I've got as much right to stay here as you have."

Miller was moving rapidly down the street to join his chief. He had already heard that there had been trouble. Clay directed him to lock up McClintock. A dozen men were standing around to watch, and he had no objection to letting them know his policy at once.

"Red does not want to leave town but insists on staying," he said. "Suits me. We'll make him a guest of the city and sock a fine on him tomorrow. After you have put him behind bars go to Winters' store and send Frenchy to the Powder Horn Hardware Company. There will be a lot of fellows coming in to cache their pistols. See that they are all unloaded and put away."

Clay made a tour of the saloons and gambling-houses. The news of what he had done preceded him. At each place there was excited talk. Opinion was divided. A good many held that he had been lucky and that his success was only a fluke. Any unarmed man who tried to take a pistol from a drunken cowboy might get away with it once, but if he continued to do so he would end in Boot Hill with a gravedigger patting dirt over what was left of him. Others were enthusiastic about the sheer daring of this coup. But they qualified their approval with the feeling that after all Clay Sanger was only a run-of-the-range cowman. Most of the famous marshals in frontier towns had been killers who shot first and asked questions later. It took a good deal more courage to bring a culprit in alive than dead, since a shooting officer could set the stage for an occasional removal of a troublesome bad man. Sanger had made a brave start, but it was very unlikely that he could carry on as well. The town was full of unruly characters, some of whom would be sure to stand up to him. Clay would either wilt under the heat of danger or he would be killed.

The new marshal was friendly but firm. "Powder Horn is getting to be quite a town, boys, and all this shooting is driving away trade," he said amiably at the Bull's Head, one of the largest gambling places. "We have got a lot of good women in town now and some fine children. It's up to us to see they have the right kind of a place to live in. All good citizens feel that. I'm asking for your support, and I feel sure I'll get it."

The proprietor was a chunky Irishman named McGuire. He believed in an open town but one that was regulated and controlled. For he was clever enough to see that if conditions went on as they were Powder Horn would some day have a reform movement that would sweep away his establishment with the other gambling resorts.

"You've got mine," McGuire chipped in. "This is too big to be a rowdy camp any more. We ought to be past the man-for-breakfast days. If you can make this stick that will be fine with me, Clay."

That appeared to be the preponderant opinion in Powder Horn. The responsible element was back of Sanger.

"A long way back of him when trouble begins," Savage commented cynically after he heard the news. "I reckon we're going to find out about that." He sent for Rock Holloway and had a talk with him.

9. The Marshal Pistolwhips a Disturber

Clay walked slowly along the north side of the courthouse square. Most of the stores were one-story houses with false fronts and wooden awnings above the sidewalk to protect them from the summer heat. Occasionally a two-story building rose above its neighbors, a more pretentious edifice constructed of lumber instead of adobe.

The town roared with life, for it was evening. Every other establishment was a saloon or a gambling-house. Dance halls were not permitted on the square. In deference to the women and children of Powder Horn they were exiled to a segregated district across the railroad tracks. But the drinking-places were doing a rushing business. In them were merchants, bummers, miners, cowboys, stage-robbers, shotgun messengers, cattlemen, and crooks. Around the roulette tables the sheriff and his Chinese laundryman brushed shoulders. Mule-skinners, rustlers, cattlemen, and professional gamblers sat side by side at poker tables, stacks of gold and silver in front of them.

Into one place of amusement after another Clay drifted. Powder Horn was an open town. It was not his duty to interfere with games of chance or with drinking unless somebody created a disturbance. He noted that in obedience to the orders he had given nobody was openly wearing a revolver. His twenty-four-hour-old campaign had been unexpectedly successful up to date. But he did not need to be told that there were rocks ahead. Somebody would go on a bender and start trouble either on the streets or in some of these resorts.

A fox-faced loose-lipped man drew Clay to one side and gave him whispered information. He was one of the fools to be found everywhere who foment trouble by carrying tales back and forth.

"Thought you'd like to know that Rock Holloway is in town packing a gun on his hip. He's at the Trail's End. Says he doesn't aim to park his hogleg anywhere but where it's at." The little black eyes of the man were quick with excitement, in them an impudent slyness. But though he wanted to start something, he also wished to protect himself. "O' course I wouldn't want him to know I told you, Clay. I knew you wouldn't say anything about it."

Sanger looked at him distastefully. He was of no importance, a mean little scalawag who went about making trouble. But men of no importance wreck lives.

"Why are you telling me this, Gill?" the marshal asked.

"Why, I figured it was my duty, so as you can arrest him."

"All right. I'll do that. Since your sense of duty has mixed you up in this I'll appoint you my deputy. We'll go and arrest him together."

"Me!" Gill drew back, alarmed. "No, sir. I'm no gunman. This isn't any business of mine. I just figured, you being marshal —"

"Don't figure so much, Gill," Sanger told him, eyes and voice as chill as a windblown glacier. "If you ever come to me with another story I'll horsewhip you. Do you understand?"

Gill was shocked. "Why, Mr. Sanger, I didn't aim — I thought —"

"Don't think," snapped Clay, and brushed past him.

He knew he could not now escape an encounter with Rock Holloway, since he had been told the killer was in town openly defying the ordinance. The Diamond K gunman was waiting at the Trail's End for him. Gill would whisper it about that the marshal knew he was serving notice to arrest him if he dared. This would have to come to a showdown. Unless he could use finesse it would be trail's end for one of them, if not both.

Clay was a good fast shot with a revolver. He had carried for years a single-action long-barreled Colt's forty-five. Like most outdoor men of the frontier he had burned a good deal of powder practicing on telegraph poles and fence posts, usually on horseback and sometimes while galloping past. Nine times out of ten he could hit a quart tomato can flung into the air. But he had never seen the day when he could use a pistol like Rock Holloway. For Rock the price of life was eternal vigilance and a swift sure accuracy with a gun. The man was uncanny in his skill. There were a lot of legends about his shooting. He could send a bullet through the mouth of a bottle at fifty yards. At fifteen paces he could drive a tenpenny nail into a wall with three successive bullets. Some of the tales seemed to Clay incredible, but enough of them had been verified to make it certain that no ordinary good shot was likely to come out victor in a duel with him.

No doubt he had come to town to pick a quarrel with Clay, probably at the instigation of Savage. The only way for Sanger to avoid it would be to hole up until the bad man had left town. This he could not stomach. He hoped to have to live with himself a long time yet, and he could not do it with self-respect if he let himself be frightened into retreat after having publicly taken a stand.

But he did not intend to be foolhardy. If he could get any break in his favor he meant to take it. Before going to the Trail's End he made sure that his forty-five, which he carried in a holster under his left arm, would slip out easily without friction and without catching on his coat. He did not have to be told that it would be practically suicide to try to arrest Rock Holloway unarmed as he had done in the cases of McClintock and Ault.

The Trail's End was in a large false-front frame building. Between it and the adjoining hardware store ran a narrow alley. A side door opened from the alley into an unfinished room which was being prepared for private poker parties. The door was not locked, and Clay pushed through it into the building. He opened two or three inches a second door, one leading into the main saloon and gambling-hall. There were probably fifty men present, and from the room came a din of voices, shuffling feet, rattling chips, and the shuffle of cards.

Clay knew the lay of the land. A long bar was on the right. Behind it and closer to where he was standing were the games — roulette, faro, chuckaluck, black jack, and poker. Those not playing were watching the others, talking, or drinking at the bar. Among those with their feet on the rail were Rock Holloway and Niles Benton. The Diamond K foreman was haranguing Jim Dall. In the noise it was impossible to make out the words, but Sanger could tell that Benton was bullying Dall and that the ranchman was defending himself stoutly. Holloway watched them silently, amusement in his cynical sardonic face.

Sanger's eyes swept the room carefully. A Diamond K puncher was sitting at the poker table, his coat on the back of the chair, a big pile of chips in front of him. Another was flirting with Lady Luck at the roulette wheel. Beside him stood Sheriff Ballard. He was playing the corners with silver dollars. Ballard was a plump red-faced man. He had a bluff hearty manner of friendliness that was not quite convincing. When he laughed, as he often did, his pale blue eyes showed no warmth.

The marshal opened the door, passed through it, and walked swiftly toward the bar. He did not much like the lay-out, but he could not help that. If Rock Holloway chanced to turn his head, if some of the men milling about the room noticed him and shouted a warning, he knew that guns would smoke instantly. Fortunately Benton was intent on bullying Dall, and his companion was leaning back with both elbows against the bar listening to the tirade. As Clay's light strides carried him forward his right hand was under his coat, the fingers around the butt of a Colt's forty-five.

"You figured you could fix up a deal with that skunk Sanger to run his place for him while he hurrahed this town and that the Diamond K would sit back and stand for it," the foreman stormed. "Well, you got another guess coming, fellow. We're clearing out trash like him. He's nothing but a damn rustler, and I'd bet my saddle you're another."

"That's not true, Niles," Dall protested. "You know doggoned well I never branded a calf that wasn't mine."

"So I'm a liar, am I?"

The foreman's figure stiffened, but he pulled up short, struck by a ludicrous expression of amazement in Dall's face. The ranchman was looking past Benton at somebody approaching.

Swinging round, the big man let out a startled exclamation. "Goddlemighty, it's Sanger!"

Clay's revolver had flashed out and the barrel of it was pressing against the ribs of Holloway. "Don't move — either of you," the marshal warned.

The eyes of Rock Holloway, fastened on the officer, narrowed to slits of glittering light.

He was too wary, too experienced, to make the least motion. His elbows were still hooked on the top of the bar and his heel was on the rail. Clay knew he was considering his chances, making up his mind what was best for him to do. No doubt he was carrying two guns. After he got into action he could be throwing bullets in a fraction of a second. But he could not make the draw in time, covered as he was. It would be better to drag out the situation and play for a break. Sanger could read the man's thoughts as well as if they had been written out in front of him.

"What's the idea?" Rock asked, out of the corner of a sneering mouth.

"I'll take your guns," Clay told him. "No, don't move. I won't trouble you to get them. Benton, you had better reach for the roof. You look like you are being tempted to commit suicide. The bullets in this forty-five will plow right through Holloway and get you too."

Though the marshal's words fell with sharp decision, his mind was not at all easy. He had to concentrate his whole attention on the two in front of him. If Benton called for help the Diamond K men at the gaming tables could get him from behind. His hope was that they would not interfere. After all, his was not their quarrel. If they followed the code of the West they would keep out.

The foreman tried bluster. "You can't do this to me, fellow. I got a right to be here much as you have. Maybe you think you own this town. Maybe —"

"Don't talk," Clay ordered, a bleak blaze in his eyes. "Stick 'em up."

The hairy hands and wrists of Benton lifted slowly into the air.

From Holloway's tight mouth a threat dripped. "You're digging a grave for yoreself. Put up that gun. You're too big for yore boots."

Without lifting his gaze from his prisoners the eyes of the marshal picked out of the watching crowd the man he wanted. They rejected Dall, because he did not want to bring his neighbor into more trouble. They did not even consider Ballard. The one chosen was a cowboy he could trust, one with whom he had shared a tarp on several bitter nights.

"Jim, collect Holloway's hardware," he ordered.

"Don't you touch my guns, Prince," Holloway snarled.

"Get them, Jim," Clay said, very clearly but quietly. "If he lifts a finger I'll blast him to Kingdom Come."

Jim Prince stepped forward. He was a wild devil-may-care young fellow who had once had trouble with Benton. "You're the law,

Clay. What you say goes with me. Nothing personal, Rock."

The sheriff moved around the roulette table toward the bar. "Now look here, Clay," he objected. "Let's be reasonable about this thing. I reckon the boys will give up their guns peaceable if that's what is bothering you. No call to —"

"Keep out of this, Ballard," Sanger snapped. "I'll have no interference. Take the guns, Jim."

The sheriff hesitated. He was a man who habitually avoided trouble when he could, but he did not like to be dismissed so contemptuously.

"If you'll let me handle this I'll guarantee —"

Again Clay cut him short. "If I have to kill these men you'll be responsible for it, you fool," he said harshly.

"All right. All right." Ballard shrugged his shoulders and fell back. "If you're trying to make a big play, why go ahead."

Prince drew from its holster the revolver at Holloway's hip. At the same moment the killer's elbows slid from the top of the bar and he swung round to get the cowboy between himself and the marshal. Swiftly his hand traveled to the left beneath his coat. But not quickly enough. Sanger's right arm went up and down. The barrel of the forty-five crashed against the head of Holloway and he went down like a poleaxed steer.

Benton started to edge away, not sure what was in store for him. Clay's crisp command stopped him. "Stay where you are."

"Hold yore horses, Clay!" the sheriff cried. "Don't get excited. No need to kill Benton too."

"Go roll your hoop outside, Ballard," Sanger told him coldly. "You are not needed here."

"If it's my gun you want, I'll give it to you," the foreman said quickly. "No need to pistolwhip me."

"Get it, Jim," Clay told the cowboy. "Make sure he hasn't two."

"Sure." Prince grinned, not without malice. "Niles and I are old pals. He won't mind giving me his gun. Will you, Niles?"

"I'll remember this, Prince," the Diamond K foreman said angrily.

"Y'betcha. Hope you do. I remember when you drove me off the Twin Forks Range, claiming it belonged to your outfit. Yore warriors took a few shots at me as I skedaddled." Prince tossed a question at the marshal. "Don't you reckon, Clay, we'd better pistolwhip this bird too?"

"Not necessary," Sanger replied. He took

a pair of handcuffs from his pocket. "You might slip these on him, Jim."

Prince snapped them on the hairy wrists. "You'll know better than to come in again and try to hurrah this town while Clay is wagon boss here," he mentioned cheerfully.

Stooping over Holloway, who was beginning to show signs of life, Sanger drew from a holster under the man's left arm a forty-five Colt's revolver. This he passed to Prince.

"He was reaching for it when I slapped him down," Clay said, for the benefit of those crowding close to see.

"That's right," Dall confirmed. "He would have had you in another second if you hadn't cut loose at him."

"They are going to jail — both of them," Sanger announced. "They came to town to make trouble. Both of them knew the rule about gun-packing. Maybe a night in a cell will do them good."

Benton protested. He had been humiliated enough already without being flung into a cell like a common drunk. "I won't stand for that," he flung out. "Get a judge tonight to hear the case. I'll pay a fine if he socks one on me."

"We'll get him tomorrow, the same as we would for anybody else," Clay told him. "If you don't want to go to jail, don't break the law."

Sanger's decision was final. Five minutes later the two Diamond K men were walking down the street to the lockup. Scores of men watched them, with varying emotions. Many exulted at the discomfiture of the men from the big ranch. Even those who did not approve his summary action admired the courage of the marshal. But they knew this was not the end. The Diamond K would fight back. It could not let this defeat stand without losing prestige.

10. The Marshal Rides His Beat

During the days that followed Clay felt that he was a man set apart. Powder Horn was watching him, wondering what the outcome of this would be. All his life the people of the town had known him. He had gone to school here and earned the reputation of an unruly boy. Later he had ridden in often with a bunch of cowboys on a spree, and more than once had raced around the courthouse square firing his revolver into the night. Since then he had put away his rollicking youth, at least as far as such adolescent follies went. But unfavorable repute once gained dies hard. In the town were sober citizens not at all sure he had not rustled calves as a side line.

Clay found a wry amusement in the perplexed doubt with which he was regarded. They thought him a tough *hombre,* these citizens, and they were not sure what lay beneath his flinty hardness. Running as he had done with a group of untamed waddies, it had been difficult to guess whether he would go right or wrong. There was in him a reckless streak common to many who later drifted into outlawry. For the time at least he had elected to stand with rather than against the better element. But on the frontier a good many peace officers had at times curious affiliations with bandits.

Public opinion made a unanimous finding in favor of his nerve. Nobody without hardy courage would have dared to stand up to the bravos of the Diamond K, and nobody lacking efficient coolness could have emerged alive. Clay was no longer looked upon as just one of fifty slim brown riders ready to gamble away in a night the earnings of half a year. He was the man who had stood off a score of the warriors of Savage, had tonguelashed the big boss to his face; dragged to jail two of his most dangerous killers, and brought the offenders into court to have heavy fines imposed on them.

Clay did not fool himself. Though he walked his beat with a light easy stride, there was no assurance of safety in his heart. He was a marked man, condemned to death, but he must wear a face that betrayed no hint of panic. When he walked into dives to quell disturbances and bullets whistled past him, he was taking only the chances that his job required. What worried him was the vengeance of the Diamond K. Often his thoughts reverted to brave Tom Smith of Abilene, always cool and cheerful and friendly, facing death a dozen times as he walked the straight line of duty, and meeting it finally at a coward's hand. He wondered if it would be so with him. This was a lonely business, waiting helplessly for his foes to strike and unable to lift a hand to prevent it. In such a situation there was no fair play. He could not go out and attack them as they could him. All he could do was to watch warily until they made their next move. Meanwhile he had to keep his chin up, to ignore as far as speech and action went the fear that was always in his mind. For if he showed signs of weakening he was lost.

Sometimes he rode his beat on the buckskin he had brought to town with him. He had several reasons for this. One was that in case of trouble he could get to the scene of action quicker. Another was that on a moving horse he was less likely to be hit when men fired at him. A psychological motive also influenced him, though he would not have used that long word to describe it. In the West the man in the saddle was always more important than the one on foot. He was given more deference. Clay knew he sat a horse well, and he needed all the prestige he could get.

It was late in the afternoon of the second day after the adventure at the Trail's End when Clay rode slowly round the courthouse square and pulled up at the sound of shots. They came from the Silver Glade, apparently. He jumped his mount to a gallop, flung himself from the saddle, and ran into the gambling-house.

Ribbons of smoke streamed across the large room. Those not involved had fled or taken cover. The bartender had ducked behind his bar. Two men were crouched back of an over-turned table. Another was crowded into a corner, trying to make himself as thin as possible in order not to intercept any stray bullets. Of the combatants two were cowboys. They were firing at a third man, a gambler from Kansas City, known locally as the K.C. Kid. He had his back to the wall, and in his hand a der-ringer. Evidently he was wounded, for the arm with the weapon hung at full length and his body was beginning to sag.

"Stop firing," Sanger shouted. He caught one of the big brown men by the coat and flung him around.

He recognized the fellow, a former rider for the K L outfit, twenty miles up the river. Yorky he was generally called. Very few knew him by any other name. His companion was a lean lank fellow with a pockmarked face. He answered to the name of Chunk, for some reason. Both of them were thought to be rustlers.

"By golly, no!" Yorky cried. "He pulled a marked deck on us, Blue Blazes."

"Cool off, or I'll take a hand," Clay warned.

Chunk took another shot at the target sliding down the wall. The marshal fired, a wild aim to serve notice. Instantly the long cowpuncher swung his revolver on Sanger. The bullet ridged Clay's left forearm.

The answering slug from the officer's weapon plowed into the man's leg. Chunk gave a yelp and clapped a hand to the wounded thigh.

Yorky backed away. "Hold on, Blue Blazes!" he shouted. "I'm through."

"Drop your gun," Clay snapped.

The forty-five clattered to the floor.

"Line up beside your partner."

Protesting, Yorky moved over to the other. "Now looky here, Clay. Don't push on the reins. We're not lookin' for trouble — not a-tall. This guy is a tinhorn gambler, and he ain't on the level. He has done cheated Chunk and me outa seventy dollars."

"You butted in and shot me in the leg," Chunk complained to the marshal. "You might of killed me, and I was only trying to get my mazuma back."

"You're lucky I didn't." Sanger spoke to one of the men emerging from back of the table: "Get Doc White. There are some men

113

here need looking after."

Chunk slumped to the floor and sat down. The K.C. Kid was already on the floor. Blood ran down Clay's arm to the back of his hand. He wondered how serious the wound was. The slight faintness he felt might be only from the sight of the blood.

Frenchy came in with Doctor White. The place was beginning to fill up with curious onlookers.

"Take the K.C. Kid first," the marshal told the doctor. "He is probably hurt worst."

"How do you know he is? I may be bleeding to death." Chunk had the frightened look of one who did not know whether he was going to live or die.

"You'll have to take a chance on that," Sanger told him. "Frenchy, collect the hardware. These boys won't want it for quite a while."

The deputy marshal gathered the weapons. He noticed for the first time that his chief was wounded.

"Hurt bad?" he asked.

"I don't think so. Only a flesh wound. My guess is that the bullet just scratched me."

"I'll help you off with yore coat and take a look at it. Maybe we ought to stanch the blood with my bandanna until the doc gets to you."

Doctor White finished with the professional gambler and gave instructions to have him taken to the hotel where he lived.

"Will he make it?" Clay asked.

"Ought to, if there are no complications. Who next?"

Clay nodded at Chunk. "Take him. He's making a lot of fuss for a man who has only one little slug in his leg."

Yorky watched the doctor dress the wound. "If I get a wagon, would he be well enough for me to take him out to the ranch?" he asked. "Or had he ought to stay in town where he can get better care?"

"Better leave him here a few days where I can look after him," Doctor White answered. "Though it is only a flesh wound and ought to heal fine."

"You'll be able to nurse him in person, Yorky," Clay said. "I'll have you both put in the same cell and you can wait on him like a twin brother."

"You wouldn't do that to us, and him a sick man," Yorky objected. "Have a heart, Clay. We wouldn't of started a fuss if this scalawag hadn't been robbing us."

"You hadn't any business to be wearing your pistols. You're going to the calaboose. If the K. C. Kid dies it will probably be worse than that for you."

Sanger was a little better than his word. He allowed Chunk to stay in a spare room at the house of the jailor, where the wife of the latter could look after him and do any nursing that was necessary.

Captain Winters hurried into the Silver Glade while the doctor was tying a bandage on Clay's arm. The big baldheaded veteran of the Civil War was relieved to find the marshal no worse hurt than he appeared to be.

"I heard you was shot into a rag doll," he exploded. "I was all ready to hire me another officer. By jumping Jehosaphat, I'm glad they didn't get you any more than they did. What was it all about?"

The bystanders who had ducked for cover were anxious to get into the picture, and Clay let them tell the story.

"Fine," Winters pronounced. "That's what you are hired for, son — to stop all this gunfighting here in town. You did right. If these brush poppers with bad reputations think they can come here and hurrah the town we'll show them different."

"As long as your marshals hold out," Clay said dryly.

"I hear that these guys are rustlers," Winters went on. "So much the better, if that's the case. It shows we're against desperadoes, no matter whether they come from the big cattle outfits or from the fellows rustling their stock."

He walked out of the Silver Glade with the doctor and his patient. Clay pulled himself awkwardly to the saddle on the buckskin.

"I reckon I'll take this horse to the stable," he said. "So long as I have only one arm in service I'll make the rounds on foot."

"Take a week off, son. Go to El Paso or San Antonio till the arm heals. You'll feel better to get out of here for a spell."

Clay shook his head. "No need for that. I'll be all right. We don't want anybody getting the idea that I've been run out."

He gathered the reins and turned the head of the horse toward Foley's Texas Corral.

11. Deputy For a Day

Clay lay on his bed reading the Powder Horn *Sentinel*. The paper was a weekly, and it usually had some reference these days to his activities. He read that William Mannon, generally known as the K.C. Kid, was recovering from wounds inflicted by two cowboys called Yorky and Chunk, the latter of whom was also recuperating from a bullet sent by our efficient marshal Clay Sanger. Another local informed the public that though the marshal had been wounded in the performance of his duty he had not lost an hour's time. The *Sentinel* was glad to report that Sanger was now feeling quite well again.

It was between two and three o'clock in the morning. Clay had just got in from his night's work, having been relieved by Bud Miller. He yawned sleepily and dropped the paper, then came to instant attention. Somebody was soft-footing down the hotel cortidor just outside of his room. Sanger had a keen sense of hearing, a characteristic of most frontier men on the range. Whoever it was in the hallway had stopped not five feet from where Clay lay listening. Only the wall separated them.

Noiselessly Clay slipped from the bed and picked up his forty-five from the table. As he tiptoed to the door the knob moved very slowly. There was a key in the lock and it was turned. Probably no other room in the hotel was locked that night, but Sanger could not afford the sense of security that others had. If he succeeded in living at all it would be because he took precautions.

Swiftly he turned the key and flung open the door, taking care to have his body behind it. The man in the passage was Clint Black.

"What are you doing here?" demanded Clay.

"I came to see you," Black explained. "Wasn't sure which was yore room and didn't want to jump up the wrong man." He walked into the room, closing and locking the door behind him.

"What are you doing in Powder Horn? Thought you were clear out of this part of the country."

"No, I'm sticking around. Got some business to finish."

"Fool around here and the Diamond K will stop your clock," Clay told him.

Black showed a set of fine teeth in a sardonic grin. "They wouldn't stop yours, would they?"

Impatiently the marshal brushed that aside.

"I'm a peace officer, as you know. If you had killed Fleagle in town I should have to arrest you."

"Yeah, but I didn't." The rustler's smile widened. "Hell, fellow, you're one of those accessory-after-the-fact guys. You hid me overnight."

"You didn't come here at three o'clock in the morning to tell me that, did you?"

"No, sir. I came to tell that you aren't going to be a peace officer long, unless you watch where you are stepping."

Clay looked hard at him. "Meaning what? Spill it."

"I been hangin' around Bill Clemsen's livery stable. In the loft. He's an old sidekick of mine. I don't show up outside in the daytime. Tonight I was out seeing a friend, and I had just got back into the loft when I heard two fellows talking at the foot of the ladder. Their voices were right low. Naturally I took a grandstand seat and listened in. One of them was yore dear friend Niles Benton."

"And what did Niles have on his mind?"

"You. But he aims to get you off it permanently tonight."

"Tonight?"

"Somewheres between eleven o'clock and midnight you are to fold up."

"Interesting if true," Clay said lightly. "Tell

me some more."

"I didn't get it all. They would lower their voices and then raise them a little. But I picked up the general idea. There's going to be a lot of shooting across the railroad tracks, at Owens' honky-tonk. Just fireworks, to bring you down there on the run. After you get there they will wind up yore ball of yarn. The annoying Mr. Sanger will be rubbed out — bumped off — planted under the daisies."

"I wouldn't like that," Clay mentioned.

"Now knowing how you'd feel about it, I thought I'd drop around and let you know what a nice send-off they are fixing to give you." Black lapsed into murmured song, apparently apropos of nothing:

"Dry bones in the valley,
I really do believe;
Dry bones in the valley.
Oh, some of them bones are mine."

"Your idea is that I had better not be among those present?"

"Well, they can't exterminate an absentee, can they?" the rustler drawled.

"Not right then, but the obsequies might only be deferred." Clay considered that for a long moment, his eyes on the worn rag rug. "I wonder if I hadn't better take a hand since they have prepared the party for me."

Black watched the marshal, pretending indifference. "I wouldn't know." He offered another stanza of his song.

"Some come a-cripple,
Some come a-lame,
Some of them bones are mine;
Some come a-walkin' with a hickory cane,
Some of them bones are mine."

"I think that would be better, rather than disappoint them," Sanger said. "I might get there early and be the chairman of a welcoming committee."

"If you are figuring on shooting up a passel of Diamond K warriors I would be interested in taking a hand." The eyes of the hunted man had grown hard and bitter. He had dropped his make-believe of lack of interest.

Sanger shook his head. "No room for you at the table, Clint. The game is full."

"I'm kinda handy with a pistol," Black suggested, with ingratiating suavity. The eagerness back of it was apparent. He did not want to be left out of this.

"Too handy. No, I can't use you. I'm the town marshal, not a guy using his office to wipe out his enemies."

"You'll be hollering for help before you are

through. They are tough gezabos."

"So they are." Clay added by way of information, "I'm a little that way myself."

The self-invited guest sat on the bed and lit a cigarette. It was a small room and contained no furniture except the bed, one chair, a small table, and a stand upon which was a basin and ewer.

"You're one hard *hombre*," Black conceded, putting the sack of tobacco back in his shirt-pocket. "But these birds will come squirting out of Owens' honky-tonk so fast you can't count 'em."

"Maybe, but I still can't use you, Clint."

Black renewed his importunities. "What's the matter with me? You act like I got small-pox. I killed Fleagle. Sure I did, but he was shootin' at me before I fired my gun. It was neck meat or nothing with me. I'd like to get a couple of cracks at that outfit, one for you and one for myself. Maybe I could get a chance to square up some of what I owe you."

"Sorry, Clint, but I can't tie up with you this time. You ought to see that. This isn't a feud. I'm the law."

"The heck it isn't a feud!" exploded the nester, but still without raising his voice. "What else do you call it? They aren't plotting to pick you off because you are marshal but because you are Clay Sanger. It's personal as the devil. You're the gink that has made them all look like thirty cents. So they aim to collect you."

"That is their point of view," Clay explained. "But mine is different. While I'm marshal I haven't got any enemies. If a fellow breaks the law I go after him. If he doesn't I let him alone."

"Yeah!" jeered the man on the bed. "And you're gonna sit around until they bump you off."

"I hope not. Don't get me wrong, Clint. I'm mightily obliged to you for giving me this tip."

"Good of me, wasn't it? Since if it hadn't been for you I would be planted in Boot Hill." Black rose reluctantly to leave. "I hate to walk out on you, but it's yore say-so. Don't make any mistakes, Clay. You could be awful dead after making just one."

Clay had the rare temperament which pushes back until tomorrow the problems that do not have to be attacked today. He slept soundly until nearly eleven o'clock. Before he rose he had worked out a tentative plan of campaign.

He breakfasted at a Chinese restaurant, and after his deputies had joined him went over the program for the evening.

"How many of them will there be?" Bud Miller asked.

"I don't know. Plenty."

"Don't you think we might be a little seldom, just the three of us against that gang?"

"I'll pick up a couple more good men," Sanger told his assistant. "We don't want too many."

As Clay moved down the street a man on horseback flung a greeting at him. "Hi yi, Blue Blazes! I heard some tenderfoot croaked you."

"Exaggerated report, Jim. Get down off that horse and rest your saddle. I want to talk with you."

Prince swung lightly from the saddle. He was a curly-haired young blond, a man nearly always cheerful and gay. "You got no right to arrest me," he sang out. "I parked my pistol at Winters' store."

"Then you had better go get it. How would you like to be my deputy for a day?"

"What's there in it?" Prince wanted to know.

Clay looked at him, a smile dragging one corner of his mouth. "Maybe a slug in your belly. I can't be sure about that, though."

"Where's the war?"

"Can't go into that until you join up. Can't even tell you who the enemies are."

"Hmp! You're mysterious as hell, Clay. But I'm so doggoned inquisitive I reckon I'll have to throw in with you. Where do we start this rumpus?"

"Whatever fighting you do, if any, will be right here in town."

"You're the darnest hell-a-miler I ever did see." Prince grinned at his friend in delight. "Here you've got me with one foot practically in the grave and I don't know a thing about who I'm fighting or what for. How do you do it?"

Clay slapped him on the shoulder. "You're three-quarters Irish, Jim. When you hear of a fight you've got to get into it."

"No, sir. I'm an innocent bystander until someone crowds me. Like you're doing now. I get a day off to see the elephant, and soon as I get to town you drag me into yore army. Last time I was here all you asked of me was to take guns away from two gents who are sudden death. I reckon you're what Preacher Barnes calls an evil influence. Maybe you don't remember the time you got me to play hooky from school with you and go swimming, but I sure do. Old Simpson wore a hickory out on me."

"On me, too," Clay reminded him with a smile. "But you didn't take any persuading to go with me any more than you do now. I've a notion to cut you out of this."

"No, you don't. Not after inviting me in.

126

I reckon it's the Diamond K outfit again."

"Right first guess. I'm to be invited tonight to a little gathering where I'm to be killed."

"Did the invite say so?" Jim asked, his eyes dancing.

Clay explained how he came by his information.

Prince accepted the warning at face value. "Clint is all right. If he says he heard these buzzards plan this, why you can bet yore boots he heard 'em. Of course they couldn't guess there was anybody in the loft at that time of night. What's yore program, Clay?"

The marshal told him. The cowboy was dubious.

"It might work out the way you hope, or it might run into a shindig with heap many shot up. Never can tell." His boyish smile returned. "But it will work out all right somehow. You're sure a whole team with a mule colt following. Yore luck will stand up."

"Whether it does or not I've got to call their bet. Soon as the Powder Horn country decides that this bully-puss outfit is just a bunch of cheap blusterers, ready to pick on the weak but not game enough to go through to a fighting finish when the going gets tough, right then Savage is through being the high mogul of this district."

Down the courthouse steps two men came.

They crossed the street heading directly for Clay and his friend without being aware of who they were.

"Look who's coming," Prince said, with a tilt of his curly head to the left. Little devils of mischief were gleaming in his eyes.

Clay turned. His jaw tightened, so that a rope of muscle showed on his cheeks. He noticed that Niles Benton was limping a little. The man walking beside him was Rock Holloway. They were talking in low tones.

The marshal and Prince were standing directly at the intersection of the crossing and the sidewalk. When the others reached them somebody would have to step aside.

Jim murmured, "I'm rooted here."

"Sure," Clay said. "Right of pre-emption."

The Diamond K men pulled up. Benton spoke to Prince harshly. "Fellow, you're headed for trouble if you don't change yore ways."

"Good of you to take an interest in me, Niles," drawled Prince. "Not the first time you have."

"Don't get funny with me," the foreman warned. "I'm tellin' you to cut loose from this bird if you know what's good for you. Right now he's swollen up like a poisoned pup because he has had a little luck. Take it from me, it won't last. He's reached the end of his trail."

Sanger had no doubt that both the Diamond K men were armed, though no weapons showed. "I'm glad you have decided to support the law, gentlemen," he said ignoring what Benton had spat out. "Powder Horn offers the right hand of fellowship to you. All converts welcomed. While the lamp holds out to burn, the vilest sinner may return."

The icy eyes of Holloway fastened to those of the marshal. His lips were a thin cruel line. "Some fools never know when to quit talking," he said in a low voice, almost as if speaking to himself.

"Not now, Rock," the foreman interposed hurriedly.

"Why be impatient?" Clay asked. "Sometime when it is dark. Tonight maybe."

There was a question in Benton's staring eyes. Did Sanger know the program? Or was this a wild shot? He couldn't know. There was no way he could have found out, for outside of Savage himself only Rock and he knew the plan.

"Let's get outa here," Holloway told his companion sharply. "I've stood all of this fellow I can."

He brushed past Prince, the other Diamond K man at his heel. They disappeared into the Trail's End.

Prince watched them go. "In reverse that would be a good idea, the one about plugging a fellow in the dark. Only make sure it's the other fellow. If I were you, Clay, I'd lay for Rock and pour a load of buckshot into him. Sort of anticipate his good intentions toward you. You picked the right time too. I'd do it tonight if you get a chance."

"No." Clay shook his head. "Nothing like that. That's why I've been made marshal: to prevent things like that. I can't touch them until they make the first move."

"Hmp! They've made a dozen moves. You'll fool around until they get you, Clay. You've chosen a hell of a way to fight varmint like them. A man doesn't sit down in a den of rattlesnakes and wait for them to strike."

Sanger was not sure that his friend was not right. Black had given him practically the same advice. He knew that in a fight the best policy was to hit first as hard as he could. But he was no longer a free agent. The marshal of Powder Horn could not go around shooting men dangerous to his own safety. That had been Wild Bill Hickok's way, but it had not been the course followed by Tom Smith. And after all, Wild Bill had been killed by an assassin just as Tom had.

A sudden heat of anger pumped through

his veins. To hell with such a job. Why must he stay with it and be killed? Or if he did stick it, why not make the breaks as his enemies were doing? It would be a smart trick to let these scoundrels fall into the pit they had dug for him. If he rubbed out half a dozen of them so much the better. The country would be well rid of Benton and Holloway and a few like them.

But he knew he could not do it. He had to fight this out as he had started.

12. Shorty Talks Too Much

As the day advanced Diamond K men filtered into Powder Horn by groups of two or three. Before dusk fell Clay knew there must be at least a dozen in town. Very likely most of them did not know why they were here.

Just before dusk the marshal met two of these riders arriving. He was on Buckskin, and the men drew up to greet him. One of them was Shorty, the cowboy who had been wounded during the raid on the courthouse.

The thick-set, freckle-faced puncher grinned at him. "How you doing, Blue Blazes?" he asked, no animosity in his manner.

"All right, Shorty. Your leg good as new?"

"Well, almost. I favor it some. You been doing a good job, Clay. Wish I'd been present when you cut the combs of Benton and Holloway. One of those roosters crows too loud."

"Which one?" Sanger asked.

"Take yore choice," Shorty answered, refusing to be drawn.

"I'll choose Benton." Clay changed the subject. "A lot of the Diamond K boys in town today. Anything doing in particular?"

"If so, I wouldn't know what," Shorty answered carelessly.

The man with him, Justin Pagett, a hard case rather recently arrived from New Mexico, spoke for the first time. "We better drift along, Shorty," he mentioned.

Shorty gathered the lax bridle reins. "Suits me. So long, you old hell-a-miler. It you win out I'll throw up my hat for you."

"Sentiments like that encouraged at The Diamond K?" Clay inquired.

"I don't reckon they are. But the Diamond K doesn't own me body and soul. I'm not knocking the ranch; yet I'm still saying good luck to you."

As the two riders swung down at the tie-rack in front of the Trail's End, Pagett growled a warning at the stubby cowboy. "You talk too much with yore mouth, Shorty. It will get you into trouble one of these days."

"Yeah? Well, I reckon I can ride what trouble it will get me into," Shorty flung back. "What does Savage ask for thirty dollars a month? I got a lead pill in my leg on one of his jobs. That ought to entitle me to say what I think. If it doesn't, to heck with the job."

"You know where the ranch stands in regard to Sanger."

"Sure I know, but I don't take my opinions from Benton and the boss any more than I take my food from a baby's bottle. I'd as lief tell them what I'm saying to you, that Clay has guts and will go through. He's paid to hold the lid down on this town. He is doing it. Fine. I hate a quitter. If Niles doesn't like that he can lump it."

They pushed through the swing doors into the Trail's End.

"Niles said for me to send you upstairs soon as you got here," the bartender told them. "The room to the right."

The Diamond K men clumped up the stairs.

"You'll have a chance to tell Benton now all about yore noble feelings," Pagett sneered.

Shorty flushed angrily. He knew he had said too much, but he was not going to back down now. "I'll do that," he answered doggedly.

Three men were in the room — Savage, Benton, and Holloway. The owner of the Diamond K sat behind a desk checking names.

"Here are Shorty and Pagett now," the foreman said. "That makes ten here."

"Shorty wants to make a li'l speech to you gents," Pagett announced, maliciously.

Nothing could be further from the cowboy's wish. He had talked himself into a jam. All

134

three of these hard men hated the marshal for affronts he had put on them. They were in no humor to listen to dissenting opinions. Shorty knew he had to carry on, but the words choked in his throat. The color deepened in his freckled face.

"Seems he's quite a friend of Sanger," the man from New Mexico explained. "Would of liked to help him cut the combs of Niles and Rock."

"I never said that," Shorty blurted.

The bleak eyes of Savage fastened on the unhappy man. "Just what did you say?"

"Why, I — I said I hoped he could ride herd on this burg so as it wouldn't be so rampagious."

"What did you say about Benton and Holloway?" the ranch-owner demanded. "Come clean, you lunkhead."

The wide-brimmed hat in Shorty's hands was being maltreated by the puncher. "I reckon I said they had ought to obey the law," he muttered.

"Anything more?"

Pagett broke in with addenda. "Only that the Diamond K doesn't own him — and that he wished Sanger luck — and Niles and Rock crow too loud, so it was fine the marshal cut their combs. When I called him on it he said he would be pleased to tell you to yore faces, so I thought I would give him a chance."

"I said I wasn't knocking the ranch," Shorty explained hurriedly.

He knew he was in for a bad time. Benton and Holloway had said nothing, but he did not like the way they looked at him. Out of the corner of his eye he noticed that Pagett was standing with his back to the door.

"So you're not knocking the ranch that feeds you," Savage said, his face cold and cruel. "You're too big for your size, Shorty. You've forgotten that you are nothing but a white chip in this game, and I reckon we'll have to remind you of it. When I hire a man he belongs to me. I don't expect him to shoot off his mouth patting my enemies on the back. He's just one of the herd. I do the thinking. I express the opinions. If he takes my money and eats my food he backs every play I make and asks no questions."

Savage was speaking more to the others than to Shorty. If there was any incipient rebellion he wanted to quell it now. As to the one who had already given his view in criticism, the Diamond K boss had already made up his mind.

"When I find a two-timer in my employ I kick him out," he continued. "Give him his time, Niles, and see that he is run out of this part of the country."

Shorty was no coward. He had been over-awed by this hard-boiled aggregation, but now he asserted himself. "You got no right to run me out. I'm a freeborn American citizen, and I don't have to light out on yore say-so!"

The ranchman did not deign to answer him. Long years of command had made him arrogant. He picked up his hat from the desk and looked round at his subordinates.

"I have an engagement with Judge Tate," he said.

Holloway and Benton had risen with him. They were watching their victim, as dogs do a cat upon which they are ready to pounce.

"I'll get what's owing me tomorrow," Shorty said, and took a step toward the door.

"Don't hurry, Shorty," Rock Holloway suggested, his voice ominously low and gentle. "We want to hear some more of yore opinions."

"About how we crow too loud and need our combs cut," Benton added.

"I don't want any truck with any of you!" Shorty cried. "I'm leaving — right damn now. Lemme outa that door, you damn tale-telling teacher's pet."

"What's yore rush?" Pagett jeered. "You just got here. Stick around a while. You wanted to tell Niles this and that, and if he didn't like it he could lump it. Don't you recollect?"

Anger surged up in the squat cowpuncher. He was in for punishment anyhow, and he might as well stand up to it and save his self-respect.

"All right, I'll tell him and the rest of you what I think of the outfit," he broke out recklessly. "It's rotten from top to bottom. No decent man ought to work for it. I'm ashamed of myself for ever having done any of its dirty work. I'll have to spend the rest of my life living this down."

There was a moment of deep silence after the tortured man's defiance had died down. When Savage spoke it was to his foreman.

"No gun stuff," he ordered. "And be careful not to kill him."

Shorty said no more. Nothing he could say would help him. He let Savage walk out of the room without protest, aware that he was going to be beaten till his body was a pain-racked mass of bruises.

They stood around the luckless cowboy in a circle.

"Tell us some more, Shorty," Benton sneered. "We don't have to hurry. We've got all day to attend to yore case."

"Hop to it, you coward," the trapped man flung at him hardily.

"Just as you say." The foreman's fist lashed at the freckled face and left an ugly wheal on the cheek.

Shorty fought back as well as he could, but he did not have a chance. They came at him from front and rear. Their fists beat against his ribs, his head, and his stomach. When at last they hammered him down the heavy boots of his assailants struck at the prone body. Benton dragged him to his feet again. He was all but out, and he could no longer make any defense against the blows ripping into him. He lurched to and fro, and though they tried to hold him up in order to punish him more he sagged to the floor unconscious.

Benton kicked him in the side. "He's playin' dead on us," the big man yelped.

"Stand back, Niles, if you don't want to kill him," Holloway snapped. "He's had a bellyful."

"No, sir. It's possum stuff."

The other two had to drag the foreman from his victim.

They left the cowboy on the floor where he lay.

When Shorty came back to life he thought a hundred hammers were beating in his head. He sat up stiffly, and a bolt of pain went through him. Slowly, an inch or two at a time, he rose to his feet and clung to the desk for support. He was very weak and dizzy. Waves of nausea sickened him. Into a chair his lax body dropped.

A quarter of an hour later he went down the stairs and lurched up to the end of the bar. The man wearing the white apron stared at him. Not an inch of his face was free of a cut or a bruise. Blood covered his cheeks and the back of his head.

"Great mother o' Moses! Who murdered you, man?"

Benton looked up from the five cards he was pinching at a near poker table. "He ran against a door," the foreman explained, mean mirth in his face. "He was makin' a little speech, Pat, and he didn't notice it."

The eyes of the bartender came back from the pokerplayer to the battered wreck leaning against the bar. Swiftly he put two and two together. There had been a lot of stamping and shuffling on the floor above when Savage came down the stairs. The Diamond K boss had explained that some of his boys were wrestling and had added that if they broke any furniture it could be charged to him. Later his three men had descended, Pagett with a cut on his cheek. Pat asked no more questions. This was none of his business.

"Gimme a drink," Shorty said thickly.

A bottle and a glass were put before him.

He drank, then fished in his trouser-pocket and tossed a dime to the bartender. Unsteadily he walked out of the saloon. Every step he took, every motion of his body, racked him with pain.

The somnolent square looked exactly as it had half an hour before when Shorty had walked into the gambling-house. There were a few drifters on the streets. The same dog was hunting fleas in the alley. But in that thirty minutes the world had changed for him. He was no longer a jaunty cocksure top rider; he had become a broken down ruin a hundred years old.

Clay Sanger was standing on the courthouse lawn talking with Jim Dall. When he caught sight of Shorty he moved across the road to find out what was the matter with him.

"Stay with me, Clay, till I get to Doc White," the cowboy said. "I'm kinda sick and might keel over."

The marshal did not ask who had assaulted him. That could wait. He tucked an arm under the elbow of the range rider and helped to steady him as he walked. Doctor White was just leaving his office, but he went back to give the patient attention. Shorty was a distressing sight. Not only were his head and face covered with welts, cuts, and bruises; the kicks given his body had broken two ribs and left livid marks on the stomach.

After the injured man had been given such help as was possible Clay put his question: "Who did it?"

After consideration, Shorty said through his pulpy lips, "I talked too much."

It was a sufficient answer. Clay knew to whom he had talked and where. He knew too that Pagett had betrayed him.

"More than one of them jumped you," Sanger guessed.

"Three."

The marshal made another conjecture by deduction. "Benton would be one of them and Rock Holloway another. You're lucky they didn't kill you."

"Savage said no guns, no killing."

"I get it. Then probably walked out while they were working you over."

"Yes. He's a cold-blooded brute."

"Want the ruffians arrested now?"

Shorty shook his head. "No. I won't testify against them even if you arrest them. Maybe I'll get a chance to settle part of this myself sometime." He added, "Savage ordered me to get outa the country."

"And you're not going?"

A flare of spirit sparked in the eyes of the beaten man. "Not on yore life."

"You'll have to go to bed for a few days,"

the doctor said. "Any friends in town?"

"No."

"Money?"

"Four dollars and two bits."

"He can get the room next to mine at the hotel," Clay suggested.

"Yeah. And what will I do for mazuma?" Shorty asked.

"I'll loan it to you. Right now I'm flush. Can I borrow your buggy, doctor, to take him to the hotel?"

"Good enough. I'll fix up some medicine and be around in a few minutes. You'll feel better after a few days, Shorty. In a week you will have forgotten all about your wounds."

"I won't forget those that gave them to me," the cowboy promised.

As Clay drove to the hotel he caught sight of Pagett on the sidewalk. The man ducked hurriedly into the store he was passing.

13. "Have It Yore Own Way, Son"

Savage left Powder Horn in the late afternoon, his buckboard loaded with supplies for the ranch. He made almost a function of his going, taking pains to explain to Mayor Winters, in the presence of several others, that he had to get back to the Diamond K to see a cattle-buyer that evening.

From the doorway of the store Clay heard him with sardonic amusement.

"Fixing his alibi for what is going to take place tonight," the marshal said to his companion Prince.

"That's right," Jim agreed contemptuously. "He'll be roosting safe at home when the fireworks start, and if you get bumped off he'll be mightily surprised and distressed."

Sanger had just returned from the Trail's End, where he had been gathering information about the attack on Shorty. He sauntered forward just as the ranchman picked up a package of rivets he had bought.

"Want to see you about that brutal assault on Shorty three of your men made about an hour ago." Clay looked at his enemy with steel-cold eyes. His voice dripped scorn. "Most cowardly thing I ever knew. Three against one. Shorty says no arrests. But I want to serve notice that if he dies there will be plenty of arrests. Four of them."

A faint flicker of alarm disturbed the Diamond K man's insolent arrogance. "The fellow isn't going to die," he asserted, boldly enough, but with a mental misgiving. He could not be sure how far his men had gone.

"I hope not. They kicked in some of his ribs after he was down. There are bad boot marks on his stomach. May be internal injuries. If they have killed him, it's murder."

"He started the fight — brought it on himself," Savage snapped.

"How do you know?" Clay flung at him. "Had it started before you left?"

"That's what my boys told me. He jumped Pagett."

"Fix up a good story," Clay advised. "For if he doesn't make it this case is coming into court."

Savage flushed angrily, "I don't allow upstarts to talk that way to me. Get out of the road and let me pass."

"After I have told you that you are through, Savage. You've bullied this country a dozen years. You've put yourself above the law. God

145

knows how many evil deeds you have buried in the hills around the Diamond K. There won't be many more of them. You're coming to the end of that rotten crooked trail of yours. Better pull up while there is time."

The owner of the big ranch was shaking with anger. There were little dots of white around his nostrils, and in his eyes a hatred that would have struck this presumptuous interferer dead if possible. Without a word he pushed past Sanger, stepped into the buckboard, and lashed the horses to a gallop.

Captain Winters looked at the marshal, a curious admiration in the deep-set eyes under the bushy brows. "You've certainly spilled the beans this time, young fellow. I don't reckon Savage ever had anybody talk to him thataway before, unless it was the time you went over to his ranch to give him what for. Keep yore eyes peeled, boy, or he'll get you."

Sanger drew him into the store office. "The plan is to get me tonight," he said.

The mayor stared at him. "How do you know?"

Clay did not give Black away. He said that a friend of his, whose name he could not give, had overheard the plotters.

"In what way do they aim to do it?" Winters asked. The marshal outlined the plot.

"By golly, we'll show 'em about that," the

old buffalo hunter cried, his faded blue eyes snapping with excitement. "I'll get my old Sharp's seventy-three out and clean it. And I'll serve notice on those birds what to expect."

The young officer shook his head. "I don't believe that's the way to handle this, Captain. My idea is to let them go ahead."

"And wipe 'em out with a posse. That what you mean?"

"No. We don't want a wholesale killing. Trick them the way they meant to trick me."

"They meant to ambush you — not give you a chance for yore white alley."

"Yes. At the bridge, I reckon. There's a bottleneck there with the river on one side and a ravine on the other. Likely Benton means to have sharpshooters among the cottonwoods to pick me off as I come down. No, my idea isn't to drygulch them, but at the critical moment to let them see they are covered."

"How many men you taking?"

"Four beside myself."

"And there may be a dozen of them."

"They will be taken by surprise, and they won't know how many of us there are. It won't help the Diamond K prestige any for them to sneak away with their tails between their legs, especially when we put it in the *Sentinel* that there were twice as many of them as of us."

"That will be fine if everything goes well. But there might be a slip-up, just as there was in their plan. Better have some more fellows down there in reserve. No use taking chances."

"I'd rather not, Captain. My idea is to get this town and county laughing at Savage and his outfit. Soon as that happens he is just another busted balloon. He has thrived on fear — the fear that people had of his vengeance if they thwarted him or even opposed him in any way."

The old soldier stroked his long gray mustache. "Have it yore own way, son. This is yore show. But whatever you do, don't underestimate these warriors of Savage's. He has some good gunmen ready to fight at the drop of the hat. No use loading yoreself with the idea they are nice Sunday-School boys. They ain't. I'm not knocking what you've done so far. It's been great. All the same you have been lucky, son. If there's any law of averages you ought by rights to have been put in a pine box long before now."

"I've come to see that danger can be greatly overfeared," Clay said. "Walk into it, and it backs away. But if you run from it, it gallops after you. These bully-puss gunfighters are only men, just as I am one."

The oldtimer waved a hand testily. "All right. Handle it yore own way. But don't go and get yoreself shot up. I don't want to have to go hunt me another marshal just because you got hell in the neck."

Clay and his deputies patrolled the town as usual for two hours after supper. The drinking- and gambling-houses swung into their usual hectic night activity. Men milled to and fro on the courthouse square and in and out of the resorts. Among them were a number of Diamond K men. Two of them stopped at the entrance to the Silver Dollar Saloon. Bud Miller, in the shadow of the alley, heard one put a question to the other.

"Seen anything of Savage, Bill? He ain't been around for quite some time."

"I heard he had some kind of run in with Clay Sanger and lit out of town like the heel flies were after him," the second answered.

"I don't reckon he need worry about Clay after tonight. I wish Niles would get going and finish this job."

Miller looked at his watch. It was time for him to be starting for the rendezvous.

14. Guns in the Night

Hell's half acre lay across the tracks, a haphazard outcrop of vice that had grown up in the form of three sides of a quadrangle. The buildings were all of wood or adobe, two-storied, the lower floor occupied principally by the dance halls. In the daytime this settlement was given mostly to sleep until the middle of the afternoon. Its hectic life was at night. Those who lived here were outcasts. When the girls crossed the tracks to shop on the square no settler's wife or daughter ever spoke to them.

The marshal's little posse did not take the usual road to the Half Acre, nor did they go in a body. Clay wanted to attract no attention. Very likely a watcher had already been placed at the bottleneck below the bridge to check on the coming or going of any of the town's peace officers. The five men went singly by a trail which swung north of town through Langer's pasture and down a deep arroyo running parallel to the railroad. This arroyo ran out in a little draw back of Jack Owens' honky-tonk.

Clay was the last of the group to arrive.

The others had been there ten minutes before he appeared.

"Sure glad to see you, old Sure Shot," Prince told him. "We thought maybe they had changed their plans and collected you already."

"Not yet," Clay told him cheerfully. "I didn't want to leave too soon. As long as they saw me drifting around as usual they would feel everything was all right for them."

From the lighted hall there came to them the sawing of the fiddles and the clump of heavy boots on the floor. Most of the dances were squares and the cowboys liked to do them with vigor. Occasionally those hidden in the draw could hear the whoop of an intoxicated patron or the singsong voice of somebody calling a quadrille.

It was a cloudy night, with neither moon nor stars showing. Clay struck a match behind a bunch of cholla.

"Time to be going to our posts," he said. "Keep back in the shadows, boys, and don't make a move till I give the word."

A mule-skinner named Beck, the fifth member of the posse, answered for the rest. "You're the doctor, Clay. We'll wait for orders."

Each member of the posse moved to his appointed place. Five nervous minutes dragged away. Two men came out of a dance hall and ran into Prince.

"Hello, Jim! What you doing here?" one of them said. "Come in and join us."

"I will after a while, Buck," Prince answered. "I'm waiting for someone."

"Oh!" Buck showed a wise grin. "Hope she isn't busy with a handsomer man."

He and his companion departed, going back into the hall.

To the waiting men came the sound of horses clattering across the bridge. Shadowy figures emerged out of the darkness and pulled up at the hitch-rack in front of one of the dance halls. The riders scattered, some going into one honky-tonk and some into another. Benton strode heavily across the porch of Owens' place and went inside.

He beckoned to the proprietor to join him at the bar.

"One on me, Jack," he said.

They drank. It was apparent to Owens that the ranch foreman was already far from sober. He had been drinking all day.

"The boys are feeling a li'l frolicsome tonight," he said. "If you hear any shooting outside don't pay any attention to it. Just some Fourth of July stuff."

"It's all right with me, as long as they do their shooting outside," Owens said. "But you want to look out for Sanger. When he hears it he'll sure come busting down."

"Yeah, we'll look out for him," Benton replied, an evil grin on his ugly face.

The ranch foreman did not leave the bar to dance. He preferred to drink. A quarter of an hour later he walked out to the porch, drew a forty-five, and fired into the air. The Diamond K men came out of the dance halls like seeds squirted from a lemon. They followed the example of their leader and sent bullets crashing into the night. Some of them did not know what was the object of this exhibition, but they obeyed the orders that had been given them. The volley died away. A few stray shots followed.

"All right, boys," Benton called out. "That will be enough."

A bullet plowed into the adobe wall just back of the foreman and sent a scatter of dirt flying.

"Goddlemighty! Who did that?" he cried. "Someone shot at me."

A man stepped out of the shadows and stood at Benton's elbow. The big man ripped out a sudden startled oath. "Sanger!" he exclaimed.

"Yes, I'm here — with a posse ready to cut loose if necessary. Weren't you expecting me?"

"A posse?"

"Y'betcha!" The exultant shout came from the second-story window of a house set at right angles to the Owens' dance hall. "I've got a rifle trained on you, Niles. My job is to tear you in two if you go crazy."

"One of my deputies," Clay told the foreman. "You can have a slug in the belly if you want it."

The Diamond K men waited, watching Benton and the marshal. Some of them did not know what this was all about. Those who had been told knew that the plans of their boss had miscarried somehow. Instead of trapping Sanger he had trapped them.

"Where is this posse you're tellin' about?" a gunman demanded. "I don't see but two of you."

"Let them know you're here, boys," Clay ordered.

Guns roared from four different directions. To the Diamond K men it sounded as though a dozen weapons were exploding.

"Is this to be a fight?" Benton asked, his throat dry.

"Up to you, Niles. Take it or leave it."

Benton tasted again the bitterness of defeat. He had been a big man in the Powder Horn country, second in power to Savage. It had pleased him to be feared, to see men who did not like him take wide detours to avoid his bullying tongue and heavy fist. Alone of all those who knew him, this man Sanger had defied him, usually with an insolent and careless scorn rather than blustering anger. Hatred burned fiercely in the foreman. There was in him a brutal desire to turn his smoking gun on the marshal and see that slim strong body slump to the ground, all the life stricken out of it. His glance slid up to the man in the window with the rifle. The long barrel was still pointed at him. No, he couldn't kill Sanger now without paying the price of his own life. Moreover, the men of the marshal were under cover, in the heavy shadows of the buildings, and his were in the open where they could be mowed down.

"You tried to kill me," he snapped petulantly at Clay, and waved a hand at the adobe wall where the bullet had struck.

Clay did not correct him, though he too wondered about that shot. It must have come from the cottonwoods opposite, and none of his men were stationed there.

"What's it to be?" Sanger demanded sharply. "Do you fight — or run away?"

From the window Jim Prince laughed derisively. "Five dollars to a dollar Mex says he sneaks out of it!" he cried.

The Diamond K men still waited. It was for Benton to decide. They were good enough fighting gunmen, but they had no fancy for a battle with the odds against them. Thirty dollars a month was not pay enough to cover the risk.

One of them, nervous at the strain, yelped a question at their leader. "What's the idea of dragging us into a trap, Niles? This is a hell of a note. I don't want any part of it."

"Nor I," another shouted. "I'm pullin' my freight, Clay."

Another shot whistled from the cottonwoods.

A Diamond K rider cried, "Is this an ambush?" He was the man Yorky, the one recently arrested by Clay at the Silver Glade, taken on by Savage because of his bitterness toward the man who had humiliated him.

The foreman rasped out an order hoarsely. "We're gettin' outa here."

He ran for his horse, reached it, pulled the slip rein, and swung to the saddle. The cowboys broke for the hitchrack, in a panic of haste to get away. The horses plunged one into another. Men cursed, pushed, hauled, and tugged, trying to mount and break away from the milling crowd. One tore out of the mêlée and lifted his horse to a gallop, taking the road that led from town toward the Diamond K. This broke the jam. Others pounded through the dust after him.

One of the horses struck Yorky and flung him from his feet. His mount tore free and ran after the rest, bridle rein flying wild.

Yorky rose and turned snarling on Sanger. Panic had gripped him entirely. His revolver lifted.

"Don't shoot, you fool!" Clay shouted.

But Yorky was beyond reason. The bark of his gun sounded twice. The bullets crashed into the wall of the dance hall back of the marshal. Yorky's knees buckled and went down, the forty-five flying from his grip as he struck the ground. Prince had fired from the window above.

Already the thud of the Diamond K horses' hoofs had died away. Clay's deputies moved forward from the shadows of the buildings, and from the honky-tonks men emerged to find out about the shooting.

Sanger stooped beside the wounded man. "Sorry, Yorky," he said. "Hope you're not badly hurt."

"In the leg," the puncher answered sullenly.

"I fired low," Prince told Clay. "He's lucky I didn't kill him, since I had to shoot fast. The scalawag was pumping lead at you quick as he could."

"Much obliged, Jim," Sanger answered. To Yorky he said: "You asked for it. That was a darn silly business, cutting loose at me."

"I figured you meant to finish me."

"You are used to Savage and Benton standards. I'm a law officer, Yorky . . . We'll get you up town to Doc White soon as we can."

"What was the fuss about?" asked Owens.

"The Diamond K laid a trap to kill Clay," Prince explained. "They had men stationed at the bridge to get him when he came down to see about the firing. We heard about it and gummed up the plan."

Owens remembered what Benton had said, and knew it was true that he had meant to kill the marshal.

15. Pagett Calls For a Showdown

The guess made by Clay that Benton would place sharp shooters to ambush him just below the bottleneck at the bridge had been a good one. This was the logical place for an attack, since the cottonwoods along the riverbank spread here to the edge of the road. A man riding down to Hell's Half Acre could easily be shot from his horse.

Rock Holloway and Justin Pagett had been assigned the task of assassinating the marshal. Both of them were gunmen who had killed for money, and neither had any scruples about fair play. The five hundred dollars offered by Savage would be a pick-up. As soon as they had made the kill they would jog on down and join the other Diamond K men at the Half Acre. There might be guesses later that they had been involved in the murder, but nobody in the world could prove it.

Pagett was a dark large-framed man, bilious and vindictive in temperament, with a raking tongue that slashed out at others roughshod. He liked the odds to be on his side, as most gunmen did, but he had plenty of raw courage when occasion demanded. Among the riders of the Diamond K there had been a good deal of speculation as to what the issue of a difficulty between him and Rock would be if they ever became involved. The majority opinion was that in such an event Holloway would be the winner. He was more cool and deliberate than Pagett, and he had an Indian cunning that would, if he could make opportunity for a scene, set in his favor.

"Time we heard from Benton," grumbled Pagett, a quarter of an hour after they had taken their posts. "This waiting gets my goat. It always did. Gimme action."

"Take it easy," Holloway advised. "Right soon Niles will start the fireworks. We got nothing to worry about."

"I'm not worryin'," Pagett answered querulously. "Point is, when I've got a job of this kind to do I like to get it over with."

To them came the crash of guns from the direction of Hell's Half Acre.

"Soon now," Holloway said. "Most any minute Sanger will come rackin' along on that buckskin."

But he did not come. The minutes dragged. Another burst of gunfire sounded, and after a time a single shot.

"I don't get this," Pagett grunted irritably.

"That came from a rifle, and none of the boys are carrying one."

"Did sound like a rifle," Holloway admitted.

There was another stretch of heavy silence, followed by three shots fired almost together, the last one certainly not from a pistol.

"I'm gonna find out what's eatin' those birds down there," Pagett said decisively. "This ain't goin' according to Hoyle."

"All right," agreed Holloway. "You go down and find out. I'll keep watch here for Sanger in case he should come. Get word back to me what's doing."

Pagett went back to the riverbank where his horse was hitched and rode down the road. The distance was less than a quarter of a mile. He was annoyed, but not alarmed. Apparently Sanger had flung a monkey wrench into the machinery by not hurrying down to quell the disturbance. That was not like him. Since he had been marshal he had never avoided trouble but had got to the scene of it as quickly as he could. The bad man felt a vague sense of disturbance. The recollection of the rifle shots puzzled him. Maybe he had better look into this a little before he made a public appearance. He had come to a bend in the road, and just beyond that lay the plaza.

He guided his mount into the brush at the

side of the road and tied it to a sapling. While still in the chaparral he made sure that both of his sixshooters rested lightly in the holsters. Though he had no expectation of being called on to use one, as a matter of routine he made sure that no obstruction would interfere with the draw.

"Might as well be thorough while I'm at it," he muttered to himself, and cut across through the brush toward the settlement.

The detour brought him to the rear of Owens' dance hall. He went in by the back door, intending to pass through the hall to the plaza in front. The dancing had stopped. Several of the girls were grouped at the foot of the stairway talking excitedly. In the room were only two men, a fiddler and a bartender.

"What's wrong?" Pagett asked the musician.

"There's been a lot of shooting outside," the man answered. "I got a crick in my back an' I didn't go out. Far as I know there's nothing much wrong. The boss told us not to worry if we heard some guns go off. Seems the Diamond K boys have been getting roostered. I quit getting excited long ago at cowboys poppin' off outside."

"Just the Diamond K boys, eh?"

"I reckon. Benton was in here a while ago and gave Owens the tip-off. Said to let the girls know it wasn't anything serious in case his riders got to burnin' powder."

Pagett walked out of the front door and felt instantly that the set-up was not right. There were only three or four horses tied to each of the hitch-racks, and one swift glance told him they were not from the Diamond K remuda. A crowd of men and some girls were crowded around some object of interest, those in the rear trying to get a view over the shoulders of the others. But none of those he knew were of the party he had seen ride down here with the ranch foreman less than a half-hour since.

"What's it all about?" he asked, touching on the shoulder a cowpuncher who was standing on his toes and craning his head forward to see past those in front.

Without turning to look at him, the range rider answered, "A guy has been shot, but I dunno who he is or who did it."

The Diamond K man had a brain flash. His companions had found the marshal down here and killed him, and then had ridden away. A flare of anger spurted in him. Why had they not let him and Holloway know what they had done?

"The dead man wouldn't be Sanger, would it?" he drawled, from the corner of his thin-lipped mouth.

"Wrong guess," another man answered him curtly. "Clay is still going wide and handsome."

The killer slewed his head, to see Jim Prince grinning at him jubilantly. His stomach muscles tightened. His eyes narrowed and grew hard. Something had gone wrong.

"Where are Benton and the Diamond K men?" he asked.

"Dragging it for home hell-for-leather," Prince told him. "Clay put it to him he had to get out or fight — so he got out."

Pagett stared at him incredulously. "That sounds strange to me," he jeered.

"You ought to have been here, Pagett. You would have enjoyed the show. Looked like some of the Diamond K warriors would break their necks getting to their broncs."

"Yeah?"

"But of course two or three of you had to wait in the brush below the bridge — to get Clay as he came down," Prince added. "You couldn't be two places at once, could you?"

"Meaning what?"

"Wasn't that Benton's plan?" Prince asked innocently. "To raise a rookus down here and pour lead into Clay as he hurried down to see what it was all about?"

"Who says so?" the Diamond K man flung out belligerantly.

Prince kept his ironic smile working. "I was only asking."

The gunman glared at him. "If you're lookin' for trouble with me you can find it any time you like."

"Not now, Pagett. Get wise, fellow. The Diamond K has been frozen out of this game tonight — lost all its chips on a busted flush. Thing for you to do is to stick yore tail between yore legs and sneak off kinda inconspicuous."

Abruptly Pagett turned from him and shouldered through the crowd to the core of it. He saw Yorky lying wounded on the ground. Sanger had been giving him first aid and was rising from his feet.

"Who did this?" Pagett demanded.

Clay turned. The eyes of the two men met and fought, cold and deadly. The marshal guessed the truth, that the man had come down from the bridge to find out why the ambush had failed.

"How much did Savage promise you?" he asked evenly, his voice low and clear.

"I'm askin' a question," the Diamond K rider returned, snarling. "Who shot Yorky?"

"Never mind that," snapped Sanger. "Better fork your broomtail and hit the road. Your friends have quite a start on you."

Pagett settled himself on feet set widely

apart, his head thrust forward. "Who says I'm to beat it?" he challenged. "And what for? Do you own this town? Or are you just a hired hand paid to walk a beat?"

"Stay if you like — and be arrested for assaulting Shorty."

They faced each other, two hard strong men, their eyes crossing like rapiers. The light shallow gray ones of the killer were stone cold, in them a glittering deadly threat. But the gaze of Clay was as steady and confident as his own.

"You can talk big when you've got a bunch of deputies hanging close to back yore play," the bad man jeered. "If I had you alone, man to man, I'd make you look like thirty cents in nickels."

Sanger paid no more attention to him but busied himself looking after Yorky. Apparently he had put the gunman out of his mind contemptuously. A door had been brought upon which to carry the wounded man into Owens' dance hall. The marshal helped to lift him onto it.

"Gangway, gentlemen," he called.

The crowd fell back to let those carrying the door through to the porch. Pagett fell back slowly with the others, his eyes still fixed with hungry hatred on the officer who had faced him down. His vanity was hurt. Like most professional killers, he was jealous of his prestige. His reputation was an asset to make men fear him, to make them sidestep him rather than take any chance of trouble. No doubt it had often saved him the need of drawing his weapon. He could not afford to lose face. Yet he knew this was not the time to push his luck.

Some instinct told him he had better go, but he could not bring himself to leave. He watched Clay pass into the dance hall and stood back in the shadow of one of the buildings. He was not sure why he was staying. Perhaps on the off chance of getting a shot at his foe, perhaps only because his simmering anger would not let him go.

Doctor White arrived and hurried into the honky-tonk. Men drifted in and out of the door. Two cowboys passed near Pagett. He caught a snatch of their talk.

"The bully-puss warriors from the Diamond K sure did climb a tree when Blue Blazes cracked the whip," one said gleefully.

"Y'betcha!" The second man laughed appreciatively. "When Clay called his bluff Pagett wilted like Benton did. Sanger has certainly got the Indian sign hung on those guys."

Pagett raged. That was what they would all be saying, that he was a four-flusher who had weakened when the marshal faced him down. Pretty soon somebody would fling a challenge at him and he would have to kill the fellow to show others he was dangerous. It had to come to a showdown between him and Sanger someday. Why not now? If he got Sanger there was five hundred dollars in it for him. Just for crooking his finger. Afterward he could ride back to the ranch and collect, lying low while he saw how much fuss was going to be made about it. If it grew too hot he could light out for Colorado or Wyoming. He was a drifter anyhow, so that would not matter.

He walked back to the ambush ground below the bridge and found Holloway.

"What did you find out?" the latter asked.

Pagett told his version of the story. "I'm going back to get that shorthorn marshal," he concluded bitterly.

"Meaning now?"

"Right damn now. I'll show him he's not foolin' with Benton this time."

Holloway shook his head. "That wouldn't be smart, Jus, not when he has all those deputies around him. We'll get him sure. But there's no hurry. We'll pick the right time."

"I thought tonight was to be the right time," Pagett sneered.

"If somebody hadn't blundered," Holloway said, thinking aloud. "Looks like somebody talked. I wonder who."

"If tonight is the night it's the night," Pagett insisted obstinately. "I'm going back to do it now, no matter how many of his men are around him. We'll see if he has got me buffaloed."

Holloway slid a long thoughtful look at his companion. He had studied this man carefully. They were like two bull moose grazing the same range. Some day the Kansas City bad man, driven by vanity, would be likely to challenge his supremacy. Rock had sized up the man's strength and his weakness, knowing that if the test ever came he must make use of the latter to his advantage. Savage had once referred to Pagett as a man in a hurry, and the words had stuck with Holloway. The fellow was too impatient to wait. Delay made him restless and nervous. Some inner urge — an irritability that grew with any call for patience — pushed him to immediate action. Rock reflected that it might save him trouble if Pagett and Sanger fought. One of them would probably be killed. That would suit him, no matter which it was.

"Whatever you say, Jus," he said. "But I'm not taking any of it tonight. I guess I'll rock along and hit the trail for the ranch."

Pagett had asked no help from the other, but this cool desertion annoyed him. His sarcastic tongue lashed out at Holloway.

"Maybe this fellow Sanger has got other guys eatin' out of his hand. He may slap 'em dizzy with his gun and drag 'em off to the calaboose. But he won't run over me."

Holloway had started for his horse, but he stopped in his tracks. A direct insult had been flung at him. He said nothing until he had mastered the cold rage that ran through him. Why let Pagett's bitter biliousness drive him to foolish action? Not now, at least, when the man was about to take on the man he hated.

"I reckon you don't mean all you say, Jus," he said quietly. "If you do, tell it to me tomorrow when you're not so busy."

Rock backed to his horse, passed around it, and swung to the saddle. A moment later the drumming of the animal's hoofs sounded from the bridge. He was heading for the town.

A wave of deep loneliness drenched Pagett as he stood beside his horse, a foreboding disaster. He pushed it from him. After having declared himself, he could not back out. Pulling a bottle from his pocket, he swallowed a long drink, one of many he had taken during the past few hours.

He rode through the brush and fastened his mount by a slipknot to a young cottonwood facing the Half Acre plaza. When he left he expected to be in a hurry. Before moving forward he eased the revolver from its holster again and made sure his clothing would not interfere with the draw. Close to the porch of the Owens' dance hall, in the shadowy gloom to one side of it, he waited for his enemy to appear.

Men came in and out. Most of them did not notice him. One of those who went in was Bud Miller. Without appearing to do so, he recognized the motionless man standing by the wall.

Sanger was talking with Doctor White when the deputy drew him aside.

"Pagett waiting close to the porch outside," he mentioned. "Want us to drive him away?"

Clay thought a moment. "On which side of the porch?"

"Left-hand side as I came in. Close to the wall."

"I'll take care of him," Clay decided.

"Better let us handle this. Two or three of us. He's one tough *hombre*."

"No," Clay answered crisply. "My job."

"Hell! Frenchy and I are yore deputies. It's our job too."

"He's alone, isn't he?"

"Yes. Far as I could see."

"I won't need help."

Clay walked out of the back door. In the darkness he tested his weapon, made sure as Pagett had that the pistol would come clean.

His approach was almost noiseless. Pagett was still hugging the corner of the building, his gaze fixed on the front door. When Clay spoke, his presence was a complete surprise.

"Still sticking around, Pagett," he drawled.

Taken aback at the unexpected challenge, Pagett whirled. His eyes stabbed into the darkness and found the dim figure standing there. The gunman was at disadvantage, since he was in the circle of light flung out by the lantern over the door. But he did not wait an instant. His arm swung up and took the revolver butt with it. The roar of his shots sounded twice. Clay's answer boomed out a fraction of a second later.

Pagett clutched at the porch post, still firing. A bullet tore into his stomach. The arm around the post slid down as he began to slump. It fell away from the support and his heavy body plunged to the ground. A long silence followed the crashing of the forty-fives. Clay moved forward slowly, his gaze not lifting from the prostrate man. The prone body twitched, then all motion stopped.

Men came out of the darkness cautiously.

"Got him clean as a whistle, Clay," a cowboy said admiringly.

"He fired frst," Sanger answered, watching the lax still figure that a minute before had been so full of life.

"You bet he did," a witness answered. "And a hell of a lot of good it did him. You ain't hurt, are you, Blue Blazes?"

"No," Clay replied harshly.

Now that the crisis was past, a queer weakness stole his strength. He had never before killed a man, and the knowledge of what he had done made him a little sick. But it was important nobody know that.

Brusquely he turned away and walked into the dance hall.

16. Bad News

Savage paced nervously his cubbyhole of an office, three steps one way, three the other. Occasionally he looked at his watch. It was well past one o'clock. He opened the door and looked into the dark night. Except for the lamp in his office there was no light in any of the ranch buildings. Clouds scudded across a moonless sky. Far in the distance a coyote yelped. No other sound disturbed the silence.

Intently he listened, hoping to catch the drum of horses' feet crossing the bridge across Skunk Creek. His men ought to have been back before this, he thought fretfully. More than once he had gone the distance from town in a buckboard under two hours and a half. On horseback it would not take so long. What was keeping the boys? Had there been some slip-up?

He resumed his pacing, this time leaving the door open. A cynic at heart, he expected loyalty from no man. His riders would give him the service he paid for and no more. The only reasons he trusted Benton and Holloway on this job were that they hated the marshal and were being well paid to get rid of him.

Abruptly he pulled up, listening. He went to the door again. To him there drifted the clop-clop of hoofs on the bridge. Out of the darkness voices came to him, an oath, the creaking of saddle leather, the stir of men in the plaza.

Someone gave a raucous bitter laugh. "Go tell the old man what a fine job you did, Niles."

Savage did not go out to meet them. That would have been to betray his anxiety, and he never exposed his hand unless it was necessary. He lit a cigar, sat down in an armchair with his feet on another, and pretended to be reading a paper. He knew that Benton would bring him the news at once. Already he had a presentiment that it was going to be a tale of failure.

The long dragging stride of the foreman crossed the porch. The door was flung open. Savage looked up to see Benton glaring down at him.

"Some fool must have talked," the big man blurted out. "We didn't get him."

"Spill it," his employer told him, between clenched teeth.

"I did it just like you said," Benton replied defensively. "I put Holloway and Pagett below the bridge and rode on down to Hell's Half Acre. We pulled off the fake shooting and that damned Sanger came out of the darkness with the drop on us. His deputies covered every last one of us."

"Two deputies," Savage said, his words dripping sarcasm.

"A whole bunch of them. More than a dozen. We didn't have a chance."

"Forgot to take guns with you, I reckon."

Benton slammed a fist on the desk. "Don't ride me, damn you! Easy for you to sit here and sneer. I tell you they had the drop on us. A guy sat up in a window of Mother Skipton's place with a rifle trained on me. I couldn't lift a hand."

"What did you do?"

"Why, one of the boys yelled he wasn't gonna stay there and be killed. They broke for the horses. Nothing I could do but join them."

"Fine. Like the French king's army that rode up the hill and then down again."

"Put it any way you like. We were trying to do yore dirty work while you sat here reading a paper and smoking a cigar."

"Dirty work for which I was to pay you well," the ranchman answered coldly. He went on, his words sharp and biting. "You must have talked too much."

"I knew that you would put that on me. The boys didn't even know why they were there, outside of those you told."

"Maybe it is your idea that Sanger is a mind-reader," Savage told him, his voice rasping like a file.

"I dunno what he is," the foreman retorted sullenly. "Someone put him wise. Who was it? Could it have been Shorty?"

"Shorty didn't know a thing about it, unless you told him."

"Find out who told. You foozled this thing, then come back bellyaching, all your tails dragging. Are you just a lunkhead, Niles?"

"I carried out orders just like you told me," the foreman snarled. "I'd say Sanger was too smart for you."

"And too tough for you," his employer countered. "Send Holloway in to me."

"Holloway and Pagett didn't come back with us. We didn't take the road to town but the cut-off from the Half Acre." Benton came painfully to another item he would have liked to omit. "Yorky's horse broke away from him when he tried to mount. He didn't catch up with us."

"You left him there? Didn't wait to pick him up?"

"We didn't notice it right away. When we did it was too late." He added, because Savage was sure to find it out, "There was some shooting about that time."

"You had a battle and ran away," the Diamond K owner suggested.

"We didn't fire a gun. Some of the boys thought Yorky was blazing away. You can't prove it by me."

"I suppose not. You were probably in the vanguard of your brave army."

"Don't talk that way to me, Savage. I don't have to take it."

The eyes of the men clashed.

"So you don't have to take it," Savage said slowly.

The foreman backed up. "No sense in you talkin' to me thataway. I wasn't in anyways to blame for this, Bert."

"I'll have some of the men in here, one at a time," the ranchman announced. "I'll find out if any of them betrayed us."

Savage grilled two or three of them severely before he gave up as a bad job the attempt to fasten guilt on one of his riders. It would be possible for Sanger to have been down at Hell's Half Acre by chance, but he would not have a dozen deputies with him unless he knew what was about to take place. Somebody bad carried the word to him. There could be no doubt about that. And of course, unless the traitor was a fool, he would not tell on himself.

Hours later Rock Holloway reached the ranch. He brought more bad news. Yorky was lying wounded at the hotel in town, a prisoner of the marshal. Pagett had been killed in a duel with Sanger.

17. Effie Declares Herself

The story of that wild night was in the *Sentinel,* written as the events occurred but with some necessary elisions. The editor had gathered the facts from various sources. He had talked with Shorty, who knew only that the Diamond K riders had been brought to town, their weapons concealed, for some purpose not divulged to them. Prince had made his contribution to the account, as had several of those who had been observers of the trouble at Hell's Half Acre. Information from Clay had tied the details into a cohesive story.

The *Sentinel* did not tell who had given Clay warning of the plot to assassinate him. The editor did not know, for the marshal had kept quiet about that, but there was a hint slipped in suggesting that one of the ranch riders had double-crossed the foreman. In the story was a mystery man. Evidence showed that two horses had been tethered on the edge of the stream below the bridge. One of their riders no doubt had been Justin Pagett. The identity of the other was anybody's guess.

Effie read the story in the pergola at the end of their garden. She let the newspaper drop to her lap and went over the facts in her mind. Nowhere was the name of Savage mentioned, but she knew he must have plotted the ambush though his hand was not in it. Of late she had been seeing less of him and his friends. Her mind was made up now. She was of Clay's party all the way, and she would no longer play with his enemies.

Bluntly she told her brother so that night at dinner when he proposed a ride over to the Diamond K next day.

"No," she said. "I'm not going — ever again."

Stanley Collins helped himself to another steak and looked across the table at his sister. He was not surprised, for he had seen the change in her.

"Have you quarreled with Bert?" he asked.

"No. Why quarrel? I'm through with him. He's . . . evil, Stan. I didn't see it at first, but I know it now. He'll stick at nothing."

"You think he tried to have Clay Sanger killed. Is that it?"

"Yes. At least that's a part of it, the last straw. I tried not to believe he was so bad, but I'm convinced now he is worse than his men."

"There's no proof of it," her brother dissented. "Even if the story of the *Sentinel* is true, it doesn't follow that Bert knew anything about it. Benton hates Clay. So does Rock Holloway. They might have been playing their own hands and Bert know nothing of it."

The girl shook her head decisively. "You don't believe that any more than I do, Stan. Mr. Savage runs the ranch. He is boss. He didn't send a dozen of his hands into town with Benton unless he knew what they were going to do there."

Stanley pointed an accusing fork at her. "You've heard only one side of this story. No telling how much of it is true."

"It's all true."

"That's what you say. Your claiming it doesn't make it so."

"No, but —"

"Maybe Clay laid the trap for them." He suggested this doggedly, without any conviction in his voice. Effie knew that he was being driven back slowly to the point of view he had held before Savage and his friends had included them in their group. But he still had some doubt, still wanted to believe that the stand he had taken was right.

"You don't think the boy we used to play with is a murderer," she said.

"What's the use of calling names? In a fight of this kind men do things they wouldn't approve of under other circumstances. Say he killed a man, and let it go at that."

"In self-defense," she flung back, her eyes bright with resentment. "I won't let it go any other way."

"You don't know that."

"The *Sentinel* says —"

"I know what it says, I read it. The *Sentinel* is against Savage. Anything he does is wrong for Rayburn."

She would not have it that way. "You must have changed a lot if you think Clay Sanger tried to trap men to murder them."

"I don't say he did. Perhaps he didn't figure on having to kill them. Anyhow, I'd like to hear what Bert has to say about it."

He heard that evening. Savage dropped in on them, on an excuse that he had brought a book for Effie.

"Thought you might like to see it," he said. "When I was in Denver last month everybody was reading it."

Effie told him, a little stiffly, that she was afraid she was not going to have much time for reading.

The Diamond K man knew that of late she had been drawing away from him. He did not need to be told that she was out of sympathy with what he had been doing to get rid of Sanger, the leader of the small stockmen opposing him. His eyes fell on the latest issue of the Powder Horn newspaper. He decided that the best defense was a bold attack.

"Of course you have read that scurrilous story about the Diamond K in the *Sentinel*," he said scornfully. "Rayburn ought to be tarred and feathered for publishing it."

"You mean it isn't true," the girl replied.

"No, it's not true. Sanger deliberately murdered one of my men and wounded another. Drew them into a trap. He'll try to sneak out under cover of law, because he is marshal. That's an old trick, for bad men to be appointed marshals in order to destroy their personal enemies."

Effie sat very straight in her chair, eyes fixed steadily on the visitor. The force and arrogance of the man had dominated her for some time, but she knew that his power over her was gone. She did not any longer want to please him or even to stay friendly.

"Clay Sanger isn't a bad man," she said, a challenge in voice and manner. "Nobody can tell me that he tried to trap men to kill them. It just isn't true."

"Justin Pagett is dead — shot through the heart by this man," he answered stiffly. "Call it what you like. The fact stands."

"I call it self-defense. That's what the witnesses say."

"His friends — rustlers, loafers, scalawags — banded together against the big ranches which have made this country prosperous." He flung out a gesture that brushed the small fry from the map. "What they say or think does not matter. All of them hate me because I'm strong and don't stoop to flatter them."

She knew other reasons why they might hate him — his brutal disregard of their rights, his overbearing pride, the ruthlessness with which he trod down those opposing him. But she did not care to go into that, since if possible she wanted to break their relationship without a quarrel. Almost they had become engaged. Now she was shocked at herself for having been so allured by what he had to offer. All she wished was that he understand she was no longer tempted.

Stanley was called out of the room by one of his cowboys who wanted to get a twenty-dollar advance on his next month's wages to send to his mother in Nebraska.

Bert Savage drew his chair nearer to the sofa where the girl sat sewing. He took in for a moment silently the soft loveliness of the dark head and the flowing lines of the light body. She was a girl who had adventured not far into life, but back of her innocence he sensed fires and passions not yet known even to her. He had a sudden sense of stilled pulses followed by a clamor of the blood. This was the woman he wanted. He felt that she was escaping from him, and a flameless anger burned in him. His arrogance resented her withdrawal. Though he did not go so far as to think of himself as King Cophetua and of her as the beggar maid, he never forgot that what he had to offer was position and power any woman ought to snatch at gratefully. He would have liked to let her know that she was a fool, but he was aware that was not the way to advance his prospects.

"Let us not quarrel about this scoundrel, Effie," he said. "He is only a show-off breezing along on a little luck that won't last. I know you knew him when you were children. That doesn't matter now. Forget it. He's gone bad."

She looked at him steadily, the light of battle in her eyes. "He isn't a scoundrel, and he hasn't gone bad. You think that anybody who opposes you must be wrong." Her feelings swept her away. "I think he is right in this all the way. He stands for law."

A dull flush beat into his face. "If he is right I must be wrong," Savage answered angrily.

She did not flinch from the conclusion. "I think so."

He rose from his seat, white dots of rage around the base of his predatory nose. "I suppose it is my fault that he wounded me and my foreman while trying to kill us, and that he shot down three of my men, one of whom I buried yesterday."

"I don't want to quarrel with you," she told him. "But we might as well face the fact that we can't be friends. We can't travel the same road. I made a mistake trying to think that we could."

"Why can't we? Because of this fellow Sanger?"

"Because you don't believe in the rights of other people. You think if they are weak you have a right to trample them down. That isn't our American way. At least it ought not to be."

He caught her by the wrist and pulled her up from the sofa. An arm went round her waist and dragged the girl close. He tilted back her head, to look down into the defiant eyes that met his furious ones.

"Listen!" he cried. "I'm going to marry you and knock all this silly nonsense out of your noodle. I'm not going to let you make a fool of yourself over this scamp. As soon as it can be arranged he'll get the punishment he deserves. If you are going to waste your sentiment it will be over a dead man. Don't forget that."

"You've tried to destroy him already," she flung up at him. "I know how bravely you send your assassins out to murder him. Maybe you'll succeed, and I'll hate you all my life. I wouldn't marry you if you were as rich as Jay Gould and as powerful as the Czar. I detest everything you stand for."

Her brother stood in the doorway, amazed at the violence of both.

"Why all the fireworks?" he asked.

The arm of Savage fell away from the waist of the girl. She turned to face Stanley.

"He has just done me the honor to tell me that he is going to marry me, whether I want to or not, but first he is going to kill Clay Sanger so as to make me a happy bride," she cried.

"The little dumbbell is in love with Sanger — or thinks she is," Savage retorted.

"If I am it is strictly my own business," Effie said, color high in her cheeks. "All you need to know is that I'm not in love with you and wouldn't marry you if you were the last man in the Powder Horn."

"Cut out the fussing," Stanley interposed. "That's no way to talk, Sis. If Bert has asked you to marry him he is entitled to a decent answer. Sanger doesn't come into this at all."

"All right. I'll give him an answer." The girl stood up, straight and slender, her head held high on the slender neck. "No — no — no!"

"You're going to change your mind," the

Diamond K man told her curtly. He set his teeth, to hold back the volcano churning in him.

"Never!" She threw the word at him as if it had been a weapon.

"We'll see about that."

Savage snatched up his hat and strode out of the house. A few moments later they could hear the beat of his galloping horse's hoofs.

Effie turned to Stanley, her face ash-colored. "What have I done?" she wailed. "Why did I have to drive him away, with another reason for killing Clay?"

She turned, sudden tears welling into her eyes, and ran upstairs to her room.

18. Savage Holds a Conference

Savage had no intention of accepting the decision of Effie as final. It had been the habit of his life to get his way, and he meant to do it now. He knew that the sentiment of the community was against him. Even the other big ranchmen, though in a measure they followed his leadership, disapproved of his violent lawlessness. He guessed that some of them were pleased at his discomfiture.

He never wavered in the determination to rub out Clay Sanger, but he realized that after the latest fiasco the time was not yet ripe for that. It would be better first to disgrace the man if possible. The fellow was vulnerable. As a lad he had been wild. Some of his early friends had swung away at a tangent from line-riding to brand-blotting. It ought not to be hard to smear his reputation. If she was persuaded he was a rustler Effie might draw back from him.

The owner of the Diamond K called on Newbolt, the county attorney he had been largely instrumental in nominating. Sheriff

Ballard was taken into conference with them. The two officials were not enthusiastic in support of Sanger. They realized that any action they might take against the marshal would not be popular.

Ballard shifted uneasily in his seat. " 'Course we would like to please you, Mr. Savage. You know that. Anything you ask we would do if it was anyways reasonable. But you got to remember that this town is hotter than mustard for Sanger right now. All of what you would call the best citizens are backing him. Don't get me wrong. I don't like him a little bit. He's a show-off. Still and all, Powder Horn is for him. You can't get around that."

"He's made plenty of enemies, hasn't he?" Savage snapped.

"Sure, and two friends for each enemy. Isn't that right, Newbolt?"

"Afraid it is," Newbolt agreed. He would have liked to complement his assent with a word about the unpopularity of the Diamond K, but he decided it would be better not to try the brittle temper of Savage too far.

"Point is," the sheriff went on, "that folks have got it in their nuts that Clay wasn't to blame for the shooting at the Half Acre. It would be a mistake to arrest him for killing Pagett."

"What you mean is that you haven't enough sand in your craw to arrest Sanger," the ranchman charged bluntly.

The red face of the sheriff grew darker with anger. "What's the sense of talking thataway?" he asked. "What I'm telling you is that it is bad policy."

"I'll be the judge of that," Savage retorted sharply. "I want him arrested and tried."

"He'll be acquitted," Newbolt told him.

"That's right," Ballard agreed. "It won't buy you a thing. His friends will get a great kick out of yore defeat."

"I'm defeated before the fight begins, am I?" the Diamond K man asked testily.

"Look at the facts," insisted the sheriff. "Too many witnesses saw Pagett outside Owens' place ready to blast Sanger. Too many watched him draw and fire first."

"I can get witnesses who will tell another story," Savage said. "And I can prove that from a kid he has been a brawler and a troublemaker. He'll be smeared with plenty of mud before I get through with him."

"What good will that do?" Newbolt wanted to know.

"I'll prove he used to be a rustler, and not so long ago either."

"By good witnesses — men who aren't prejudiced?"

"By better witnesses than his rustler friends."

"Even so, that will not hurt him." Newbolt shrugged his shoulders, a wry smile on his saturnine face. "The good people will like him better because he is a brand snatched from the burning. I've noticed how popular repentant sinners are. There's something likable about this fellow. I reckon it's his dash — or his cool hard nerve. If you were to prove he was a rustler it would not hurt him with a lot of his admirers. They would say he had reformed and bygones were bygones."

Savage was not thinking of the public, but of one member of it. He wanted to discredit his enemy in the eyes of one girl.

"It'll be the way I say," he announced with decision.

Benton walked into the office of the county attorney. "Heard you were here. I been down at the depot. Tate tells me that bull you're having shipped didn't come in on the afternoon freight. It will sure be along tomorrow he claims." The foreman rolled a cigarette, lit it, and glanced from one to another of the seated men. "Hope I didn't interrupt," he said a touch of jealous sarcasm in his heavy voice.

"Doesn't matter," Savage told him. "I'm giving orders to have Sanger arrested for killing Pagett."

"What good will that do?" the foreman said derisively. "He'll be out of the calaboose again in a few hours."

"I'm not asking for your opinion," his employer answered coldly. "I'm telling you."

"Suits me," Benton responded sulkily. "You're the doctor. If that's the way you want to play it, fine. But it doesn't make sense to me. The proper medicine for that guy is a lead slug in his belly."

"How about making the arrest today, Ballard?" the ranchman asked.

The sheriff did not relish his job. He did not know how Sanger would react to this move, and he was sure that even if he pulled off the arrest successfully the town and county would resent his action. But he was under obligations to Savage and expected further favors. "All right," he assented, plainly because his hand was forced. "But I think you are making a mistake."

"It will be my mistake, then," Savage cut back, annoyed at his unwillingness.

"Yeah, and I'm the guy that will have to pay for it," Ballard complained. "But that's all right, I reckon. Have a warrant sworn out, and I'll bring him in. Then about twenty of our best citizens will bust a trace in their hurry to sign a bond to get him out."

Savage rose and looked at his watch. "Six-fifteen now. He'll be coming down from the hotel about this time to start his night's work.

Might as well get him now as later."

"Order him to reach for the sky, Ballard, and if he doesn't get 'em up *prontito* pump about four bullets into him quick," advised Benton.

"Not me," demurred the sheriff. "I'm no killer, and I don't aim to start any gunplay with that bird. I mean to talk him into it, after I have broke it to him easy. He's got sense enough not to raise a rookus when I show him the warrant."

"I still think my way is the best," the foreman sneered. "Plug him first and then arrest him."

"If you would like to be appointed deputy and try yore way —" Ballard began, and let the rest of the sentence hang a question.

"You'd like that, wouldn't you, Jim?" In Benton's heavy voice a jeer rode. He always enjoyed seeing another man in a difficulty. "But you're sheriff. I'll let you go ahead and make a rep. All I'll do is watch from the side."

The sheriff said, an edge of sarcasm in his words: "Too bad I can't get you to handle this, Niles, because I know if you did everything would be jake. You've certainly made Sanger climb a tree every time you have bumped into him."

"I'm not through with the guy yet!" Benton cried with an oath, black anger in his face.

"Stop your scrapping, boys," Savage ordered, and led the way from the office. "And let Ballard alone, Niles. I'm telling him to arrest Sanger, not to kill him."

Benton followed his chief, an evil grin on his face. "I expect it would worry you a lot if somebody shot Sanger to rag dolls," he said.

"Politics is a rotten game," Newbolt said in disgust after the Diamond K men had gone. "Sanger may be a rustler for all I know. He is certainly bull-headed and rambunctious. But I'd rather be on his side of the fence than to be tied up with these two buzzards."

The sheriff agreed with him.

19. A Shot in the Night

Clay dropped into his favorite Chinese restaurant for supper and ordered a steak, fried potatoes, and coffee. He was well through his meal when Sheriff Ballard stepped into the eating-house and gingerly took a chair opposite the marshal.

"How are things coming, Clay?" he asked, most amiably.

Sanger decorously concealed a smile. He was amused, for he knew Ballard had not joined him because he liked his company. The sheriff always appeared a little uneasy in his presence. Perhaps he did not actively dislike the marshal, but he did not feel comfortable with him.

"Can't complain," Clay said, and called for another cup of coffee.

"Kinda nice weather we've been having. Not too hot for this time of year. 'Course we could do with some rain."

That he was making talk because of an embarrassed difficulty in getting to the point, Clay knew just as well as if it had been printed on his breast. Sanger was in no hurry, and he rather enjoyed seeing the man flounder.

"Had supper yet, Jim?" he asked.

"Yes, I just finished."

"Better have a cup of coffee with me?"

Ballard said, to make time, "Don't mind if I do."

The coffee was hot. He swallowed too large a mouthful, burned his mouth, and made a painful face before he could get down the liquid.

"Fact is, Clay," he began at last, "I got an unpleasant job to do."

"We all have sometimes," Sanger agreed, and asked no questions.

"I hate to do it, and I said flatfoot I thought it was a crazy idea. But it's up to me. I got to serve a warrant for arrest on a man who won't like it."

Clay's cool eyes rested appraisingly on the man. He could guess upon whom the warrant was to be served, but he did not give the sheriff any help. Ballard could worry awhile, since he was serving Sanger's enemies.

"Most generally fellows don't like to be arrested," he said, glints of mischief in his eyes. "Sometimes they drag a gun out and go to smoking."

"No occasion for that," Ballard said hurriedly. "This is a friendly sort of an arrest."

"Better be sure he understands that," Sanger replied, deviling the other. "From the way you talk I gather this is a pretty tough *hombre*. You can't tell what he'll do, especially if he gets excited. Maybe you had better take two or three deputies along with you." Clay came to an afterthought with apparent innocence. "Or do you want to deputize me to help you get him?"

"No-o. That's not it. Fact is — I don't want you to get sore at me, Clay, seeing the warrant was given to me against my wishes — but the fact is I got a warrant for you."

"For me? Well, doesn't that beat the Dutch! Perhaps I could arrest myself and save you the trouble." Clay finished his piece of dried apple pie before he made inquiry as to cause. "What the dickens have I been up to, Jim?"

" 'Course you can get out on bond," Ballard said apologetically. "No trouble at all about that. Looks to me like this is just a kind of formality, but Savage thinks —"

"Oh, Savage thinks," Clay interrupted. "He has pointed a finger at me and you trot up nice and obedient. Well, what does Savage think?"

"He has sworn out a warrant to have you arrested for killing Pagett. I told him there was no sense to it. All the witnesses are on yore side. But you know how bull-headed Savage is."

Sanger leaned forward and fastened a hard and steady gaze on the man opposite. "What's back of this, Ballard?" he asked. "Is this another trap? Are three-four Diamond K men waiting in some alley to riddle me as we pass it?"

"No. Clay. Nothing like that. I swear to heaven there isn't. He couldn't make me a party to such a thing. His idea seems to be to throw mud at you so folks will lose confidence in you."

"How can he do that on such a trumped-up charge? Several witnesses saw the whole business. Pagett was waiting to kill me. He drew and fired first. You know that."

"I told him so, but he's hell bent on having his own way. Nothing I can do about it."

Seated at the next table were Red McClintock of the Bar B Bar and Mike McGuire, owner of the Bull's Head gambling-house. They had been surprised to see the sheriff sit down opposite Clay, knowing that he did not feel friendly toward the marshal, and they had heard the conversation between the two men.

McGuire rose and walked over to the adjoining table. "Forty men in this town will be glad to go bail for you, Sanger," he said. "I'm one of them."

"Much obliged, Mike," Clay said. "I'll sure call on you if necessary. This is some of the Diamond K dirty work, but it won't get Mr. Savage a thing, as far as I can see."

"I don't want to hurry you, Clay," the sheriff said, "but any time you are ready I expect we had better mosey along. Just so this will look right, maybe you had better give me yore pistol."

Sanger smiled, a little grimly. "No, I don't think so, Ballard. I'll keep the gun handy in case I might need it tonight."

"All right, if you don't trust me," the sheriff answered, with some annoyance. "I'm trying to make things easy for you. It's not my fault I have to serve this warrant. I might have done it in a whole lot more unpleasant way than this if I had wanted to make you sore."

"It's some of your friends I have in mind," Sanger told him. "They are a little quick on the trigger, and if they thought I didn't have a gun with me their fingers might get to itching."

"They say everything comes to a guy who waits," Red McClintock chortled. "It wasn't so long ago you flung me in the calaboose. Now it's yore turn, Mr. Marshal."

"So it is," Clay assented lightly.

"They socked me twenty-five dollars. Maybe you won't get out so easy."

Sanger did not bother to answer that triumphant bit of repartee.

"I'm ready, Ballard, whenever you are," he said.

The two officers walked out of the restaurant together and turned toward the courthouse square.

"We'll stop at Winters' store for a minute," Clay told the sheriff. "I want to see him."

Ballard consented. He was glad enough to have the marshal submit to arrest without making him any trouble. There was no harm in humoring him a little. No doubt he wanted to arrange with the mayor about getting him released on bond.

Winters was sitting in the store talking with some oldtimers, his chair tilted back against the counter. "Hello, son!" he called out, with an attempt at humor. "You haven't arrested our sheriff, have you?"

"You've got the reverse English on it, Captain," explained Clay. "He has arrested me."

The old Civil war veteran suspected a joke, but gave up that thought after one searching look at Sanger and another at Ballard. "What's the idea?" he asked.

Ballard told his story smoothly, taking care to make it plain that personally he disapproved of the arrest but was as an official helpless to avoid it.

Winters mopped his bald head with a bandanna hand kerchief. "Savage can't get away with it," he snapped out promptly. "Not in this town while I'm mayor. I'll have you out inside of two hours, Clay."

"That will suit me," Sanger replied cheerfully. "I haven't been worrying about it."

"Well, don't you!" Winters roared, the light eyes in his red face snapping angrily. "We'll show the Diamond K right now where it gets off."

"It looks as if Savage was slipping when he pulls a trick as silly as this," Clay said. "He used to do better than that."

"I see you are still packing yore gun," the mayor mentioned. "You look pretty pert for a fellow arrested for murder."

"The sheriff is letting me keep my side arms," Clay responded, grinning. "Just in case."

"He's scared this is a frame-up to have him shot," Ballard protested. "He'd ought to know me better than that. I'm sheriff of this county, and I'm not in cahoots with anybody to have citizens ambushed. If he has any other notion he is crazy. Far as keeping his gun goes, that's all right with me. But I notice that when he arrests anybody he's mighty particular to strip him of his weapons. I reckon that is a horse of another color."

Sanger cocked an eyebrow whimsically at the sheriff. "I'm still marshal, Jim. Maybe on the way to jail I might have to quell some kind of disturbance. You never can tell.

You're going to take me to the calaboose and lock me up. Isn't that enough?"

"Let's go, then." Ballard was irritated at Clay's gay derision. He took himself and the job seriously and he did not like to have his dignity ruffled.

"I'll be seeing you in an hour or two, Clay — soon as I can get this fixed up," Winters called after them. "This is a nice how-d'you-do. The fellow that ought to be arrested is that scalawag Benton. He is responsible for Pagett's death, and not you."

The sheriff and his prisoner crossed the square and turned down Texas Street. As they passed the Bull's Head Shorty Pierce and Jim Prince came out of the gambling-house. The face of Shorty was still a map of bruises from the beating he had been given.

"Hello, Blue Blazes," he called. "Where you headin' for in such a hurry?"

"The sheriff is taking me to jail," Clay said.

"Quit loading me, fellow, I ain't the kind of a guy that buys wooden nutmegs."

"Cross my heart," Sanger assured him. "Ask Ballard if you don't believe me."

"What for?" Prince asked.

"For killing Pagett."

"Great jumping Jehosaphat! He was fixin' to bump you off, wasn't he? His gun was smoking before you let him have it."

"Mr. Savage isn't quite satisfied," Clay explained.

"So that's the way of it." Shorty glared at the sheriff. "He has given orders to his hired men to attend to yore case. Like he did with me. Only a licking won't be enough for you, seeing you have made his whole bunch of four flushers look like plugged nickels."

"Ballard promises it isn't to be that way."

"He promises, does he? What good would his promise be after you have had about fourteen buckshot plunked into yore back?"

"That's no way to talk, Shorty," Ballard reproved severely. "I'm not an assassin."

"Say," Prince cut in, "why don't I get into this jam? I was in the posse and wounded Yorky. I want to be arrested too."

"All right," the harassed officer flung out. "Swear out a warrant against yoreself. I'm just doing a job, one handed to me against my wishes. Eyerybody acts like I started this. What in Mexico have I got against Clay? Not a thing. No sense in you fellows getting on the prod."

"That's right," agreed Clay. "He's just obeying orders."

"Whose?" asked Prince.

"A gent by the name of Savage." Clay's smile was grim. "Don't obstruct the law, boys. I'll be seeing you later."

"We'll push along with you and see you don't stumble on the way," Shorty announced.

"No, boys. I don't need an escort. Ballard is all right. He wouldn't lead me into an ambush . . . *Buenas noches.*"

"No harm in us making sure," the squat cowboy insisted.

"Do I look as if I needed a nurse?" the marshal asked. "Nothing doing, Shorty. Much obliged, but — no thanks."

His friends gave way reluctantly, because they knew it would annoy Clay for them to insist.

"Something about this I don't like," Shorty said, watching the two vanish into the darkness. "I've a notion to follow them. But hell's bells! Every man has a right to say how he wants his hand played!"

"That's right," Prince agreed. "We can't baby Clay. He won't stand for it."

The sheriff and his prisoner left Texas Street to take the road leading to the jail. It had been opened recently and brush still pushed close to the edge of the narrow road. Clay did not like the density of the chaparral. It would make ideal cover from which to ambush a passing man. The jail building loomed up in the starless gloom, a dark mass about twenty-five yards in front of them. The ground was a little more open on the left side of the path, and Sanger crossed in front of the sheriff to take that position to protect himself against possible drygulching. He did not distrust Ballard, but there were probably others who knew he was to be arrested.

A moment later he knew that his unease was justified. From behind there came the crack of a revolver. Clay swung round, dragging out his weapon. The slap of running feet sounded on the road. He caught sight of a shadowy figure vanishing in the darkness, took aim, and fired, not with the expectation of scoring a hit but to discourage further attack. His first thought was to race after the man, but a groan from Ballard stopped him. The sheriff was staggering forward like a drunken man, his body twisted with agony. He stumbled as if his foot had struck an obstacle, and plunged to the ground.

Clay ran to help him, just as the front door of the jail was flung open. A man moved toward them, the jailor Mark Atchison. Behind him came a tall gaunt woman, his wife. What the Atchisons saw was the sheriff lying on the ground and Sanger advancing toward him, smoke filtering from the barrel of the revolver in his hand.

Jane Atchison was a woman of the frontier, one who had met danger without flinching many times. "Why did you kill him?" she demanded.

Clay pushed his weapon back into its holster. "I didn't, ma'am. Someone shot him from behind — came out of the brush beside the road. I had just moved across to Ballard's left. The fellow must have meant to get me." He knelt beside the wounded man. "Jim isn't dead. We'd better carry him into the house."

They did so, and laid the wounded man on a cot in a downstairs room. To all of them it was plain that the life was ebbing out of Ballard. It would be a question of only minutes.

"Run and get Doctor White," Jane told her husband. "Hurry, Mark."

The jailor looked from his wife to Sanger. He hesitated to leave her alone with the killer.

"Don't be scared," she told him sharply. "I've met murderers before. They only shoot from behind."

"I'm no murderer, madam," Clay protested. He took the forty-five from its scabbard and put it on a table beside Mrs. Atchison. "If you'd rather I would go for help, Mark —"

"Mark will go," his wife decided. Already she was busy trying to get the coat from the dying man's back.

"Try to slip his arm out of the coat," she ordered Clay.

Sanger knew that at last he had walked into real trouble. He would be accused of shooting Ballard in the back. And it would be impossible to prove his innocence.

20. "Any Friend of His is an Enemy of Mine"

Dall turned in to the Collins place from the road and yelled, "Hello the house!"

From the house Effie came out to the porch and said, "Hi yi, Jim!"

The fat ranchman was an old friend of the family. He had dandled the girl on his knee when she was a baby. "Doggone, I wish I wasn't married. I'd give some of these young galoots a run for their money, Miss Effie. You sure get prettier ever day."

"Nice of you, Jim. It's too bad you are so happily married. A man would be crazy to divorce Bess Dall. No girl could ask it."

"That's right." He met her derisive friendly smile with a wide grin. "I'll have to make out the way I am, I reckon."

Stanley Collins joined his sister. " 'Lo, Jim," he said. "We need a rain mighty bad. You didn't meet one on the way down from the hills, did you?"

"No, sir, I didn't." Dall eased his plump body in the saddle and settled himself for talk. "Say, Stan, have you heard about the trouble

Clay Sanger got into last night?"

It seemed to Effie that the blood drained out of her heart.

"What trouble?" her brother asked.

"He's in jail for killing Sheriff Ballard."

Something inside the girl tied itself into a knot, a cold tight shuddering tangle of fear. She waited, her very being suspended.

"For killing Ballard," Stanley repeated. "Why did he do that?"

"Nobody knows how the trouble rose exactly. Ballard had arrested him for the Hell's Half Acre business and was taking him to jail." Dall rubbed a calloused hand along the crisscross wrinkles at the back of his neck. He was greatly disturbed at this development and he did not understand it. Clay did not seem to him the kind of man to go crazy and kill a law officer for such an inadequate reason. But maybe there were extenuating circumstances.

Effie's voice came in a croak that she did not recognize. "Are they sure it was Clay did it?"

"He claims he didn't, that someone came outa the brush and shot Ballard from behind."

"From behind?" the girl echoed.

"Right spang in the middle of the back."

"Clay didn't do it!" Effie cried. "Not that way. He couldn't shoot a man in the back."

"That's how it looks to me," Dall agreed.

"Trouble is that Mark Atchison ran out from the jail and saw Clay standing over Ballard with a smoking gun."

Stanley asked a question. "What does Sanger say about that?"

"Says he fired at the killer as he was running away."

"Of course that's what he did!" Effie cried. "Clay just couldn't do such a thing. I'm as sure of that as that I am alive."

"I don't get this, Dall," said Stanley, his forehead furrowed in a frown. "The coroner's jury decided Clay killed Pagett in self-defense. Two or three witnesses said so. Why was Ballard arresting him for that?"

Dall flung out a fat hand disclaiming knowledge of the reason. "Folks say Savage is back of it. Looks to me like there is dirty work somewhere."

Effie was white to the lips. "Of course there is. Anybody but an idiot would know that."

"It's hard for me to swallow any story about Clay shooting Ballard in the back," Dall said. "He must of known the sheriff was just obeying orders. But it certainly looks bad for Clay. When he was arrested by Jim he wouldn't give up his gun — said he might be needing it a little later."

"Of course he had to keep his gun," the girl explained, "since he had so many enemies ready to kill him. If Clay says he didn't do it, then he didn't. That's all there is to it."

"Except that he is locked up charged with murder," her brother differed. "Who told you about this, Jim?"

"I just got back from town. I never did see a place so excited as Powder Horn. Naturally everybody is talking about this. The sentiment is against Clay, account of Ballard being a kind of inoffensive bird and him being plugged in the back. But I think you're right, girl. There's something back of this we don't know."

"Of course there is. It's Bert Savage." Effie had a dreadful feeling of life closing in on her. She felt that his enemy had trapped Clay to his ruin.

"Let's wait till we know more about this," Stanley reproved. "Let's not accuse anybody until we are sure, Sis."

Effie turned on him, a little wildly. "Do you think Clay would shoot Jim Ballard in the back for no reason?" she demanded.

"No," he answered. "I think there's some shenanigan about this, but I don't know what it is yet. I'm going to town soon as I can get off."

"I'm going with you," she said.

They were just leaving in the surrey when Savage rode into the yard. "I've just heard about this dreadful business of Sanger murdering Ballard," he told them. "I can't think what in the world made him do it."

Effie looked straight at him, her slim body erect and her eyes a fierce challenge. "He didn't do it. Some of your ruffians did it."

"Don't talk that way," Stanley warned. "You don't know who did it. All we know is that Clay didn't shoot the sheriff in the back."

"I'm afraid there is no doubt about it," the Diamond K owner replied gravely. "He was caught in the act, his gun still smoking."

"Because in trying to defend the sheriff he had fired at his assassin," the girl flung back. "Nobody who knows Clay will believe he is guilty of this. You don't believe it yourself. You know better. It's a trick to destroy him."

"A trick?" Savage said, his cold face set like a block of cement. "You can't trick a man into committing murder. The fellow is a killer. Why fight against it?"

"You've got him wrong, Mr. Savage," Stanley replied. "I'm no friend of his, but Clay is no killer. The only man he ever shot to death was Pagett, and he was forced to do that."

"I see," sneered Savage. "You've gone over to his side — decided to throw down on your friends."

The younger man flushed angrily. "I reckon

214

I ought to have been on his side all the time. You go too far for me, Mr. Savage. I don't hold with you that anything you do is right just because you do it."

"What do you mean? Are you claiming that I killed Ballard?" the Diamond K man demanded. He was holding in his brittle temper by an effort. His fingers gripped the pommel of the saddle so tightly that the knuckles stood out white and bloodless.

"I don't know who killed him," Stanley answered. "I'm going to town to see Clay and get his story."

"Any friend of his is an enemy of mine," Savage told him curtly.

"I'm not an enemy to you unless you make me one," Collins said.

"This is a fight to a finish. You can't straddle a fence. Either you are for me or you are against me. Take your choice."

Stanley's eyes were bright with defiance. "You won't get anywhere trying to bully me. I'll do what I think best."

He took the whip from the socket and touched the flank of the near horse lightly.

Savage watched them go down the road, his furious eyes barometers of the rage churning in him.

21. A Horse at Foley's Corral

A bombshell dropped on the courthouse square could not have stirred up more excitement in Powder Horn than the killing of Ballard. It was a blow to those who had been looking to Clay Sanger for leadership against the dominating influence of Savage. They had felt that he was a bulwark for law and order. The shooting of Pagett had been justified on the ground of self-defense, but no such excuse could be offered in the case of the sheriff. He had been murdered in cold blood.

The story Sanger told of an unknown assassin firing from ambush was too improbable for acceptance except by the minority who knew him well and were friendly to him. The majority rejected it as a fabrication made up by him to escape punishment. His reputation in earlier years was against him, as was also his known opposition to the political group with which Ballard had been associated. Though the town had supported him after the trouble at Hell's Half Acre, what Sanger had been forced to do there was now used against him. Once a killer, always a killer. So men said. Moreover, the evidence against him was strong. Atchison had caught him bending over the sheriff, a smoking gun in his hand. Mike McGuire and Red McClintock had testified, with evident reluctance on Mike's part, that Clay had refused to give his weapon to Ballard on the ground that he might need it later. The prosecution felt it had an invulnerable case, though the coroner's jury had returned a verdict specifying no killer by name.

When Winters called at the jail to see Clay after the killing he brought with him a young man Sanger was surprised to see, Stanley Collins.

Collins was embarrassed and blurted out without delay the object of his visit. "About time you and I stopped this foolishness and shook hands, Clay," he said impulsively. "Of course I know darned well you didn't shoot Jim Ballard in the back. Effie asked me to tell you she wouldn't believe it if half the county testified against you."

Stanley's words warmed the heart of the accused man. He held out his hand and gripped that of his restored friend.

"I'd rather have you two on my side than anybody else in the county," he said.

"You'll need all the friends you can get," Winters told him bluntly. "You've certainly got yoreself into a jam, boy. If every angle had been fixed up by an enemy to make it look bad for you it could not have been done better."

"Maybe that is just what was done," Clay said.

"You mean they killed Ballard so as to make it look like you did it?" the mayor asked.

"Might be that way, but I don't think so," Clay answered. "Remember that it was right dark. Whoever was waiting in the brush could not see too well. When he slipped out for his shot he might have mistaken Ballard for me. I had crossed to the other side of Ballard after we passed where he was crouching. Or he might not have aimed straight. We must have been fifteen yards from him or more. So he got the wrong man."

"Could be," nodded Winters. "But it is going to be hard to show any set-up like that. It's a lot easier for folks to believe that you dropped behind him and plugged Ballard in the back. Atchison's' story is damning. He almost saw you do it. And there is backing for it too, because when Doc White and the boys reached the jail one cartridge in yore sixshooter was empty."

"I took a shot at the assassin as he was running."

"Hmp! Pity you didn't hit him. If a dead

man had been found there yore story would stand up fine."

"You didn't recognize the fellow?" Stanley said. "Didn't have any idea who he was?"

"No. He was just a shadow in the distance." Sanger turned to the mayor. "You sound as if you needed a little convincing yourself that I didn't shoot Ballard, Captain."

"No, sir. I'm convinced some of Savage's skunks did it. I was just pointing out the argument folks are using. If you had gunned Benton, say instead of the sheriff, there wouldn't have been any complaints to speak of. But Ballard was a kind of a decent old coot, not a bad sort even if he did let Savage use him to pull his chestnuts out of the fire. And he was shot in the back. It's a doggoned nasty business to be charged with, especially when you are not guilty. We've got to find the man who did it."

"Unless he was seen coming or going I don't know how we can do that," Clay said. "Can you learn by making inquiries whether the Diamond K men were in town?"

"Savage and Benton were here Thursday. They may have left before the killing. I can probably get the time they left. Of course Savage did not do this himself."

Clay did not look at Stanley, but he felt a little awkward about discussing Savage before him. "Collins is rather friendly with Mr. Savage," he suggested to the mayor.

"Forget that," Stanley said, flushing. "We've broken with him. He's too ruthless for me."

"Glad to hear it," the old soldier said brusquely. "Time has come when a good citizen has to take a stand. Savage is a menace."

They talked of ways and means to bolster Clay's case. One of these was to check up on Benton and Holloway's whereabouts at the time of the killing. So far as was known Holloway had not been in town, but nobody had seen the foreman leave either before or after the shooting.

"He brought his horse to town," the mayor said. "It's still where he left it at Foley's corral. That's queer. Where is Benton? He hasn't been seen since. Did he somehow sneak back to the ranch? If not, where is he holed up at?"

"Why should he be holed up anywhere?" Collins asked. "His name hasn't been mentioned in connection with this."

"That is what I would like to know," Winters went on. "One thing is a cinch. He didn't ride to town and then walk home."

Clay's eyes narrowed in thought. "Benton might be the man who killed the sheriff, meaning of course to get me. He would know

Ballard was arresting me, and he could have hid in the brush and waited for us. But if he had been the fellow he would have hurried back to some saloon to build up an alibi, unless there was some reason why he couldn't show himself."

"What kind of a reason?"

"I can think of one reason. My bullet might have hit him."

"By thunder, you've got something there, Clay." The oldtimer stroked his mustache as a help to concentration. "That might be the reason why he couldn't be seen. For him to be found wounded would have been a give-away. Maybe he went to Doc White to be fixed up. I'll find out about that."

The doctor quashed that hope. He had not seen Benton as a patient since he had bandaged his leg after the courthouse fracas. Winters reported to the prisoner.

"I reckon we were too optimistic," he told Clay. "Probably Benton got a lift home in a buckboard or a buggy, but you would think he'd have tied his horse behind. By the way, a fellow came in from the Diamond K and got the horse an hour ago. Foley asked him where Benton was, and the man said he didn't know a thing about it. I guess he had instructions not to talk."

Yet it struck in Clay's mind that there was

some connection between the killing and the horse left overnight at the corral. Later he was more sure of it when Jim Prince mentioned a circumstance to which he had given no weight. This was three days after Ballard's death. He had dropped in to the jail to find out if he could do anything for his friend.

"Saw Clint Black last night," he said. "Clint is still roosting in Bill Clemsen's loft. He won't leave on account of that girl he's daffy about. Stays holed up all day and comes out after dark. Clint says he almost took a crack at Niles Benton Thursday night. He was heading down past the depot to where Nelly Cline's folks live when he saw Niles buying a ticket at the window. Said he had a mind to call the son-of-a-gun out to settle things right there."

"Thursday night!" Clay exclaimed, and through him there tingled a hot excitement, the sense of being close to an important discovery. "The train leaves at five minutes to eight. Why, that was just after the sheriff had been shot. Where was Niles going? And why?"

Prince shook his head. "Search me. I wouldn't know." He woke to sudden interest. "By jinks! Do you think he was running away?"

"I don't quite know what I think, except that you've got to find where he went and why."

"You mean that Niles killed Ballard?"

"I won't go that far yet. But he was in it somehow. If we can learn why he had to get out so suddenly and where he went we'll be nearer the truth than we are now."

Prince said: "That's easy. I'll run down to the depot and ask Tate where he sold Benton the ticket to."

Clay frowned at the barred windows of his cell. "I'm not sure he will want to tell you. We're a little late. Benton has probably got into touch with Savage before this, and my guess it that Tate has been told not to talk."

"Bribed, you mean."

"Perhaps you can get it out of him anyhow. You might try."

The cowboy grinned. "He'll talk for me." Swiftly, he added, to forestall an objection Clay seemed about to make: "We're pals."

"Have you any money, Jim? You'll probably have to buy a ticket for the same place in order to find out why Benton went."

"Money? Nary a dollar. I got in a faro game at the Bull's Head. If I'd only known —"

Clay handed his friend a roll of bills. "On your way, boy. There's an eastbound local leaves in half an hour. You'll find me right here when you get back."

"Keep up yore chin, old scout," Prince told him. "I'll be back right soon."

From the window Clay saw him walking to the station. At the corner of Texas Street he was hailed by Stanley Collins. They stopped to talk for a moment, after which the two walked away together.

22. Collins and Prince Cut Trail

"Where you going so fast, brother?" Collins called to Prince. "No fire, is there?"

The curly-headed blond stopped and grinned at Stanley. Ten years ago they had been schoolmates. "I'm going on a choo-choo train," he said.

Collins eyed him with simulated suspicion. "Getting married to that biscuit-shooter at the Sawbuck eatinghouse?" he asked.

"No, sir. This is a pleasure trip — with some business mixed in." Knowing that Stanley and Clay had made up their quarrel, he told his friend what he had in mind. "Better come along with me," he urged. "They say two heads are better than one."

As they walked down to the station Stanley decided he would. There was an urgent impulse in him to help get Sanger out of this trouble if he could. This looked like a good lead.

"I'll handle Tate," Prince told him.

The office window was up, ready for the sale of tickets to any passenger who might want to take the local. The cowboy did not stop at the window but walked through the door into the office. Collins followed him.

Tate looked up from the table where he sat working. A telegraph set was clicking in front of him. The operator was a big man in his early thirties. He had been an athlete once, but he was running to gross fat. He was in his shirtsleeves, his vest open.

"See you in a minute, boys," he said, sealing and addressing an envelope. This done, he asked what he could do for them.

Prince sauntered toward him. "Niles Benton bought a ticket from you Thursday night," he said. "I'd like to know where to."

"I can't give out information of that sort," Tate replied. "It's against the rules."

The cowpuncher noticed that the man's eyes had gone blank. He had been warned not to answer that question.

"Whose rules?" Prince wanted to know. "Savage's?"

"You can't talk that way to me," the railroad man snapped. "I don't have to stand for it."

Stanley sat on the edge of the table. He had picked up a newspaper and was reading it. Apparently he was not interested in the conversation of the other two.

"Savage can't make all the rules," Prince said cheerfully. "I'll make one today. All information given gladly to patrons of the railroad. The rule is now in effect. Cough up."

The station agent rose, swelling with indignation. "You've got no right in this office. Get out of here."

"We want to buy tickets to wherever friend Benton went Thursday night. I'm talking turkey, Tate. You look kinda soft to me. I'd hate to start working you over." Jim prodded a finger deep into the fat stomach. "Gosh, I hope you haven't got a bad heart. Too bad if you kicked off on me."

Tate appealed to Collins. He was furious but helpless. "Get this fellow out of here."

"I see they have had a fine rain up at Summit," Stanley mentioned, still engrossed in the paper's news. "Wish it would do as much for my range."

The brown fingers of Prince gathered up a handful of bulging fat and closed on it with an iron grip. The agent let out a yell of pain. He tried to break away and the cowboy crowded him against the table, increasing the pressure on the tortured flesh.

"Lemme go, you — you —"

"Yes, I know I'm a big cowardly bully," Prince said pleasantly. "We'll take that for granted, the same as we will that Savage slipped you a bill to keep mum. The point is, do you talk or don't you?"

Tate escaped from the sinewy fingers and edged along the table. The range rider followed him closely, driving him into a corner. An approaching train whistled.

"I got to meet that train," Tate gasped.

"So have I," Prince said. "No time for monkeying now. Do I have to whale the stuffing out of you? Last call. Speak fast."

Tate knew a hard fist would crash against his face in another moment if he did not surrender. Taking the advice of Prince, he spoke fast.

"The ticket was for Palo Verde."

"Anything funny about Benton? Did he seem hurried or worried?"

"He just asked for a ticket like anybody would." The words came sulkily. Tate objected to having his person and his dignity outraged in this way.

Collins tossed aside the paper. "I hope your information is correct, Tate. Because if it isn't — if the ticket was for some other place — you'll have two whalings coming to you when we get back."

"I'm giving it to you straight," the agent said, massaging his bruised flesh tenderly. "And if it's the last thing I ever do in this world I'm going to have the law on this ruffian."

"Two return tickets to Palo Verde, Mr.

Tate," Prince said. "I'm sorry I mussed yore feelings, but the fact is we had to find out. Too bad I had to get kinda personal with you. Tell you what I'll do. Soon as I get back I'll give you a free sock at me. You can tell the boys you handed me a black eye and I took it like a lamb without a word. How's that?"

At Palo Verde the two men left the train. They walked uptown to the hotel and took a room.

"Number 16," the clerk said. "Right upstairs and along the hall. Seeing as you have no grips, maybe you wouldn't mind paying in advance."

"Money on the barrelhead," Prince said, and paid for one night.

Stanley slid in a casual question. "Gent by the name of Niles Benton staying here?"

"No, sir."

"A big broad-shouldered guy who looks meaner than a bear with a sore paw?"

It was not necessary for the clerk to answer, for at that moment Benton came downstairs into the lobby. At sight of the newcomers he stopped in his tracks, startled and stared at them.

"I'll be doggoned if it isn't my old friend, Sure Shot Benton!" Prince cried. "Lemme see. Last time I saw you was the night you 'most killed a horse running away from a fight, wasn't it?"

"Any time you are lookin' for trouble with me, Prince, you can find it *pronto*," the Diamond K man snarled.

The cowboy noticed that the foreman's left arm was not in the sleeve of his coat. The shoulder of the garment on that side was draped over the collarbone like a cloak.

"You know I wouldn't want any trouble with you, Niles," Jim said, a gleam of mischief in his eyes. "Not with an old sidekick like you, especially when you are wounded."

"Who says I'm wounded?" Benton flung out harshly.

"Fine if you're not, oldtimer." Unexpectedly Prince dropped a hand heavily on the foreman's left shoulder.

Benton let out a cry of pain, stifled it, and drew in a hurried breath sharply.

"What's the matter, Niles?" Prince asked, raising his hand to clap the shoulder again.

Benton stepped back, his eyes wincing. "Don't do that, damn you," he growled.

"You hurt yoreself?" the cowboy asked. "Busted yore shoulder maybe when a horse threw you."

"Yeah," the foreman agreed sulkily. "Smashed it up some."

"You ought to have Doc White fix you up,"

Collins advised, an ironic smile on his face.

"Don't worry about it, Stan. I don't need any help from you." The Diamond K man flung out a question. "Since when have you started running with birds like Prince here?"

"I began twenty years ago when Jim and I were kids. Have you got any objections, Niles?" Stanley inquired frostily.

"Me, no. But I know somebody who won't like it."

"Then tell him from me to go jump in a lake," Collins retorted.

"You're gettin' mighty brash all of a sudden. What's bitin' you, fellow?"

Uneasily Benton wondered what these two men were doing here. His instinct told him that they had come on some business threatening his safety. If so, they must have found out from Tate the point to which he had bought a ticket. But he could not see what reason they had to run him down, since in the darkness nobody could have recognized him as the killer of Ballard. That had been a piece of bad luck. He had waited too long before firing. Of course he had been drinking. He still did not know whether he had been confused as to which man was Sanger or had in the murky night made a wild shot. His plan had been to hurry back to the Trail's End for an alibi, but he had been forced to give up that idea. Passing the station, he had seen the train ready to start and had decided on a temporary retirement at Palo Verde. Apparently he had made a mistake in buying the ticket from Tate. He could just as well have got it from the train conductor.

Benton had been cut off from news of Powder Horn since his hurried departure, and he was anxious to find out how the land lay.

"No use of us fussing, Stan," he said with false heartiness. "We always been friends. I been here three-four days and haven't heard a word from Powder Horn. Anything new doing there?"

"Let's see," Stanley replied. "It was a few minutes before you left that some yellow coyote shot Ballard in the back. You know about that, of course."

"Why, no!" Benton showed shocked surprise. "Who would want to hurt good old Jim?"

"You tell me," Collins answered. "Some think he didn't mean to kill the sheriff but the man beside him."

"And who was that?"

The eyes of the two young men did not lift for a fraction of a second from the face of the foreman.

"Clay Sanger."

Benton took time to consider that. "Didn't

anybody see this guy?"

"How did you come to think of that?" Prince asked.

"Why, you didn't mention his name. Was it — someone I know?"

"We think so."

"Who?"

"We're not telling his name yet," the cowboy said curtly. "Let's go, Stan."

The young men brushed past Benton and went to their room. As soon as the door was closed Prince told his friend what was in his mind. When he saw that Benton's arm was not in the sleeve of the coat he had guessed that Clay's bullet had struck him in the shoulder. That was why he had clamped his hand down on it, to smoke the fellow out. The killer had come to Palo Verde to get a doctor to dress the wound, since he knew that if White took care of him all Powder Horn would know he had been shot. The thing for them to do was to see at once all the doctors of the little town. Probably there were only two, possibly only one. If they could prove the Diamond K man had been shot by a revolver Clay Sanger's story would stand up.

They wandered down Main Street and inquired about doctors from a pair of old men who sat in front of a livery stable on a bench. There were, it appeared, two doctors in town,

Doctor Katz and Doctor McCord. The offices of both of them were on the other side of the street, one block down. They found the first in his office reading Goethe in the original. He was leaning back comfortably in a chair, his heels on the desk. When his visitors inquired about Benton it developed that he had never heard of the man and that he had not taken care of a gunfight victim for six months.

"Must have been McCord who looked after him," Katz suggested. "Down the street a half a block, in a little one-story frame building with a false front. Someone told me that a stranger with a hurt shoulder has been going in to see him. Might be your friend."

They drifted out into the broad unpaved street, the road of which was two inches deep with a fine brown dust that rose in a cloud whenever a wagon passed.

Doctor McCord was a shrewd dry little Scotchman, and he viewed the two young men with suspicion. Assuming that he had such a patient, though he did not at all admit it, what was their object in trying to get this information?

They told him the story of the killing of Sheriff Ballard.

"It was cold-blooded murder," Collins said. "We have reason to think the man you are treating is the killer."

"I'm treating naebody of the name Benton," the doctor evaded.

"He is passing under the name of Brown. That is how he is registered at the hotel."

"This is a wild God-forsaken country," McCord told them bluntly. "Nae doot you are carrying weapons this very minute. You tell a plausible tale, but for all I ken you may be bitter enemies of this man ready to do him a mischief."

"The only mischief we want to do him is to turn him over to justice if he is guilty. Since you believe in law you won't want to shield a murderer," Stanley said.

"I do not," McCord answered promptly. "But we'll put it hypothetically that I'm serving this man professionally. I'm in a confidential relation with him. You're giving me no proofs of what you say. You dinna even claim to be officers of the law. I gather you are far from freendly to him."

"An honest man's life is at stake," Prince insisted. "We'll face this man down before you. How will that do? I suppose he comes in every day for treatment."

"He might," the doctor conceded cautiously.

"Say we drop in at that time. What harm can it do? If he is innocent he will have a chance to prove it to your satisfaction."

Even before meeting these young men Mc-Cord had had his doubts about this patient. The man was a tough-looking specimen and he had lied about the cause of the wound. His story was that he had shot himself by accident while cleaning a revolver he had thought to be unloaded. From the position of the hurt and the direction the bullet had taken the doctor knew this could not be true. For the lead had come in from the rear and struck the collarbone. Moreover, there were no powder marks. And if the wound was due to misadventure why did the man have to go to a strange doctor in another town for treatment?

"I'll agree to that," McCord said. "But there is to be no violence, gentlemen, no shooting in this office. You'll get your information if it seems best to me, and you'll then walk out and leave me alone with my patient. Have I your word for that?"

They accepted the terms of the doctor. What they wanted primarily was proof that Benton had been shot.

"Tomorrow morning at ten, then," the doctor said. "I hope I'm doing right."

"You are, sir. Don't worry about that." Stanley added a word of caution. "Of course it would spoil everything if Benton heard of this in advance."

"He won't," McCord promised.

At precisely ten o'clock next morning Collins and Prince walked into the office of the doctor. McCord was changing the bandage on the shoulder wound of a patient, a big raw-boned hairy individual passing temporarily under the name of Brown.

Benton glared at them angrily. Back of the anger was doubt. He felt sure they had come to call for some kind of showdown.

"What you doing here?" he rasped.

"Just dropped in to find how yore arm is getting along," Prince told him, "the one you busted when yore bronc threw you."

The foreman ripped out an oath. "If you birds have come to crowd me I'll blast you both off the map," he threatened. "I know why you are here. That scoundrel Sanger sent you."

Prince took the offered lead. "You don't have much luck with Clay, do you? This is the second time he has pumped lead into you when you were trying to kill him."

"That's a lie."

"Sure enough," the cowboy replied amiably. "Then I'll bet you shot yoreself, accidentally, with a gun you didn't know was loaded."

"It's none of yore business how I shot myself. But that's how it was. I got careless."

Prince shook his head reproachfully. "They oughtn't to trust you with a gun till you've had more experience, Niles."

The doctor made up his mind not to support the fiction of his patient. "You couldn't have shot yourself, Mr. Brown, since the bullet came in at the back of your shoulder."

Benton's narrowed eyes slid from one to another of them. He knew that he was being trapped and began to feel the cold clutch of fear. His thoughts raced, searching for an out.

"I promised Savage not to tell how I got this wound," he said. "But I reckon I'll have to talk now. I was shot by a rustler trying to drygulch me. The boss wanted me to keep my mouth shut until we got the fellow who did it. That's why I didn't have Doc White fix me up. The whole town would have known it. So I came here."

The cowboy laughed derisively. "I believe he has made up his mind at last, Stan. That's the story he aims to stick to. Of course a fellow could throw a cat through the holes in it. A dozen fellows saw him in town Thursday night looking right hearty. We'll see if he can get away with that fairy tale."

Collins and his friend walked out of the office and back to the hotel.

23. Newbolt Reconsiders

Captain Winters was selling a pair of boots to a cowboy when Stanley Collins dropped into the store. The sale was a complicated affair, for the range rider wanted a close fit and the certainty that the boots would not pinch his feet. He stamped around in them, cast an admiring eye at the fancy decoration, and found it more difficult to decide than a lady of fashion. A cowpuncher's boots are the most important item of his wardrobe. He is as fussy about them as he is about his saddle.

Collins sat on a counter and gave derisive advice. "Better take 'em on trial, Buck. If you don't like them you can bring them back in about six months. All goods guaranteed. Money cheerfully refunded to unsatisfied customers."

Buck finally bought the boots. "You can throw away the old ones, Captain," he said, and teetered proudly out of the store.

Winters carefully wrapped up the discarded footwear. They were dusty and run down at the heels. The leather was cracked in a dozen places.

"Saving them for some poor banker?" Stanley asked.

"I'm saving them for Buck," the merchant answered. "In about three hours he'll be back yelling bloody murder because his feet are scalding like fire. He'll want these old tried and true friends forty times while he is breaking in his new ones."

Stanley lowered himself from the counter. "Like to see you alone for a minute, Captain."

Winters led the way to the office. "Shoot, son," he said after he had closed the door.

"I just got back on the afternoon train with important news," Collins told him.

"Back from where? Didn't know you had been gone."

"From Palo Verde."

"What kind of news?"

"The kind that Clay Sanger would appreciate most right now — evidence to prove he didn't kill Jim Ballard."

"Do you claim you have got evidence like that?" Winters demanded eagerly.

"I don't claim I have positive proof. But I'm dead sure I know the man who did it, even if it isn't enough yet to hang him."

"Who is he?"

Stanley told his story. To confirm it he had brought with him a written statement from Doctor McCord to the effect that he had been treating a man named Brown, alias Benton, for a gunshot wound in the back. Prince, it appeared, had stayed at Palo Verde to keep an eye on Benton lest he try to run away.

"Is it yore notion that Benton will try to cut his stick?" the old soldier wanted to know.

Stanley shook his head. "No. He'd be caught and dragged back. My guess is that he will slip into town and out to the Diamond K. Savage will give him protection. He can hide out in the brush back of the ranch if officers come out there looking for him."

The captain was much excited. "You've uncovered something good there, boy!" he cried. "I'll get a pass for us to see Clay. He'll be plumb tickled with you. What first put you on to Benton?"

"A fellow saw him buying a ticket right after the shooting. He mentioned it to Jim Prince, and Jim passed it on to Clay. It seemed funny Benton had to beat it away on the train at that particular hour, so we checked up on him. He is as guilty as the devil."

"Looks like. That story he told you is too thin. Savage will have to patch that up."

Stanley agreed. "Yes, sir. Bert won't like it. There's no doubt in my mind that Benton killed the wrong man by mistake. He was waiting in the brush to get Clay. Savage doesn't like failure. Until Clay crossed his path he hasn't had any worth mentioning. But it's been different lately. If he dared he would feed Benton to the wolves. But he can't. Niles knows too much. He'll have to get indignant and throw a fit about how outrageous it is to accuse his foreman of such a crime."

The mayor and Collins dropped in to see Newbolt at the courthouse on their way to the jail. What they had to tell the county attorney disturbed that official a good deal. He had built up what he considered a convincing case against Sanger. Back of it had been a personal belief in the guilt of the marshal. But this evidence against Benton was a knockout blow to the case. It substantiated completely the story Clay had told, and it deflated Newbolt's assurance. The lawyer was not a scoundrel, and he had no intention of prosecuting a murder case against an innocent man. If he thought Benton guilty — and it began to look very like it — he knew he would have to break with Savage and indict his foreman for the murder.

"Clay can't have shot Ballard," the mayor insisted. "Atchison was with him from the moment of the killing until he left to bring help, and Mrs. Atchison did not leave him until he was arrested. He had no chance to tamper with his pistol, and there had been only one shot fired from it. That shot hit Niles Benton while he was running away after killing Ballard. There's no other explanation."

"We'll hear Benton's story before I decide," Newbolt said.

Collins laughed scornfully. "I've heard three stories from him about his wound. First, he was thrown from a horse and busted his shoulder. The second was that he had shot himself accidentally. Then he shifted to another, that he was hit by a rustler out near the ranch."

"We're going to hear a fourth one after he gets back," Winters prophesied. "One that Savage fixes up for him."

The mayor's guess was a correct one.

Two men descended from the afternoon train a few days later. One of them was Benton, the other Prince. They had been sitting at different ends of the same car. Savage was at the station to meet his foreman. The Diamond K men walked up town and disappeared into the hotel. What talk occurred between the two men nobody knew, but an hour later they emerged from retirement and went to the office of the county attorney in the courthouse.

Many curious eyes watched them as they passed down the street. There was more than curiosity in the fixed regard of the onlookers. A wave of disapproval beat upon the ranchman and his foreman. Savage disdained to pay any attention to it, but Benton was visibly disturbed. His nervous eyes slid to the right and left, measuring the condemnation which had the force of something tangible. He realized that Powder Horn had listened to the stories of Sanger and of Collins, the testimony of Mark and Jane Atchison, had weighed them and made up its mind. The town had not waited to hear his story. It had judged him and the marshal on their records and on the facts available, and it had found him guilty. The beginning of panic fear was choking up into the man's throat.

Savage detected instantly a change in Newbolt. The county attorney's eyes looked straight into his. It was not necessary for the prosecutor to tell him that he intended to try this on its merits. The Diamond K man knew it before a word had been said.

"I hear you released Sanger today on bond," Savage accused.

"Yes."

"Why?"

"Because I don't think the evidence against him is strong enough to justify holding him. New evidence has come out."

"What evidence?" demanded the rancher.

"Testimony implicating Benton. I'm glad he has come back. I was going to send for him."

"Of course he has come back. Why

wouldn't he? As another witness against Sanger. He was there when this marshal killed Ballard."

Newbolt was aware of a surprise coming. He waited, without speaking.

"On the way to jail they met Benton, and Ballard asked him to go along with him as he was afraid of his prisoner. Niles agreed. When they were close to the jail Sanger dropped back a step, drew a gun, and killed the sheriff. Knowing this killer had the drop on him, Benton started to run. Before he had gone a dozen steps he was hit, but he kept on going to save his life. Because he had not liked the way Doctor White took care of him before, he boarded a train and went to Palo Verde. He had heard Doctor McCord was good with wounds and had gone to him. That is all there is to this story young Collins started about Benton. The object of it of course was to draw the attention of people from the obvious guilt of Sanger."

"As I look at it," Newbolt contradicted, "this story of Benton's practically clears Sanger. While his gun was still smoking the Atchisons were on the scene. They were with Sanger until he was arrested and his weapon examined. Only one shot had been fired. Since he wounded Benton, he could not have killed the sheriff."

"That makes me a liar," Benton charged angrily. "I say I saw him do it. What about that?"

The county attorney knew that the Diamond K foreman was a bully given to violence. It had been only a short time since he had led a brutal attack on the cowboy Shorty. But Newbolt was no coward.

"I am not now making an accusation against you, Mr. Benton, but pointing out a fact," he said incisively. "But since you are asking for plain talk I'll say that if it comes to a trial you have told too many stories about your wound for your testimony to have much weight."

"You're telling me again that I'm a liar!" the foreman shouted.

"No," Newbolt denied. "I'm telling you the effect your story will have on a jury. After Collins and Prince and Doctor McCord have testified it won't be believed."

Savage brushed Benton aside with an arrogant gesture. "Keep out of this, Niles. I'll do any talking that's necessary." He turned to the lawyer. "About the single shot fired from Sanger's gun, my contention is that after hitting Benton he slipped another cartridge into his revolver."

"I don't think he would have had time, even if he had thought of it," Newbolt objected.

"He would have had plenty of time. It wouldn't take him a half a second. But after the Atchisons heard the first shot they would sit a minute discussing it. As a reasonable guess I would say they didn't get to the place of the shooting for at least three minutes."

"The gun was still smoking."

"Just imagination on the part of Atchison. It was too dark to see that anyhow."

"Both Mark and his wife noticed it. About the time it would have taken them to come out, you would have a valid point except for one thing. They were just opening the door to come out and go to prayer meeting."

"Got it all fixed up to clear this fellow Sanger, haven't you, Newbolt?" Savage sneered.

Newbolt said, again looking directly at the ranchman: "I'm trying to look at the facts honestly. I don't say Benton is the guilty man. But I do say that he has a lot of explaining to do before I am satisfied he is innocent."

"Rats and a sinking ship," Savage flung at the attorney contemptuously. "But I'll show you this ship isn't sinking. A time will come soon when you will wish you hadn't lined up with my enemies."

"I haven't lined up with anyone," Newbolt replied firmly. "I am prosecuting attorney of this county and I intend to do my sworn duty."

He called in a clerk. "I want you to answer some questions, Mr. Benton. Of course you don't have to do this if it would incriminate you."

Benton jumped up from the chair in which he sat. He ripped out an oath and said he would not stand for it.

"What are your questions, Newbolt?" Savage wanted to know, silencing the foreman with a wave of the hand.

"I want to know exactly what his movements were the night of the killing."

"I'll tell you. He was at the bar of the Trail's End drinking with some friends. Somebody came in from the street and said that Ballard had arrested Sanger. Knowing the marshal was a bad man, Niles thought the sheriff might have trouble with him. So he walked down Texas Street and joined them just after they turned off from it."

"How long after? How far had Ballard and the prisoner gone from the corner?"

"I should say about ten yards," Savage answered.

"Let Mr. Benton do the answering, please," Newbolt suggested. "He isn't dumb."

"Ten yards," Benton growled.

"As you went down Texas Street you must have passed the Bull's Head. Was there anybody standing in front of it who can substantiate your story?"

"It doesn't need any backing. I'm telling you how it was."

"I understand that, but of course if anybody happened to be there and saw you it would make your story stronger."

"I didn't notice anyone," the foreman said sullenly.

"There wasn't anybody standing under the lamp then? That's too bad."

"Why do you harp on that?" Savage demanded suspiciously.

"Wouldn't it help Benton if there were witnesses to support what he says?" the lawyer asked.

He did not tell the real reason. Jim Prince and Shorty Pierce had been standing in front of the Bull's Head at this time. They had talked with Ballard and his prisoner and had watched them go down Texas Street and turn from it toward the jail. But Benton had not seen them, according to his story, and what was more important, they had not seen him. It followed that somebody was not telling the truth. Newbolt had no trouble in deciding who this was.

He took Benton over the rest of the journey to the scene of the killing, the story of it, and of the foreman's retreat to the station and his decision to go to Palo Verde for treatment of his wound. The big man had a bad enough half-hour. He perspired freely, contradicted himself, cursed, got angry. If Savage had not been there to protect him it would have been a great deal worse.

"You're not thinking of leaving these parts, are you, Benton?" the lawyer asked at last, rising from his chair.

"No," stormed the foreman. "Why the hell should I?"

"I'll want to talk with you again one of these days."

Savage looked at the attorney. "Don't make a mistake and get off on the wrong foot," he warned, his face set like granite and his voice cold as steel.

"I'll try not to," Newbolt retorted.

He did not expand or explain the answer.

24. Clay in Circulation Again

When Mark Atchison told Clay he was free to leave the jail the marshal packed his telescope grip and went downstairs into the kitchen to say good-bye to the wife of the jailor.

"I want to thank you for the care you have given me," he said. "Even though you think I am a murderer you have fed me well and been good to me."

She was washing a shirt, and she stood up tall and gaunt after she had dried her hands. On her dry weather-beaten face there was a friendliness he had not expected to see there.

"I don't think now that you killed Jim Ballard," she said. "I did, and after I got to know you I couldn't understand it. You didn't look like . . . that sort of man. But your story was true all the time. Of course that Benton did it. We came out of the house just a minute too late to see you shoot at him. I'm sorry for misjudging you."

In his smile there was forgiveness. "How could you help thinking what you did? I'm the luckiest man in the world. If I hadn't chanced to hit Benton folks would have thought to my dying day that I was guilty — and I reckon my dying day wouldn't have been very far away."

She offered him the rough hand she had just dried. "Take care of yourself, young man. Get a nice wife — and settle down — and stop offering yourself as a target for the bullets of bad men."

"Can you recommend a girl, ma'am?" he asked innocently.

"Go along with you!" she snorted. "I daresay you have her all picked out."

He shook his head cheerfully. "They won't look at me. I'm too wild a coot. I reckon I'll have to rock along alone."

Clay's passage down Texas Street and along the square was in the nature of an ovation. He had been a town hero, and they had believed him guilty of a cowardly murder. In their regret at having fallen away from him so easily they felt ashamed and at his exoneration greatly pleased.

"If we'd had a lick of sense we'd of known you wouldn't do a dirty killing like that," Foley said, expressing the feeling of many. "Trouble was it looked so open and shut we got fooled by it."

As soon as he could escape Clay went to

the hotel. A girl who had trusted him and been sure of him all the time was staying there, and he wanted to see her before she went back to the ranch.

Effie was startled at seeing Clay, since she had not heard yet that he had been released. She stood for a moment looking at him, lips parted, eyes shining. Almost breathless, she waited for him to speak. It was disturbing to be so moved by his presence, to feel this queer weakness steal over her, and she felt that at any cost she must not let him know how intensely he stirred her.

"I just got into circulation again," he said, "and I came to thank you for your message."

"I'm glad," she said. "It was so silly of anybody to suspect you. Of course all your friends knew you didn't do it."

He gave her his strong brown hand. "I'm pleased one of them knew it," he told her.

The soft color beat into her face. He thought he had never seen anybody more lovely than this girl. "I hope you'll be more careful now," she urged. "He meant to kill you and not the sheriff. Some of them will try again." She hesitated, and then continued: "Mr. Savage hates you. He as good as told me that he meant to destroy you. If you had seen his face!"

He laughed. "I've seen it, and I don't like it. But don't worry about me. I'll be all right.

One of the good things about this is that the Collins family are my friends again. It was Stan and Jim Prince, you know, who dug up the evidence against Benton."

That night Clay dropped around to Bill Clemsen's livery stable.

"Like to have a talk with Clint Black," he told Clemsen.

Bill was a small man with a face like a wrinkled red apple. He put on a good act. "Like to see him myself," he said innocently. "Don't you reckon maybe he is in Mexico?"

"No, I reckon he is up in your loft," Clay hazarded, grinning at the little man.

"Well, I'll be dogged. You figure he slipped up there when I wasn't lookin'. It don't look reasonable to me."

"Nor to me, Bill. Come off of it. I know that's his hideout. I'm not going to do him any harm. Is he nesting up in the hay right now? Or is this his evening out?"

A voice came down from above. "I'm here, Clay. Step right up." Black's face peered down from beyond the ladder.

Clay ascended. The fugitive lit a lantern and led the way to a small room where harness, tools, and odds and ends were kept. Black's blankets lay in one corner of it.

"I don't know as I ought to associate with jailbirds and killers," the rustler mentioned.

"This won't do my rep any good if anyone finds it out."

"Nor mine," Clay replied. "Here's a guy roosting in the hay to keep from being arrested. Probably I ought to do something about that."

"I've heard tell of the pot calling the kettle black," Clint admitted. "Maybe we'd better call it quits. How you doing, Blue Blazes? I'm right glad you got the goods on Benton to clear you."

"Perhaps you don't know that we got the evidence through you."

"Through me?" The man in hiding stared at his friend. "Why, I didn't lift a hand, Clay."

"No, but you saw him buying a railroad ticket, and you told Jim Prince. That gave us our first hunch. So Jim and Stan Collins followed it up."

"Jiminy! Don't that beat the Dutch! I did see him at the depot, and I came mighty near calling him out to settle once for all our fuss."

"That's what I came to see you about, Clint. I won't have you pot-shotting at him. You tried it once before."

"Who told you so?"

"Nobody. I used my head. That's why there are brains in it."

"When was it I took a crack at him, then?"

"On the night we had the shindig down at

the Half Acre. There were a good many shots fired that night. A lot of them came from the guns of Diamond K men, one volley from my deputies, an extra blast from Jim Prince addressed to Yorky, and one bullet from my forty-five aimed at Pagett. That leaves one rifle crack unexplained. I dug the bullet later out of the adobe wall of Owens' dance hall. That lead pellet missed Benton's head by not more than four inches."

"The fellow that fired it ought to be lynched — for missing," Clint commented.

"It was a little too dark to see well," the marshal explained. "Benton wasn't standing right in the light. What I have to say is this, Clint: If that shot had killed Benton you would not be sleeping in this room but down in the jail. You have done me two favors and I did you two. We'll call the score even. But whether it is or not isn't important. I'm marshal in this town. You let the law take care of Niles Benton. It's hard on his heels. I won't have you settling private scores with him. Understand?"

Black nodded. "I could claim I didn't take that shot at him the night of the big rookus, but you wouldn't believe me. And by gum, you would be right. Why shouldn't I bump him off? He was getting ready to rub you out without giving you a chance for yore white alley. Anybody who killed that bird would be doing the country a service. If I had done it I would of saved poor old Jim Ballard's life."

"He'll pay for that before he is through. I'm telling you not to butt in. This isn't your job. Sure as you do I'll put you behind bars."

"All right," Clint conceded sulkily "I'll leave him lay, and very likely he'll shoot up a lot more good citizens."

"All right. That's settled." Clay shifted to more friendly conversation. "How do you spend all your days, Clint? Don't you get lonesome?"

"I sleep some. And I'm going in for education. Three-four years ago my sister sent me a book called *David Copperfield*. I was sorta keeping it to read some time when I busted my leg after being throwed from a bronc. But seeing I'm tired up here I figured I would get it outa my system now. A fellow ought to read a book every ten or fifteen years anyhow so as not to let his schoolin' rust. It's quite a chore, but after you get into it you get real interested. You'd ought to try it some time, Blue Blazes."

"I think I shall," Clay said dryly. "I can't have you getting too far ahead of me." He added, returning to the subject on his mind: "But I think you ought to complete your education elsewhere. By this time a lot of people must know you are sticking around. One of these nights there will be another shot from the brush and Mr. Black will turn up his toes. Quit fooling around and hit the trail for Colorado, say."

"I'm aiming to leave in a day or two," Black defended. "I had a little unfinished business, but it looks like I'm getting it taken care of." He grinned, a little sheepishly.

"That's fine. All I've got to say is that after you get married and have a little Clint and a little Nelly I'll be expecting to hear that you have quit helling around and are a respectable citizen."

"Y'betcha," Black agreed. "I aim to have a little ranch of my own with a bunch of cows bearing the C B brand."

"Be sure too many of those cows don't have twin calves every year or two," Clay advised meaningly.

"No, sir. No more rustling. I'll probably be a deacon in the church."

The two men shook hands on that.

25. The Net Tightens

On the courthouse steps, just after the talk with Newbolt, the owner of the Diamond K said in his cold precise voice, "None of my business of course, but I presume you have made your plan to get out of this country before they put a rope around your neck."

Benton turned on him a startled gaze. "What you talkin' about?" he exclaimed. "I'm going back to the ranch. The law hasn't got a thing on me, but if any deputy sheriffs show up I'll slip back into the hills till they have gone."

"No," Savage told him. "I'm through with you. I'll not lift a hand to save you. You're not working for the Diamond K anymore."

"You can't do this to me!" the foreman cried, the angry blood pouring into his face. "I've got too much on you. I know enough to put you out of business."

"I'm telling you that you have drawn your last Diamond K check," Savage explained, his flinty eyes fixed without mercy on his employee. "I told you my plans for Sanger, and you went ahead on your own in spite of what I said. You wooden-headed fool, I thought you knew me better. When I hire a man he can't grind his own corn in my mill. He takes orders from me. If you know what is good for you, don't show up at the ranch."

The big foreman glared at him, alarm struggling with rage. "Talk about rats leaving a sinking ship. You take the cake, Savage." The man's fury overrode for the moment his fear. "I'll show you if you can get away with this, you double-crossing scoundrel. For you I've done things no decent man would have touched. If it comes to a showdown I'll tell everything I know."

Savage laughed cruelly. "Go ahead and see how far you get," he taunted. "You can tell plenty that you have done, but you can't prove I ordered you to do any of them. Take this killing of Ballard. I can show by Newbolt that all I wanted was to have Sanger legally arrested and that you were urging me to kill him. I can prove that you swore a dozen times to kill him. You are tied hand and foot by your own words."

He turned away abruptly and left the discharged foreman on the steps. Benton watched him go, a bitter resentment in his heart. That he had many enemies the big man knew, and most of them had been made while doing dirty work for Savage. Now he was cast off, without a real friend in the world, to face alone the consequences of his last crime.

There would be no safety for him in this country. He must get across the line into Mexico and hole up. But he had to make careful preparations for a getaway. It would be better to show a bold front, allay suspicion, and slip away unexpectedly. He would have to buy a horse secretly and enough supplies to carry him across the desert. It would be better to avoid the towns, since a hue and cry for him would go out probably if he disappeared. Maybe it was not that bad. After all, it was his word against that of Sanger. There was no positive proof of his guilt. He would very likely have plenty of time to escape. No need to get panicky.

But when he walked into the Trail's End he knew that he had made a mistake. There were not more than a scattering of patrons in the house. The place would not fill up until after supper. Of the dozen or so present five were playing stud and three faro. The rest were at the bar. Benton was aware instantly that his entrance had created a tension. Red McClintock stopped riffling his chips to stare at him. Shorty was one of those at the faro layout and he instantly lost interest in the king he had coppered.

"Look who's here," he said aloud, a drawling insolence in his voice.

Benton ordered a drink before he answered the stumpy cowboy. "Don't try to run on me, Shorty," he warned. "I won't stand for it a minute."

"That's right," the cowboy replied. "You're a big shot. When you're around small fry have to sidestep softly on their toes. Of course you can't get Pagett to help you now, but Holloway is still on deck."

"I don't need anyone to help me handle a shrimp like you, Shorty."

"I aim to be right careful not to wander around the edge of town where there is a lot of brush around," Pierce answered.

"What do you mean by that?" Benton demanded, and ripped out an oath.

Jim Prince, at the poker table, took another look at his ace in the hole and shoved in chips. "Raise it a buck," he said, and let his gaze rest on Benton.

"Maybe you haven't heard the rumor going around, Niles," Shorty responded.

"What rumor? If anybody says I had anything to do with killing Ballard he's a liar."

"I was speakin' of the rumor that you got throwed from a horse and busted yore shoulder."

Most of the men in the room laughed raucously. They had never liked Benton, and it pleased them that he had fallen into Shorty's trap.

"Seems the bronc was mighty well educated," Prince said, dragging his words a little to convey an insult. "It up and plunked a bullet into Niles' shoulder after it had made him take dirt."

"Some think that broomtail might put a rope round his neck kinda soon," a poker player mentioned.

"Or round the neck of Clay Sanger," Red McClintock offered as an alternative. "Funny how his friends have got folks minds turned another way now."

Benton nodded gratefully to Red. "You're right about that. Sanger not only killed Ballard, but pretty near got me too. He's a bad *hombre,* that man."

"That's a damn lie," Prince said very clearly, leaning forward, his arms on the table.

Two of the others who had been playing poker hurriedly vacated their chairs and ranged themselves along the side walls.

"Don't disturb yoreselves, gents," Jim continued. "Mr. Benton isn't going to make any trouble. He's plumb tame. Aren't you, Niles?"

The ex-foreman slid troubled eyes around the hall. Nearly everybody in the room was watching him with a grim steadiness that shook his nerve. He knew what they were thinking — that he had shot Jim Ballard from behind, and that something ought to be done about this. They represented a cross-section of Powder Horn. Given a very little impetus, a leader to get it started, a mob might hang him to a telegraph pole before morning. A swift cold fear drenched him. He knew he was a fool to be inviting more trouble now.

"If you mean when you say tame that I'm not a bad man, Jim, you never spoke a truer word," Benton whined. "Most of the time I don't carry a gun. I didn't have one with me Thursday night when Sanger shot me. A guntoter is asking for trouble, and that never was my way."

"That's right," Shorty agreed. "It's trouble for the other fellow you specialize in. What you enjoy most is to be one of three jumping on a single guy. You're good at that. I'm still carrying bruises to prove it."

"Now, Shorty, you hadn't ought to hold a grudge about a little scrap we all got into when we were roostered up," Benton reproved, with a thin smile intended to show friendliness. "Still, I'll say I was sorry about that. I been wantin' to tell you so."

"No guts," Shorty gave verdict, looking with disgust at the man who had been his boss for three years. "When he's ridin' high and handsome he's a bully-puss son-of-a-gun, but when he gets in a jam he quits like a yellow dog."

"I'm not in any jam," Benton blurted out. "No reason why I should be. It's this fellow Sanger who is making all the trouble. No use foolin' yoreselves, boys. He's gone bad. If he hadn't of been a killer he wouldn't have shot Ballard and me."

"Don't try to pull that stuff," Shorty snarled at him. "You're caught in a trap and you'll never get out of it alive. Right now you are scared stiff, and you have a license to be. They are watching you. If you try to run they will drag you back with a rope round yore throat. Pretty soon you will be arrested and tried and hanged. If the law fools away any time there are plenty of folks ready to fix up a necktie party for you any night. If you ask me, you are in one hell of a spot."

Prince had a few words to say. "This country doesn't stand for shooting in the back. Savage can't save you, even if he tries. Today — or tomorrow — or next month — you'll hand in yore checks just as sure as you're standing there now shaking in yore boots, Benton."

"I'm not scared!" the harassed man cried, trying to make his words sound big and brave. "I got no need to be, seeing as I have done nothing wrong. Don't you fellows get on the prod. I got as much right here as any of you, and I aim to stay. My money's good, ain't it?"

"Not at the Trail's End," the proprietor denied. "Your trade isn't wanted here, Mr. Benton."

"Why not? I'm innocent, I tell you. You boys got no right to crowd me."

A cowboy named Warren who had once worked for the foreman of the Diamond K spoke up. "No, you're guilty as the devil, Niles. You've done sold yore saddle.[1] You've come to the end of yore crooked mile. What's the use of waiting? Why not do the job tonight while he is in town?"

The suggestion met a yell of approval.

"Not tonight," Prince objected. "Clay is digging up new evidence against him. Let the fellow sweat awhile till we're dead sure."

"I'm sure enough right now," Warren insisted. "How about you boys?"

There was another shout of assent.

The mouth of the killer was a thin tight slit. His pale shifty eyes darted from one to another of these men who were surrounding him as a pack of wolves do a wounded elk they are about to drag down. Lines of worry

---

[1]In the West a man was said to have sold his saddle when he had lost his self-respect.

were bitten deep into his ugly lupine face. A dreadful sense of doom weighted his stomach muscles.

If Rock Holloway had been in his place he would have known that the danger was not immediate, that it was a growing one which had not yet come to an explosion point. For Rock had not only a catlike patience but that sixth sense which warned him when to strike and when to sit quiet. But Benton lacked the cool courage that can judge a peril surely. He was a bully, with a red-hot devil of malice in him, but he had no touch of the gay recklessness that set Jim Prince's pulses dancing when the call to action came, nor of the dogged self-respect that made Shorty Pierce see a situation out to a fighting finish. That yell of the pack brought Benton close to panic.

"You damn buzzard-heads!" he cried. "Touch me, and hell will start to cough for you."

He had dragged out a forty-five and was waving it wildly in front of him.

"Put that gun up," Prince ordered sharply.

"You stay back, or I'll riddle you."

Benton backed toward the swing doors. At that moment somebody pushed through them into the room. The gunman slewed his head to see who it was, and the bartender reached for a sixshooter from the shelf close to his hand.

Twice Benton's gun sounded. The man behind the bar gave a choking groan and dropped out of sight.

The killer pushed through the doors, revolver in hand, and ran to the hitch-rack. He pulled the slipknot that tied the nearest horse and vaulted to the saddle. In a cloud of yellow dust he went clattering out of town.

26. Wanted — For Murder

Benton left Powder Horn at a gallop. Frequently he looked back, half-expecting to see a posse at his heels. A wild despairing fear rode with him. Why had he ever returned to the town? Why had he gone into the Trail's End? He had not been looking for any more trouble. It had been forced on him by his enemies. Through no fault of his own he had been driven into another killing.

Though he had been a bold and hardy ruffian, he had never been a courageous man. Now he was filled with self-pity. It was hard to believe that he was a hunted man fleeing for his life. Three months ago he had been a big man in the community. The merchants of the town had solicited the ranch patronage which he in part controlled. He had hired and fired cowboys at will. Nesters and small stockmen were careful not to annoy him. So sure of his place was he that there had been no need to conciliate. His rough harsh ways had made foes for him, and he cared not a snap of his fingers for their resentment.

He was the same man today as then, but all his power and prestige were gone. The man who had wrecked him was Clay Sanger. Looking back, Benton could trace the beginning of the change to the day when Sanger had frustrated the hanging of Clint Black. The fellow must have been born lucky to be still alive. At least a half-dozen times with any kind of break he would have been rubbed out. Yet the marshal was still top dog and he, Niles Benton, was scuttling into the hills to hide.

When he recovered from his panic enough to take stock of his situation, he discovered that the horse he had taken was headed for the Diamond K. Probably unconsciously he had been guiding it in that direction. Savage had cast him off, but at a pinch he would be forced to aid him. As foreman of the ranch during the years when Savage had been on the make, he knew too much of the Diamond K high-handed lawlessness to be refused food.

For a time he must hole up. Already word must have gone from Powder Horn to the rangers and to all the border authorities to apprehend him. If he could get food he would nest in the hills back of the ranch until the hunt for him had died down. After that he could cross the desert to Mexico, riding by night and lying low during the day.

The fugitive did not ride up to the ranch house as any casual traveler might do. Too many of its riders hated him. They were a wild lot, but most of them held to the code of the West. You could not shoot a man in the back. Benton dared not trust them not to betray him.

He swung round by a ridge trail that brought him to the back of the horse pasture. This he entered by a wire gate. There were lights in the big house and in the bunkhouse. As he wound forward through the brush his nerves were keyed to a high pitch. It was certain that Savage would not be pleased to see him. He wanted, if possible, to find him alone, so that he could remind the ranchman he would be a danger if help was refused.

After tying the horse to a mesquite he crept through the wire fence and came on the house from the rear. He heard voices and soft-footed up the side steps to look through a window. Rock Holloway was in the office with his employer. They were going over some accounts together.

Niles opened the door and walked into the room. The ranchman looked at him, a cold and hostile surprise in his eyes.

"What are you doing here?" he asked.

"Listen, boys." The discharged foreman spoke hurriedly, to forestall criticism. "I'm in trouble. I had to come here, Bert, so as to get grub and beat it to the hills."

The hard gaze of his former boss did not

lift from him for a second. "I told you I was through with you — that I didn't want ever to see you on this ranch again," he said.

"I know," Benton explained, his voice humble and ingraitating. "But I got into another jam, kind of. I was crowded into it, and I knew you would want to help me out of it."

"I'm not helping you out of anything. I gave you orders, and you disobeyed them. You're a fool for coming here. Didn't I tell you I would set the dogs on you if you showed up?"

"Still and all, Bert, we been friends for twenty years. You wouldn't throw me down when I need a horse and a little grub."

"I've never been your friend," Savage told him implacably. "I paid you to do a job. Your head got too big for your hat, and I gave you your time. That's all there is to it. I'm not going to stand the gaff because you are a jugheaded idiot who tries to kill a man, gets the wrong one, and leaves sign all over the lot so that he is caught."

"I got to hole up for a while," Benton reiterated, tiny beads of sweat on his forehead. "All I'm asking is some grub and a bronc. I'll pay for them if you're as tight as all that."

"No, you won't get them free, and you won't pay for them either," Savage answered with blunt cruelty.

Holloway spoke for the first time. "You

272

mentioned getting into some fresh trouble, Niles. What do you mean?"

"Well, it was this way." The worried man's glance swept the room in search of liquor. "My nerves are all shot. Gimme a drink, Bert, before I tell my story. I've had a hell of a time."

"No drink," Savage said in curt refusal. "If you have anything more to say, spit it out and then hit the trail."

"I wouldn't treat a dog thataway," Benton pleaded. "Let alone a man who has done all I have building you up."

Savage drew out his watch and laid it on the table. "I'll give you three minutes. If you are not out of here by that time I'll have the boys arrest you and drag you back to town."

"Better talk fast, Niles," advised Holloway derisively. "Looks like the boss is in a hurry."

"I was in the Trail's End and some of Sanger's friends got to running on me. Prince and Shorty Pierce and some others. They pushed in on me and talked about a necktie party. One of 'em drew a gun, and I had to kill him." The badgered man stopped, licked his dry lips, and gulped out a plea. "I was druv to it, Bert. So help me, I couldn't help it."

"Who did you kill?" Holloway asked.

"The bartender, Pete Doyle. My gun kinda went off."

"Doyle," repeated Holloway. "But he is not a friend of Sanger. If anything, he leans our way."

"He had his gun pointed at me. It was him or me."

Abruptly Savage rose. "I don't believe it. I'm going to have you arrested right now and sent to town."

His former foreman snatched out his gun. "You won't be alive to see me go, you rat," he cried, his face a map of rage and terror.

Holloway lifted the palm of his hand. "Wait a minute, Niles. Sure as you start the smoke I'll drill you. Listen to me, both of you. This can be fixed up."

"No," Savage flung out.

"Yes. This is how it will be. We'll all three walk out to the corral. There I want to talk with Mr. Savage alone for a minute. If I can't change his mind we're no worse off than at present. Put up yore gun, Niles."

Benton glared at him, suspicions racing through his mind.

"How do I know you're not aiming to double-cross me?" he snarled.

"You don't," Holloway replied coolly. "All you know is that if this goes to a showdown now you'll be a dead duck inside of two minutes. Even with yore gun out you can't keep me from killing you."

"All right. But no monkey business, Rock."

"Not unless you start it." Holloway rose from the chair. "I'm not going out that door first," Benton declared flatly.

"Play it safe," Holloway advised sarcastically. "Mr. Savage will go first, you next, and I'll bring up the rear. You'll be in no more danger than you would at church."

They filed out of the house and walked across the plaza to the corral. Holloway drew his employer a dozen yards to one side. While the two talked in low murmurs the former foreman watched them warily, his fingers on the butt of the revolver.

"What's the point of all this, Rock?" Savage demanded impatiently. "I know my own mind."

"The point is that there's no use hunting for trouble. If you send Benton back a prisoner he'll spill all he knows, and that won't be so good for you."

"I can take it. He can't prove a thing."

"He won't have to prove it," the gunman said dryly. "Anything he says about you will be believed if it's bad enough. Don't fool yoreself about that. Whatever happens, you don't want him flung into jail where all he has to do is lie there and think up a way to get even with you. That's out. Nor you don't want him rubbed out — not here tonight on the ranch. That would make a lot of talk — which is unnecessary."

"You seem to know exactly what I don't want," Savage jeered. "Now go ahead and tell me what I do want."

Holloway said, in a low voice that was almost a whisper, "You want him removed in such a way that there won't be any kick-back on us."

"Meaning how?"

"Give him grub tonight, enough to last him for tomorrow. Tell him to come down to the Five Mile cabin Friday night and we'll have a pack made up ready for him and a couple of blankets. The idea is that he is to come and steal the stuff, so that you won't be implicated. When he comes, blast him off the map. You'll get credit all over the Powder Horn for getting rid of him."

Savage thought this over. "That's not a bad idea, Rock. The fellow is a menace as long as he is alive. Yes, I reckon you're right. But I'm not going to give him a horse. He'll have to hoof it. If he should be caught with a horse carrying a Diamond K brand the story would be that I was helping him."

"Better act as if you think maybe you'd been a little hard on him. We don't want him to get suspicious."

The ranchman nodded. They rejoined the outlaw.

"Rock says I've been too hard on you, Niles," Savage said sulkily. "Maybe so. I don't want you around. I don't want ever to have anything more to do with you. But if you're up against it I don't mind letting you have some grub. But no horse."

"I can get along without a mount," Benton admitted. "I jumped the first horse I saw outside the Trail's End. What I would like to do is turn it loose to go back to its own range. But I can picket it out in the hills somewhere if you won't let me have another."

"I won't. That's flat. I'm not going to have you captured with a Diamond K horse in your camp. Grub can't be identified, but a horse can." Savage went on to explain the plan. "I can slip you enough food to last you a day or so without Chin Lee's missing it. Tomorrow I'll have a supply taken down to the Five Mile cabin for the boys to use when they are camped down that way. I'll send some blankets too. There won't be anybody staying there Friday night. I'll see to that. If you should come down and help yourself to what you need I can't help it. But don't show up around here. I won't lift a hand for you."

"That's fine," the ex-foreman approved.

"I'm much obliged. It didn't seem like you would throw me down so cold after you had thought it over."

"This is the last thing I'm going to do for you. Don't forget that."

"I can make out with that. Gimme enough to last a week. I aim to cross the desert and get down into Mexico."

"Stay here. I'll get the stuff for you. Beans, flour, bacon, coffee, a fry-pan, and a pail. Anything else?"

"Some chewing tobacco."

"I haven't any. The best I can do is a pipe and some smoking."

Savage left the other two alone. He was gone several minutes. The hunted man was extremely uneasy. A man came out of the bunkhouse with a bucket, filled it at the pump, and caught sight of the figures at the corral.

"Who's there?" he called.

"Rock Holloway," the owner of that name answered. "Tote your water, Bill. I'm talking with a friend."

"All right with me," Bill shouted back.

Ten minutes later Benton mounted his stolen horse and rode out of the pasture. He turned the head of the animal toward the hills.

27. Benton Chuckles

Jim Dall swung from the saddle and called to a Mexican lad. "Is Miss Effie to home, Juan?"

"*Si, señor.* In the house, I theenk."

The fat ranchman waddled forward and up the steps. Effie had seen him coming and reached the front door just as he did.

"Come in, Jim," she invited. "How is Bess?"

"Not so good, Miss Effie. She fell and hurt her wrist. It's swollen to beat the band. Looks to me like it might be broken. I'm on my way to town for Doc White."

"Did you leave her alone?"

"I had to. My wagon's busted, or I would have taken her to the doc. Bess said she would be all right. But you know how she is. She'll run around and do this and that, and like as not do her wrist a lot of harm."

"I'll have my palomino saddled and ride right over there."

Dall beamed. "I hoped you would say that. 'Course I hate to trouble you, but —"

"I'm glad to go. It's no trouble."

"Worst of it is I may not get back tonight.

If the doc is out of town seeing someone I'll have to wait for him. Could you fix it to stay all night?"

"Of course. Stan isn't here, but I'll leave a note and tell him. Chances are the wrist is only sprained and not broken. Don't worry about it, Jim. I'll stay till you get back."

Dall took the road to town feeling much better in his mind. He knew that Effie was more competent in emergencies than most girls of her age, even on the frontier, where women have to be prepared to give first aid when accidents occur.

Juan saddled the palomino while Effie packed the saddlebags with the simple remedies she knew and with the necessities she would require for an overnight stay. She did not take the road but followed a short cut which led across a saddleback to a wooded gulch cutting into the hills. Up here the air had a pleasant warmth. The sun beat down through a blue cloudless sky and flung long shadows across the floor of the cañon. The girl drew a long breath of pleasure. It was good to be alive in this primeval world of beauty. It was good to feel the lift of bouyant youth coursing through her arteries. There were times of late when she had known unhappy hours. The man she loved walked a perilous path. Any day his enemies might destroy him. And if he lived she had no reason to expect his thoughts would turn to her when he chose a mate. But on such a day it was hard not to let her hopes soar. Surely since she loved him so much, held him so near and tenderly in her dreams, he must come in time to care for her.

The horse picked its way down in the rubble to the bottom of the gulch and took the winding path that led up it into the hill cleft. Toward the top the walls almost met. She came out at last from between two cliffs not far enough apart to have driven two wagons abreast into the opening.

In front of her a plateau stretched, a thin little stream trickling through it. Effie followed this for a distance, then deflected with the path. This turned sharply to the left, to take an easier descent to the valley below. She caught sight of wild roses blooming at the edge of the bluff where the mesa terminated. Bess Dall was a lover of flowers. The girl decided to cut a few sprays to take to her.

She rode close, swung from the saddle, and grounded the reins. From the edge of the cliff she looked down. There was a nearly sheer descent of almost a hundred feet. The rosebushes clung to the upper face of this, their roots sunk in slight crevices of the rock wall.

Effie broke off one or two branches. One bush particularly tempted her, but it was one she could scarcely reach. Used to mountain-climbing, the height did not disturb her. Balancing herself carefully, she leaned far out to break off the twig. A dry rattle at her feet gave warning. She looked down, to see a diamondback coiled among the leaves, its head lifted to strike.

She lost her balance, gave a cry of terror, and went over the precipice. As her body plunged down, she caught at the thorny bush to save herself. She had time only to think that she was lost before she struck hard and lost consciousness.

When she came to herself it took a moment to realize what had taken place. She had fallen over the cliff and had landed on a sloping shelf about fifteen feet from the top. The bare smooth wall rose above her for ten to twelve feet, and above that grew the fringe of rose-bushes.

Though badly jarred from the crash, she did not at first think she was seriously hurt. One of her hands was bleeding from deep thorn scratches, but that was a minor mishap. It was not until she rose to look for a way up the wall that a sharp pain from an ankle notified her she had not escaped more important damage. Hurriedly she sat down to relieve the pressure on the leg. That she had either sprained the ankle or broken a bone was clear. Taking off the boot, Effie examined the leg. She massaged it very gently with her fingers. All the information she gained was that this was painful. She could not tell whether it was a break or a sprain.

Very few people came this way, but on the chance of aid she called for help. No answer came. During the next hour, at short intervals, she shouted again and again.

It was plain to her that she was a prisoner until rescue arrived. Even if she had been uninjured she could not have clambered up the sheer wall above her. There were no hand- or footholds. Below the ledge there was a straight drop of sixty or seventy feet to a boulder bed at the foot of the cliff.

Her heart sank at the long wait which lay before her until there was any likelihood of being found. She had told her brother in the note that she would probably spend the night at the Dalls. He would not begin to wonder about where she was until late the next day. She must school herself to endure pain and cold and anxiety, as well as hunger and thirst, for many hours and perhaps for several days. For they would never think to look for her here.

The only thing she could do for herself was

to cry out for help, and presently she discovered that she must do this sparingly or she would lose her voice and be able only to croak. The sun sank lower. It would be night soon, after which there would be no chance of a traveler until morning.

After each shout she listened for a response. An hour must have passed before she heard the sound of something moving above. She raised her voice in another cry.

Eyes peered down at her. Evidently the owner of them was stretched at full length, his head in space. "Who are you? What are you doing there?" he demanded roughly.

"I fell and landed on this ledge," the girl explained. "I'm so glad you have come. I was dreadfully afraid nobody would. I'm Effie Collins."

She saw now that the man was Niles Benton. Though she never had liked him, that made no difference now. He would throw her a rope, pull her up, hand help her to mount. No doubt too he would carry a message to Bess Dall explaining why she could not come.

"I don't get it," the man said suspiciously. "How come you to fall? What were you doing here? Who was with you?"

"I'll tell you all about that after you have pulled me up," she told him. "I'll tie the rope around my waist when you lower it."

"You'll tell me all about it now," he corrected. "And you'd better make it good. If I don't like yore story — no rope."

There was something cruel and malevolent in his face, a look she had never seen before on any human countenance. It gave her a queer shock. She could not guess the cause of that feral expression. No word had come to her of the latest killing at Powder Horn, and she did not know that he was like a hunted wolf, ready to strike back savagely at any opportunity, more dangerous because he was filled with the fear that he would never get out alive from the trap in which he was caught.

Effie told her tale, beginning with the arrival of Jim Dall and her promise to stay with his wife until the return of the rancher from town.

"You're not lying?" he snarled down. "Nobody knows you took the cut-off over the saddleback?"

"No, I didn't think of coming this way until after I started. . . . But it doesn't matter now, since you have found me. You have a rope with you?"

He did not answer immediately. His mind was busying taking stock of the situation. If he hauled this girl up from the ledge she would spread the word that he was hiding in the hills. Before twenty-four hours posses would be combing the ravines and pockets in search of him. It was as much as his life was worth to rescue her now. To justify himself he built up the grievances he had against her. At the dances where they had met occasionally she had always ignored him, as if she was too good to step a quadrille as his partner. Once she had declined to dance with him on a flimsy excuse. He did not know that she had been aware of his greedy eyes watching her before he crossed the floor. Also, she was the sister of Stanley Collins, who had gone out of his way to help pin the Ballard murder on him. Now it was his turn to laugh. He suspected too that she and Clay Sanger were lovers, and he hated Clay more than any man alive.

It would have given him pleasure to gloat over her openly and leave her where she was, but there was peril in that. If she should be found and that known, every nester within thirty miles would help the ranchmen hunt him down. No, he had to play safe, as far as there was any safety for him in a world where his life was already forfeit.

"Sorry, I got no rope with me except a short tie one."

"Is my horse still there? There's a rope tied to the saddle."

He squirmed round and saw her horse grazing fifty yards away.

"Can't see it," he said. "Must have gone

home, I reckon."

"That's queer. He usually stands after the bridle rein is grounded."

"Mebbe I'm a liar," the man sneered.

"I didn't mean that," the girl answered, and at the same time felt a queer sinking of the heart. She was afraid she would have trouble with him after he had pulled her up. "I suppose you'll have to knot your belt to the tie rope."

"Not long enough," he vetoed. "Besides, the knot might come loose. Couldn't risk having you fall down the cliff, seeing as you are the most popular young lady in the Powder Horn — and Stan Collins' sister to boot."

She understood the jeer. He was telling her indirectly that he would do as little as he dared for her. "How are you going to get me up then?" she asked sharply.

"I'm wondering some about that." A malicious chuckle of triumph rode in his voice. "You see, I had a piece of bad luck yesterday at Powder Horn. I had to kill a fellow who drew a gun on me. Plain self-defense, if ever there was a case. But my enemies won't see it that way. I reckon I'm a hunted man."

His words filled her with dread. She had a strange sensation as if her heart were turning over. He had killed a man — and his worst enemy was Clay Sanger. She put into a question the fear in her breast.

"Who did you kill?"

"Never mind about that. I'm just explaining to you why we're both in a kind of a fix. If I was to get you up from that ledge somehow you would spread the word that I was in the hills. That wouldn't be so good for me. They would get me sure."

"I asked who you killed!" she cried. "Was it Clay Sanger?"

"Clay Sanger." He rolled the name on his tongue with a bitter virulence. "How come you to think of Clay, my dear? Would I want to gun a man like him who has always acted so friendly to me?"

"Why don't you tell me?"

He laughed, with no mirth in his eyes. "No, ma'am. Not Clay. Never mind who. It's none of yore business."

She felt no assurance that he was telling the truth. It might have been Clay. He was trying to torment her.

"I'm talkin' about you and me, girlie," he continued. "Of course I haven't got any way of getting you up right now, and I'm fixed so I can't go running around asking the neighbors for a rope. Looks like circumstances are sorta pushing me around."

"You're going to leave me here. Is that what you are driving at?"

"What else can I do, with no rope long enough to reach you? For the present, I mean. Besides, when you are free what is to stop you from giving me away?"

"I would give you my word not to tell."

"Yeah! Do you take me for a sucker? You'd let it out inside of five minutes."

"Until you had got away I would never tell it to a soul."

"Don't try to load me, girl. I wasn't born yesterday. Take it from me that it won't be like that. After I have pulled you up you'll stick around with me till I've made a clean getaway. I know I'm a rough customer, not nice enough for you to dance with, but I reckon I'll have to inflict myself on you for a day or two."

Effie did not argue the point. The first step was to be helped from the ledge. "I'm not very heavy," she said. "You can make a line strong enough to bear my weight from your belt, the bridle reins, and the tie rope."

"I won't do it," he told her bluntly. "If it broke, yore friends would sure tell it that I killed you. Listen. I'm headed down to a ranch to get a sack of grub. On my way back, if I can fix it to get a rope, I'll stop and get you. But I'm not going to stand any funny business. I don't aim to let you out of my sight until I'm safe. Get that straight. I'm not one of those soft guys who would stick his head in a noose for any woman."

"And if you can't get a rope, what then?"

"I'll get a rope, all right. Don't worry about that."

"How long will you be gone?"

"About three-four hours, I reckon."

She made one more attempt to persuade him to help her now. "The line won't break if you tie the parts together right. Pull me up now, Mr. Benton. I think I have broken my leg. I'll promise this. If you'll take me home to my brother he'll give you five hundred dollars and help you to escape."

"If you promised me a million I wouldn't take you to him," he answered brutally. "Think I'm a fool? Soon as you were safe you would round on me. I know women. And I know that double-crossing brother of yours."

Nothing she could say would move him. Effie gave up. She was not sure that he would return at all. She heard him moving about on the bluff for a minute or two. Then there was silence.

Once or twice she cried out, in the hope that somebody else might be passing. Darkness fell. The moon rose. Stars filled the sky. Loneliness pressed on her. She was a thousand miles from the nearest friend.

And then a horse nickered. The rider might

be Benton, or he might be somebody else. She shouted, "Help! Help!"

No answer came, though she repeated several times her call. The horse neighed again. Effie was hoarse before she stopped calling. She could not understand why the rider had not answered, whether he was Benton or another man.

Later the explanation came to her. There was no rider. The horse that had neighed was her own mount. It had been within a hundred yards of her all the time. The outlaw had tied it in order that it might not go home and start a search for her. She could not be sure that it was as she guessed, but it seemed to her likely. Probably he had lied to her when he said he had not seen her horse. If it was true that he had killed another man and was being hunted, he might never come back to rescue her.

28. Clay Cuts Sign

Jim Dall hunted up Clay Sanger while he was in town to report that the Diamond K riders had burned a barn on the Circle S.

"Leastways somebody did it, and I don't know anybody else would want to do you a meanness like that," the fat ranchman added.

"I'll give Savage the credit for it," Clay agreed. "Think I'll ride out with you and Doctor White. Like to have a look around and see how things are going. The town is quiet right now and my deputies can look after things till I get back."

After supper the three men rode out of town. They discussed the killing of Pete Doyle and the disappearance of Benton. Since they did not know of the quarrel between Savage and his foreman, they were of the opinion that the fugitive was hiding either at the ranch or in the hills back of it. With the Diamond K supplying food and one or two of its riders keeping Benton informed of the movements of any posses in the vicinity, the chances of arresting the murderer did not look bright. Though he did not say so, the main object of Sanger's trip was to pick up any news of the outlawed foreman that might be circulating among the ranchmen. Clay had been appointed a deputy sheriff and was empowered to capture the man if he found an opportunity.

At the Collins place they heard from Stanley that Effie had ridden up to help Mrs. Dall. He was a little uneasy when he learned that a murderer might be loose in the tangle of gulches and hill pockets adjoining the Dall homestead, especially one who just now held an active grudge against the girl's brother. It was extremely unlikely that he would meet Effie, but the hundredth adverse chance disturbed both Stanley and Clay.

"Think I'll ride up with you, Jim, and bring her back," Collins said.

"I'll bring Miss Effie down with me," the doctor suggested. "Save you the trouble of going."

But Stanley decided he would go anyhow. Doctor White was not a fighting man in case there should be any trouble. Collins admitted that he was making a mountain out of a molehill, but thought it better to go in person rather than sit at home and worry even a little.

Clay left them at the Circle S. "Wish you would stop a minute on your way down, just so I'll know Effie is all right," he said to Collins.

"If there is still a light in your house, we'll

do that," Stanley promised. "Of course there is nothing wrong. We know that. Still, a fellow wants to make sure."

An hour later Collins was hammering on the door of the Circle S ranch house.

Clay stepped to the door but did not at once open it. "Who's there?" he asked.

"It's me — Stan. Let me in." A moment later his frightened eyes stared into those of his friend. "Effie isn't at the Dalls'. She never got there."

"Didn't get there? Then where is she?"

"I don't know. She's been over the road twenty times. She couldn't have got lost. Something has happened."

The two men looked at each other. Both were guessing at what that something might be.

"No, Stan," Clay said. "We're jumping to a crazy conclusion. Even if Benton met Effie he wouldn't hurt her. He's not such a fool. He would know that this country never would rest until it had hanged him and riddled his body. He couldn't get far enough away to escape."

"I've been telling myself that, Clay. But look at it this way. He meets her, and he knows she will tell he is up here. His life is forfeit anyhow if he is caught. So . . . he takes steps to protect himself against her."

"It is not likely he would be on this road," Sanger comforted. "He would be farther west — up in the maze of gulches and draws over Round Top way."

"Yes, unless he was on his way to or from making contact with the Diamond K. It's easy to say she's all right. But where is she? We did not pass her on the road. She isn't at our place or at the Dalls'. What has happened to her?"

Clay thought for a moment. "She wouldn't have taken the saddleback cut-off, would she?"

"Why would she? It's a little shorter, but the trail is far steeper than the road."

"Yes, but Effie always liked to take trails rather than main-traveled roads. It rained some last night. I could ride down and see if a horse went up over the saddleback today. You had better round up the neighbors and comb the country. We'll find her." Clay stopped, struck by another possibility. "You don't think that Savage could be in this, do you?"

"No. Savage wouldn't hurt her. He swears he'll marry her no matter what she says. He is daffy about her."

"That's the point. He is a tough hard scoundrel. If he met her might he not take her with him to the Diamond K?"

"She wouldn't go. She is through with him."

"No, but Savage wouldn't be above a little coercion if it served his end."

"What good would it do him? Effie wouldn't marry him."

"I don't know. Maybe it is a silly idea. I'm just suggesting it. Well, let's go. I'll try the cut-off while you are getting out the neighbors."

Cutting trail by moonlight on the saddleback trail Clay found to be a very difficult task. Here and there he picked out tracks, but he could not be sure how recent they were. Half a dozen times he dismounted to look the ground over at places likely to show the imprint of a hoof, yet he was not at all certain whether a traveler on horseback had or had not climbed the ascent since the rain.

None the less he took the path that angled up to the saddleback, and from there dipped down to the gulch of live-oaks. On the hillside was a grove of sahuaro. Under the sky of stars the desiccated giant cacti, drilled full of holes by woodpeckers, had a strange ghostly look. They gave the desert the appearance of a graveyard of dinosaurs, a cemetery of unlighted candelabra as ancient as Egypt. He took the gulch trail that wound up to the gorge above and came out on the plateau. As he crossed it his gaze searched the terrain carefully. It was possible that Effie might have been thrown from her horse, though he thought this not very probable. She was an excellent rider, as much at home in the saddle as the average cowboy, and it was likely if she had been thrown and hurt that the animal would have wandered back to the ranch head-quarters.

As he veered to the left, to drop down from the plateau into the valley below, his eyes swept the cluster of trees above him to the right. A tenderfoot would have seen nothing unusual in the dark mass of live-oaks, but a cattleman develops unusual keenness of vision. He can read brands at a distance so far that a townsman could scarcely tell there was one there. What Clay saw in the vague gloom of the grove was a patch of lighter color.

He swung up the hill and rode closer. Tied to a young tree was a saddled horse. The animal was a palomino. Instantly he recognized it as Effie's favorite mount.

Sanger looked round, but saw nothing of Effie. He raised his voice in a shout.

29. A Notch for His Gun

Benton hung around in the foothills until after dark, holed up in a pocket screened by heavy brush. It was not likely anybody would come that way at this time of day, but he was a man exceedingly careful of his own skin. His horse he tied to a mesquite, and he lay on the sundried alfilaria smoking a corncob pipe.

A slow-witted man, he was fumbling in his mind for a way to make capital of his ace in the hole. Suspicion was so much a part of his character that he found it difficult to trust anybody. In the course of many years of high-handed bullying he had made enemies of nearly all the small ranchers and the nesters. Stanley Collins could not be considered, since he had been one of the two men who had pinned the murder of Sheriff Ballard on him. Moreover, he would resent so strongly the postponement of the girl's rescue that he would probably turn him over to justice.

His thoughts kept coming back to Savage. The Diamond K owner was very much interested in the girl, and it would give him the inside track if he could save her from the ledge. Bert ought to be grateful to anyone who would show him how to put the Collins girl under obligations to him. The thing for him, Niles Benton, to do was to make a bargain with Savage. His life in exchange for information about the plight of the girl. The question was whether the ranchman would stick to his agreement. Savage was a cruel man, cold as a dead fish, with no glow of human kindness in him. The hunted man could think of no pressure he could bring to bear on the fellow to make him keep his word.

But it was worth trying. At least he would be no worse off than he was now, not if he kept a watchful eye on Savage. After darkness had fallen he mounted again and rode down to the Diamond K. As he had done when he had slipped back to the ranch after his flight from Powder Horn, he came to the house by way of the horse pasture.

Savage was startled when Benton walked into the office and closed the door behind him, so startled that the look in his eyes would have betrayed him if his former foreman had been an observant man. He had been thinking about Benton at the moment of his entrance. A picture of the man had been in his mind, moving forward through the semi-darkness toward the cabin at Five Mile Camp. From the shadow of the cottonwoods had come a flash, the crash of a rifle, and the big body of the fugitive

299

had plunged to the ground. And at the opening of the office door he looked up to see Niles Benton there as large and as ugly as in life. For a moment he thought his imagination was tricking him.

"What did you come here for?" Savage asked sharply. "I told you the Five Mile cabin."

"So you did, and that's where I'm going later," Benton replied. "But I got news for you that might be interesting."

The thin lips of Savage tightened. His ice-cold eyes held fast to the other. "I'm listening," he said.

Benton showed his stained teeth in a grin. "A friend of yores is stuck on a rock ledge up in the hills and cain't get up or down."

"I'm not interested in riddles," the rancher told him. "Who?"

"The Collins girl."

"Are you lying to me?"

"Take it or leave it," Benton grunted. "All one to me. She can stay and starve far as I care."

Savage rose to his feet, erect and rigid. "If this is some trick of yours, you muddleheaded idiot —"

"Don't get on the peck with me, Savage," the big man interrupted. "I'm giving it to you straight. If you're not interested, like you claim —" Benton did not finish his sentence but turned as if to leave.

The Diamond K boss caught him by the lapel of his coat. "Don't *you* get funny with me," he warned bluntly, "or I'll throw you to the wolves. Tell me what you've got to say and be done with it."

"Not quite yet." The ex-foreman helped himself to a drink from a bottle on the table. He poured half a tumbler of whiskey and downed it at a gulp. "I'm ready to make a trade. You can do what you like with this girl, providing you fix me up with a horse, grub, and rifle to light out for the border, *and* promise to keep yore mouth shut for twenty-four hours."

"What do you mean when you say Miss Collins is stuck and can't get up or down? How did she get there?"

"She fell while picking roses to take a sick friend," jeered Benton.

It was an improbable story, but possible. "Why didn't you help her?" snapped Savage.

"First off, I didn't want her running all over the Powder Horn telling where I was. Then I thought maybe you would like to be the rescue committee yore own self."

"All right. I'll get a couple of the boys. We'll get up there quick as we can."

Benton shook his head. "Not on yore tintype. We'll go alone. I don't aim to have everybody in this range meet up with me." He added, with heavy emphasis, "And we won't go till you get me a good fast horse and plenty of grub, plus that rifle I mentioned."

The Diamond K man was white with anger. He was of half a mind to call in his men and string up the killer until he came through with information of the girl's whereabouts. But the bad man might turn stubborn. Better to let him have his way, perhaps.

"All right. We'll go alone." Savage spoke curtly, imperiously. "I'll get you a horse and a rifle. The food is waiting for you at Five Mile. I can't get you more here without making my cook suspicious."

"I'll pick the grub up at Five Mile," Benton agreed reluctantly.

There were mounts in the corral. They roped two. One of these Savage saddled. The other they led into the horse pasture where the killer had left the one he had ridden down from the hills. This horse they turned loose, to return to its own range.

As they traveled up a draw toward the shadowy mountains Savage let his anger rip loose in a threat. "If this is a trick you had better chortle now," he warned, "for you won't live long enough to have much fun about it later."

"What would be the sense of me trying to

load you with a fairy tale?" the other asked with sour impatience. "You'd find it out inside of an hour anyhow. I tell you the girl is there."

For the most part the trail was steep and the going rough. Often they had to travel in single file. At such times Savage took care to see that the other led the way. He did not trust the man who had worked for him twenty years, though he could not find a reason why it would be of advantage for Benton to destroy him. After the one sharp outbreak he fell to silence. It would do no good to quarrel with the fellow unnecessarily. He would be taken care of when he appeared at the Five Mile cabin to get the food that was not there.

Though he tried to argue it out of his mind, Savage was oppressed by a keen sense of danger. He had arranged a trap to wipe out his former foreman, since the man had become a killer and if cornered would spill all he knew. Was it possible Benton could have found out what he had planned? Not unless Rock Holloway had betrayed him. That did not seem likely. Rock had never been friendly with the foreman and he was not likely to throw away the chance of five hundred dollars' easy money. Moreover, Holloway had the reputation of being true to the side that hired him.

They emerged from the gulch and rode across the plateau beyond. It was not until they were close to the live-oaks that Benton realized something was wrong. At first he would not believe it. His eye searched the grove, looking for a palomino he had left tied to a tree.

"What's the matter?" Savage rapped out.

"The horse." Benton's voice was sharp-edged with worry. "I left it tied to that tree. It's gone."

All the suspicions Savage had tried to banish swept through him again.

"So you are trying to trick me," he said in a voice low and ominously cold.

"No!" Benton cried. "I swear to heaven I'm not. The horse must have broke loose. We'll find the girl right where I said."

"I hope so," Savage said. "Or it will be too bad — for you." His lean jaw had set tight. The gray eyes narrowed and wary, held a hard and cruel glitter.

Benton slid a sidelong look at him. He knew the fierce explosive nature of the man, his heady arrogance that would brook no frustration. If Effie Collins was not still on the ledge he would jump to the conclusion that this was a trap and he would reach for his sixshooter. The cold feet of mice ran down the spine of the outlaw.

They walked to the top of the precipice, each watching the other.

"She must be there," Benton said, tiny beads of perspiration on his forehead. "No way she could have got away, unless someone helped her."

Savage did not step close to the edge of the precipice. He shouted Effie's name, and when no answer came called again. Before the echo of his shout had died his gun leaped out. He spat out two furious words: "You fool!"

The heart of Benton died under his ribs. "She may have fainted," he cried hurriedly.

"Look and see," the ranchman ordered.

The hunted man moistened his lips. He knew that he was very close to death. Unexpectedly something had gone wrong. He had to play for time, for a break in the luck.

"Sure," he said, trying to keep the fear out of his voice.

He knelt and looked down the face of the wall. The ledge was empty. "She's there!" he cried. "On the shelf. Looks like she has fainted. One of us will have to go down by a rope to get her." Benton rose. "I'll get the rope from my saddle," he continued.

"I don't believe she's there. You're lying."

"You can see for yoreself, Bert. It's gonna be a job to get her up."

Savage moved closer to the precipice. For an instant his gaze lifted from the intent frightened eyes of the fugitive, to look down the rock wall.

It was Benton's chance, the only one he would have. His fingers swept up and dragged out the forty-five. A flash of yellow fire ripped the darkness.

Savage turned, staring at the murderer, a look of dreadful surprise in his face. He fired twice, even as he slid to the ground, the darkness closing in on him.

The ruffian, panic choking his throat, poured bullets into the prone body. He moved forward slowly, not lifting his eyes from the figure slumped in front of him. He kicked his victim in the ribs, to make sure there was no life left. Hysterically, he laughed.

"Claimed he was gonna throw me to the wolves," he snickered. "I'll have my foot on the rail pouring 'em down twenty years after he's forgotten."

He helped himself to the pocketbook and the revolver of the dead man and then flung the body over the cliff.

Niles Benton's exultation did not last long. Miss Collins had been rescued and no doubt had told her story. Vengeance would be riding hard on his heels. He must get down to the Five Mile cabin, collect the grub left there for him, and begin the long desert ride to the border. Given a long night's start, if luck was with him, he ought to make it all right.

30. Clay Makes a Discovery

After Benton had left her on the ledge Effie had to fight back a wave of self-pity. She was trapped on a shelf not three feet wide in a deserted mountain region where no traveler might pass for days. Night was close, and before morning it would be bitterly cold. Then there would be another day and still another night, perhaps several of them, before the . . . end. Her ankle would probably get worse. She would be without food or drink, and as the hours lengthened they would bring a sense of desperate loneliness.

She pushed from her these thoughts. There would be a search for her, but since her brother was not expecting her home tonight it would not begin until late tomorrow. At first they would not think of the cut-off. When they did her friends might pass within fifty yards of the cliff and miss finding her if they did not happen to hear a call for help. It would have been better to have worn her small revolver and ammunition belt, so that she could fire at intervals to attract the searchers. She laughed a little at that. She might as well say that it would have been better to have brought a store of provisions with her, or that it would have been best not to have fallen at all.

Clay was in her mind a good deal. About now he would be starting his usual patrol of the town, unaware that she was in this dreadful plight. Would he care much if . . . if . . . ?

She supposed that she was foolish to love him when he showed no interest in her. A nice girl was expected to fold her hands and wait until a man made it clear he was in love with her. Some deep instinct in her rebelled at that. When a woman knew the man she wanted for her mate it could not be right to lose him without his even knowing that she cared. If Clay were here now . . .

Out of the silence came a shout. Effie was so startled that for a moment she could not answer. This was the voice of Clay Sanger. It could not be real. She must already be getting light-headed.

But she cried wildly, "Clay!" and again, "Clay!"

The answer was no fantasy. It came clear and ringing. She heard running footsteps. He stood on the cliff above and looked down.

"Are you hurt?" he asked.

"My ankle — a little. When I fell." Her throat choked up a bit. "Oh, Clay, I am so glad you came."

"I'll get my rope," he told her.

He brought the reata from the saddle and arranged a loop by passing one end through the hondo. The lariat was a long one because like most riders of his district he used some of it for a dally.

The girl caught the loop he lowered and put it around her waist. A minute later she was on the cliff beside him.

When her weight rested on the injured ankle she would have fallen if his arm had not slipped round her waist.

"Steady," he said, and held her close.

She felt her heart beating wildly against his body. "I think I've broken it," she said, to cover her emotion. She meant her ankle, not her heart.

"I'll have a look at it," he told her. "How long have you been down there?"

"Several hours. It seemed forever." She began to sob, clinging close to him. "It was just coming dark when Niles Benton left."

He let her cry, his arms tight around her. Presently she stopped. "I'm acting like a baby. Give me your handkerchief, Clay." She wiped away the tears.

Gently, Clay took up the story, trying to piece it out. "So Benton was here. He didn't put you down there?"

"No, I fell. I was gathering roses for Bess Dall and a rattler startled me. He came later."

The voice of Sanger grew grim and hard. "Do you mean that he saw you down there and didn't pull you up?"

"Yes. He said he hadn't a rope."

"There is one tied to your saddle not fifty yards away. He must have left you there deliberately."

"He told me he had killed a man and was being hunted, that he could not free me because I would tell he was in these hills."

She had never before seen such anger in his face. "And he left you here to die," he said, repressed passion in his low voice.

"He told me he was going to help me when he got back from a ranch where he was going to get supplies. But he couldn't let me go home for fear I would talk, so I was to stay with him until he could make what he called his getaway."

"I'd like to be here when he comes back, if he does, but I reckon I'll have to postpone the meeting." Clay drove that thought from his mind. Just now he must give his full attention to helping his friend. "I'll take a look at the ankle and bind it up. Then we'll head for your home. Doctor White is still up at Dalls' ranch. We'll have him down to your ranch as soon as he can come."

Like many plainsmen, he was deft at giving first aid to men with broken limbs and damaged heads, for accidents among the riders were frequent. He bound the ankle neatly with his bandanna, his fingers moving gently and efficiently.

Effie thanked him, a little curtly. She was afraid she had made too much fuss about the injury. "I'll be fine now. Sorry I was so soppy. I had got to thinking how bad it was going to be in two or three days if nobody came. But that's no excuse for crying all over you."

"Best thing you could have done," he differed casually. "Relieved the nervous tension. Fact is, I've seen times when I would have liked to howl myself if my sex hadn't debarred me. We'll get going now."

He brought the palomino and lifted the girl into the saddle, disregarding her protest that she could pull herself up without help.

"You've got to be careful of that ankle," he warned. "Rest the foot in the stirrup without putting any weight on it."

"Yes," she assented meekly.

Clouds had come out of the north and were scudding across the sky. The moon disappeared behind them as Clay and the girl he had rescued rode across the mesa. They had not gone more than a couple of hundred yards when Sanger reached across and put his hand on hers.

"Wait," he said in a low voice.

"What is it?" she asked.

"Somebody over to the right."

She listened. To her drifted the faint sound of moving horses, a rumor almost lost in the stillness of the night. It came again.

"Are you going to call to them?" Effie asked in a whisper.

He decided against it. The travelers could not be members of a party searching for her. It might be Benton on his way back from the ranch, but just now his job was to get the girl back home and not to arrest the murderer. He could come back and try to pick up the trail after daybreak.

Clay did not give the word to start until he was sure they could not be heard by the other party. He and Effie were not halfway across the mesa when there came to them the booming of a gun from the rear. Almost before the echo had died away there came several more shots.

They drew up to listen, but after that there was only silence. Both of them felt a sense of shock, a certainty of evil in the sudden explosion. The moon slid out from behind a cloud at that moment, and Sanger saw that the girl was staring at him with frightened eyes.

"Some cowpokes shooting at the moon," he said cheerfully. "Let's go."

She rode a little closer to him. It was a comfort to feel the pressure of his knee when occasionally they jolted against each other on the narrow trail. His explanation did not convince her, but she let it go at that.

They rode for the most part in silence. Clay had been very matter of fact about her adventure, except for that moment when she had seen anger burning in his eyes. Skillful and kind enough, she thought, but not very sympathetic under the circumstances. He had a face which he could freeze to immobility. She had noticed that often even when he was a boy, and she had guessed when she saw that look he was on guard. It would have made her happier if he had let himself go a little more. She did not fall over a cliff every day. But if he did not care very much what happened to her, there was nothing to do about it.

Her ankle pained a good deal, but when he inquired about it she told him lightly that she was doing nicely, thank you. If he was going to be so stuffy about this, she felt, she would help him build the wall between them.

It was surprising, she reflected, how long a short ride could be if one counted every fifty yards of the way. When her pony jolted down slopes or jumped across little gullies a sharp reminder was telegraphed to her brain of the need to favor the ankle. The sight of the Collins ranch was very welcome. During the latter part of the trip Sanger had seen signs of her distress. He talked, to distract her attention and he was much relieved when they drew up in front of the house.

"I'm going to carry you in," he said.

The color beat into her face, for there had flashed into mind the old custom of a young husband carrying his bride across the threshold of their home. "If you'll help me a bit I can walk," she told him.

"Maybe, but you are not going to put your weight on that foot." He reached up and lifted her from the saddle, climbed the porch steps, and walked into the house with her in his arms. "Same bedroom as you used to have?" he asked.

"Yes. Afraid I'm a lot of trouble."

"You always were a nuisance," he told her, and smiled a warm boyish smile that belied the words. "And I always liked you."

"That's nice," she commented. "I thought you disapproved of me. Now if you'll put me on the bed and call Mary."

He did not put her down at once but looked long into the flushed charming face, a strange excitement tingling through his veins. Her shy eyes went into hiding beneath the lids that fluttered to the hot cheeks.

"Look at me," he ordered.

"I've just been looking at you." She laughed, not very convincingly. "It's the same homely phiz I've seen off and on ever since we learned at school out of McGuffy's Reader.

'It was the schooner Hesperus
That sailed the wintry sea.'"

"Mine is the same, but yours isn't, unless I've been blind all these years," he amended. "Did anybody ever tell you, Effie, that you are as pretty as a painted wagon?"

She flashed one quick questioning look at him. "If you would put me down you could stand back and see if I really do stack with a nice new wagon. I weigh one hundred twenty-five pounds, you know. Besides, I have a ricked ankle. I'd like it to have some attention before it gangrenes — if that is what broken ankles do."

"A sprained ankle can wait. I've just made a tremendous discovery. Don't push on the reins while I consider it. I've been a fool."

"Interesting, but not news," she told him. "I found that out about myself . . . once or twice."

"Yes, but this is important. I want to share it with you."

"That will be nice. Now if you will lay me on the bed and call Mary you can tell me all about it while she bathes the ankle."

"I can't wait that long." The near warm dearness of her set the blood pounding in his veins. "I love you. Very likely I always have and didn't know it."

Effie said, looking at him with incredulous eyes still shy, "Men get ideas like that in the moonlight and wonder at it next day."

"The only wonder I'll have is why I've been a Rip Van Winkle so long. I'm going to kiss you — now."

A drum of joy was beating in her, but she warned herself that this might be a fancy of his, a delusion of the moment. She did not want any mistakes that would have to be corrected later with grief and embarrassment.

"Wouldn't that be taking advantage of a girl who can't help herself?" she asked, still fighting against the sheer ecstasy rising in her.

"It wouldn't if — if she cared too."

"I could talk more reasonably if you would put me down and sit in that chair," she urged.

"I don't want you to talk reasonably. We'll have fifty years together to do that later, I hope. I'm asking you to marry me."

"How can you be sure in just a moment,

Clay? I'm the same girl you taught to ride almost as soon as I could walk. I'm the long-legged freckle squealer whose pigtail you once cut off and got licked for doing it. I'm the bad-tempered vixen who quarreled with you not so long ago. That's what you called me, and you said I ought to be spanked. Now, all of a sudden, because I fell and hurt my ankle, you get notions."

"No," he contradicted. "It's all clear in my mind now. I want to be with you all the rest of my life."

That was what Effie wanted. She felt herself melting into his being, as if she were a part of him. The drum was pounding in her faster. She had no faith in the arguments she had raised, for it had been that way with her also. She had learned in one flashing moment that she had loved him, and there had never been a doubt since. But she carried on, weakly.

"A teacher I had when I was away at school in Denver said that most of our little love idiocies were caused by contiguity. It's a nice long word, isn't it? What it means is —"

"I know what it means," he interrupted bluntly. "I'll bet that teacher wasn't married."

"No, but —"

"Quit dodging, girl. I want an answer. Can you learn to love me?"

"No," she answered quickly, and flung her

318

arms around his neck. "You dear goose, I can't learn what I've known a long long time. I think I've loved you ever since I was a little girl, Clay. It was you who wouldn't ever look at me."

"I'll look at you plenty now," he cried exultantly, and lifted her to the threatened kiss.

Ten minutes later Clay passed into the back of the house shouting for Mary to come and look after her mistress. He gave instructions to bathe the ankle in hot and cold towels alternately. To Effie he promised that he would be back with Doctor White inside of two hours.

Effie felt incredibly light-hearted. A broken leg was nothing. "It doesn't matter about the doctor if you will come soon," she assured him.

He kissed her before Mary's astonished scandalized eyes.

31. A Bad Man
Checks Out

Benton rode out of the hills with an ugly sinister exultation bouying him up. He was leaving behind him one debt paid in full. After twenty years of service, part of the time as top rider and part as foreman, the owner of the Diamond K had cast him adrift to fend for himself at a time when he was in great need of aid. It was, he felt, a shabby way to treat a man whose troubles had come upon him because of the overbearing ranch policies. If he was hated by scores of people the reason lay in the faithfulness with which he had done the crooked work of Savage. The cattleman had come within a hair's breadth of destroying him. He had outsmarted the fellow by quick thinking. That was all to the good.

None the less he was a worried man, and as he dropped lower into the ranch country the glee died away in him. He knew how the minds of the settlers would react to the killing of Savage, despite the fact that he was very unpopular. Though Benton did not blame himself, he realized that public opinion would not stand for the shooting of three men in a month by him. Also, there was his refusal to help Effie Collins, which would be considered worse than his other crimes. If caught, he would be hanged at once.

As soon as daylight came posses would be combing the hills and the desert for him. It would be a race against time. He must gather the provisions Savage had ordered left at the Five Mile cabin and strike into the desert. Before dawn he ought to be forty miles from the Diamond K. Even if he reached Mexico the rurales might find him and drag him back to punishment with a rope around his neck. The best chance would be to throw in with José Saliveras' band of outlaws after changing his name.

After he struck the road running down to the valley he traveled warily, since it was important he not be seen and recognized. Lights showed in the Collins house. He tied his horse in the brush and crept forward to look through the window of one of the side rooms. There was little risk. He wanted to find out if the Collins girl was home yet. If anybody came out of the house he could duck behind a cottonwood.

He tiptoed up the porch steps and looked through the lighted window. Effie Collins was lying on a bed, and a woman was kneeling beside it. The maid was drawing gently a stocking from the girl's foot. Beside the bed stood Clay Sanger smiling down at the wounded young woman.

A wild surge of hatred flared up in Benton. The marshal was still riding wide and handsome, and he was skulking out of the country like a hunted wolf. A spasm of rage contorted his face. His hairy hands tightened on the rifle. With a crook of one finger he could blow the man from the map.

Why not? Sanger had brought him to ruin. His life was forfeit anyhow. Even if he should be caught they could kill him only once.

Sanger stooped down and kissed the girl. Her arms went around his neck and clung to him. When at last she released him the man outside could see the happiness shining in her eyes. The reflection of it lit Clay's face as he started to turn away.

Something snapped in Benton, drove his anger to a white heat. He was not going to leave this man to enjoy a future of happiness and success. This last lucky chance had been given him to even the score. He could get him now, with no risk to himself.

At that instant the gay laughter was sponged from Sanger's face. It froze to immobility. The marshal had looked out of the window and caught sight of the feral eyes glaring in at him.

For a fraction of a second Clay stood there, his gaze fixed, but before the killer could get into action he plunged for the door.

Benton leaped from the porch and ran for the shelter of the cottonwoods. He raced through them to the road. A bullet struck the trunk of a tree beside him. Without stopping to answer it, he ran across the road into the brush beyond. That Sanger was hard on his heels he knew, for he could hear him tearing through the bushes. It did not occur to him to stand his ground and fight. His only thought was to get away from the vengeance crashing toward him.

He dragged so furiously at the slipknot he had tied that the horse was frightened. It reared. Jerking at the bridle rein, Benton flung himself into the saddle just as Sanger burst into the little clearing.

Clay caught at the bridle of the dancing horse.

"Let go!" Benton shouted.

He had not time to shoot but brought the barrel of the rifle sweeping down on the marshal. The blow was aimed for Clay's head. It struck his shoulder, for the officer ducked. In doing so, Sanger loosened his grip on the reins. The rearing horse tore it free, leaped to a gallop, and ran wildly into the chaparral. Mesquite branches whipped at Benton's face and hands. He covered up and gave the animal its head. An urgent desire possessed him to get away from there.

The fugitive did not strike the road again for a mile or more. When he did at last come out on it he traveled fast. No doubt Sanger had sent word to the neighbors to be on the lookout for him. Frequently he glanced back over his shoulder. He was a man very much in a hurry. Blue Blazes himself might have guessed where he was going and be following him into the valley.

He swung away from the road to the right and dropped down through the low hills to the draw in which the Five Mile cabin lay. As he drew closer he saw that there was no light in the hut. Savage had promised him that none of the Diamond K men would be spending the night there. He hoped the dead man had kept his word and sent down supplies for the trip. If he had been double-crossed he would have a hard time to make it across the desert, since he dared not show his face at any settlement this side of the line.

Fifty yards from the house he tied his mount to the post of a barb wire fence and moved forward cautiously. There was no sign of any other life about the place. He opened the door of the house and walked into the only room. Several times he had spent a night in the cabin, and he knew there was a coal-oil lamp on the table. Striking a match, he put the flame to the wick and replaced the glass chimney.

Before lighting the lamp he had laid the rifle on the floor. He was stooping to pick it up when a mocking voice hailed him.

"Don't bother with that Winchester, Niles. You won't need it."

Rock Holloway was sitting in a chair. He was leaning forward, forearms resting on thighs, a forty-five calibre Colt's revolver in the fingers of his right hand.

Benton's stomach muscles collapsed. A chill went shuddering through him. He knew that the man he had left dead at the foot of the cliff far up in the hills had arranged this for him. The Diamond K hired killer had been promised money, probably five hundred dollars, to rub him out.

"You . . . kinda scared me, Rock," he croaked, from a throat dry as cotton. "I . . . I didn't expect to see you."

Holloway laughed, but there was no comfort for the condemned man in the sound of that cruel mirth. "No, I reckon you didn't. I expect I'm a pleasant surprise. Savage sent me as a welcome committee."

"Did you bring the grub?" Benton quavered, and knew the dreadful answer.

"No grub. You won't need it where

you're going, Niles."

The hunted man flung out a despairing hand. "Don't talk thataway, Rock. We been good friends, you an' me. You wouldn't do me a meanness when I'm up against it."

"Not friends, Niles. You have no friends. Long ago you wore out all human kindness. You couldn't treat even a dog or a horse right. I never liked you. Neither did anybody else. There won't be any complaints when you are buried."

"Now looky here, Rock," Benton whined. "You can't do this. You can't kill me in cold blood, without a chance for my white alley. Why —"

"How did you kill Ballard?" Holloway interrupted. "No use crawling on yore belly, Niles. The fact is you're worth quite a bit to me as dead mutton and not nearly as much alive. There's a reward of two hundred and fifty plunks for you, and I got another nice pickup for the job from Savage."

The barrel of the revolver tilted up till it pointed straight at Benton's heart.

"Wait!" the foreman shrieked. "Savage is dead. You'll never get that five hundred. Listen, Rock, I —"

"What do you mean, Savage dead?"

"I had to kill him, an hour or so ago, to keep him from gunning me."

Holloway did not believe him. He thought the man was snatching at a straw to save himself. "Where did you pull off this killing?" he drawled.

"Up in the hills. Listen. I'll tell you all about it."

"I'll give you one minute. Keep yore hands folded right where they are now. Get going. Shoot, and when you're through I'll shoot."

Benton told his version of the trip into the hills and its result.

When he had finished Holloway told him that he did not believe a word of it. "And if it is true, do you reckon I'll stand to let you beat me out of five hundred dollars that was as good as in the bank for me? Besides, by yore own story you're too dangerous to let live. Three men in a month. That's too many."

"Rock, if you'll let me go, I swear —"

The crash of the revolver cut short the words. Benton's hand clutched at his heart. His body twisted halfway round and went down like a falling sack of grain. He was dead almost before he hit the floor.

32. Guns Out, Little Red Schoolhouses In

The death of Savage marked the end of an era in the Powder Horn country. The Diamond K had led the fight against homesteaders for the big cattlemen. Its war against them had been fierce and ruthless, just as had its treatment of settlers with small herds. Boldly the riders of the big spread had disregarded the law, obeying orders given to them by Niles Benton to hold the range for cows carrying the ◇K◇ brand.

With Savage out of the picture the owners of the larger ranches modified their claims. Reluctantly they recognized the rights of the little men to their share of the open range. The days when running cattle was an adventure were passing, giving way to a more businesslike system. Landowners began to fence, to breed up their stock, to raise hay for winter feed. The little man joined the big one to help stamp out rustling.

Yorky and Rock Holloway discussed the situation.

"The Diamond K won't ever be what it has

been," Yorky admitted. "I reckon you read the story in the *Sentinel* about how Miss Savage aims to sell the ranch. It's to be split up and sold in parts. Seems she is a schoolmarm at Chicago. Looks like to me this spells the end of the good old days. Pretty soon a cowpoke will be following a plow and hoeing corn. All this barb wire coming in means raising feed for stock. Pretty soon there won't be enough open range left to graze a jackrabbit."

"That's right," Holloway agreed. "Far as the Diamond K goes it doesn't matter whether the schoolmarm sells or holds the ranch. There won't be any fight left in it. Savage was as cold-blooded as a snake. But I'll say this for him: he had the guts to stand up and tell the law to go to hell."

"Yep. But he's dead and buried. Question before the house is, where do we go from here?"

"I go to Wyoming," Holloway said. "That's still a country with the bark on where a he-man can play his own hand."

"Maybe I'll throw in with you," Yorky suggested. "When do you hit the trail?"

"Not till the commissioners pay me that two hundred and fifty dollars for bumping off Benton. Say a day or two after that. I've got one job to do before I leave."

Yorky looked at his companion, speculation

in his eye. He did not ask what the job was. Something in the way Rock had mentioned it told him that it would be better to put no questions. If this was the gunman's private business the cowboy had no desire to push into it.

The handwriting on the wall was so plain that impending changes were argued about at every hill cabin. In the town of Powder Horn the general opinion was that except for sporadic outbreaks law would now rule the country.

Clay walked into Captain Winters' store and handed in his resignation, to take effect the following Saturday night.

"What's the idea?" demanded the Civil War veteran.

"There are two of them in my noodle," Clay answered. "The first is that my job is done. Powder Horn has made up its mind to be a good town. The ladies organized a temperance society last night, and there is a piece in the *Sentinel* about the Reverend Sam Johnson arriving to start a Methodist church. Looks to me like guns are out and little red schoolhouses are coming in."

"Is it yore view that Powder Horn doesn't need a marshal any more?" Winters asked belligerently.

"My opinion is that it doesn't need me. I've

made enemies. A new man will start with a clean slate. There won't be any grudges against him. That will be good for the town. Besides, I've got to get back to my ranch. I have a lot of plans. Want to do some fencing. I aim to breed up my herd and winter-feed. A settled married man has to look out for the future."

"When did you become a settled married man?" Winters grunted.

"I haven't yet, but I aim to *muy pronto*. I've found a girl crazy enough to throw in with me. No more helling around. No more gunplays. I'm a sure enough reformed character."

"If I know that young lady — and I reckon I do — she's taking a whale of a chance in marrying a wild coot like you." Winters got out of his chair and beat the marshal on the back with a hand as big as a small ham. "You're a lucky fellow, Clay, and you'll sure have to keep on yore toes to deserve a girl like that. But I'll say this. I don't know any man in this town who will give her as exciting a life as you will."

Clay shook his head. "No excitement. The hurrah stuff is all in the discard now."

"Hmp!" snorted the mayor. "We'll see about that. Unless you get religion there will always be some kind of a breeze where you're at. A leopard can't change his spots, can he?"

"I might do just that — get religion and become a deacon in the church, like my father was before he came out here where there wasn't a church in forty miles."[1]

"You'd certainly be a ripsnorter of a deacon. If the boys didn't hit the sawdust trail you'd drag 'em down the way you do roostered lads to the calaboose." Winters flung up his hands. "All right. I'll get me another marshal. And you tell yore young lady to come in here and pick her the best piece of goods in the house for a wedding dress, compliments of an old fool who thinks you are the best marshal ever hit the Southwest. Now get outa here. I got to work."

Clay departed, a warm spot in his heart for the rough old man. Winters' bark was a great deal worse than his bite.

---

[1]Clay could not know that his jest was prophetic and that within ten years he actually would be a deacon in the church.

33. End of the Road

As Clay covered his beat that last Saturday he felt a curious sense of regret. One phase of his life was coming to an end. He had lived carelessly, almost recklessly, ready for whatever adventures the day might bring forth. Ever since he had been the leader of the small cattlemen against the aggressions of the big ranches he had walked with danger, a peril that had increased when the feud between him and the Diamond K became personal. As marshal of a wild little cow town he had been in the thick of all its recent gunfights, propelled into them because of the star he wore.

Now all that was past. Savage and his foreman were dead, each a victim of the other's suspicion. The Diamond K belonged to a Chicago schoolteacher as mild as milk. Powder Horn was getting excited about its new baseball team. And more important than any of these changes, from Clay's personal viewpoint, he was about to take on the responsibilities of marriage.

He would not have had it any other way. He had found his mate, and he had to follow the law of life that had obtained since Adam and Eve. She was a girl sometimes brittle and often proud, used to having her own way, with a temper that could easily flare to anger. But he knew too her great capacity for tenderness. He still felt her strong warm arms clinging tightly to him, her lovely face all broken with emotion. Without her, life would be empty and purposeless. Yet there was in him a nostalgic wistfulness for the youth upon which he was turning his back.

Twenty men stopped him on Texas Street or on the square to tell him they were sorry he was quitting and to wish him luck. He told them all that Bud Miller would make a good marshal and deserved the support of the town. If he had been a drinking man it would have been too bad for him, since at nearly every saloon he passed somebody invited him in to have just one.

It was after supper, when the town was just beginning to get lively, that Jim Prince drew him aside and dropped a dissonant note into the general felicitations.

"Rock Holloway is in town with Yorky," Prince said. "He got his two hundred and fifty dollars today from the commissioners for rubbing out Benton. Says he is leaving tomorrow for Wyoming. But I got a tip that he is laying for you. I don't know whether Yorky is in it or not. Maybe I had better drift along with you, just so Yorky won't get notions."

"Where did you get your tip?" Clay asked.

"Well, it wasn't what you would call definite. He stopped at the Trail's End and settled a little bill he had there. Red McClintock asked him if he was paying up all his bills. He looked at Red for a long time without answering, as if he was sorta churning over his private thoughts, and then he said, in that low hard voice of his, 'Yes, Red, all of 'em — all of 'em.' "

"Was that all?"

"You needn't laugh, fellow. I heard him say it. And it wasn't all either. Red grinned and piped up, 'Sayin' goodbye to yore friends and enemies, I reckon.' Rock came back, slow and deliberate, kinda drawling it, 'Especially to my enemies.' I'm not a goosey man, Clay, but it gave me the shivers to hear him. He's only got one enemy here — the man who pistolwhipped him and dragged him to jail. I wish you would lie low till he leaves town. He's sudden death with a gun."

"What d'you mean lie low — crawl into a hole?"

"Hell! I knew you wouldn't. But don't get the idea that this is my imagination. Red McClintock hooked on to the pair, and now there are three of 'em, all with nice fat grudges against you they have been nursing. What do you reckon that spells?"

"I don't know. Maybe they will take it out in cussing me."

"Two of the beauties might, but not Rock Holloway. He's aiming to kill you, Clay." Prince pulled up, struck by an idea. "Say, I could get Winters, with about a dozen other responsible citizens, all armed, to serve notice on Holloway to light a shuck out of here immediately if not sooner."

"On what grounds? Winters isn't a mind-reader. He and his friends can't touch Holloway until he has got into action. No, Jim. There isn't a thing to do but to try to be ready for him if he means business."

"I'll stick around with you, then."

"Not with me, Jim. Behind me, thirty or forty yards back, so as to warn me if they come at me from the rear. You're not armed, are you?"

"Is it the marshal or Clay Sanger asking?" Prince wanted to know.

Clay laughed. "I won't arrest you tonight. Keep out of this, Jim. It's not your fight. All I want you to do is to shout out if they are coming up on me from behind."

The officer sauntered down Texas Street and into the courthouse square. All the pleasant sense of well-being that had warmed Sanger had been frozen out of him. This was

336

not a world where friends slapped you on the back and congratulated you on winning the prettiest girl in the Powder Horn district. It was one where enemies, deadly as rattlesnakes, lurked in doorways or back of corners to fling death at you unexpectedly.

He caught a glimpse of Holloway, flanked by his two allies, walking into the Cowboys' Rest. Apparently they did not see him. Prince moved up to join him.

"See who just went in there?" he asked.

"Yes," Clay answered. "None of them noticed me."

Presently they met Frenchy. Clay mentioned to him that Holloway and Yorky were in town and might be looking for trouble. After a few words the deputy passed on his way. But he did not get by Prince. The cowboy stopped him and explained the situation. After that two men trailed the marshal.

They circled the courthouse. It was just nine o'clock by the clock in the tower when Clay passed the Trail's End.

He saw his enemy again, still with his satellites. They were coming down the board walk toward him. When they were about thirty paces distant they deflected, moving across the road and the courthouse yard. Clay was sure they had recognized him, and their refusal to meet him at the moment made it clear to him that there was trouble ahead. The Holloway party had been in the light and Clay in the shadow of an unlit building. Rock did not intend to be at a disadvantage when they met. He would maneuver for a favorable break if possible.

Clay pushed through the doors into the Trail's End and walked through to the back. The place was well filled, and there was a good deal of noise. Snatches of words, the rattle of chips, the shuffling of feet on the floor, rose above the droning of a fiddle. He ran against Foley, and they stopped to chat for a moment. Before they separated the wagon-yard owner dropped a remark casually that was meant to be significant.

"Rock Holloway is in town."

"I've seen him," Clay replied. "Much obliged."

That was all. A warning had been given. It was not necessary for either to say more.

Clay went out of the back door into the alley and moved along it. Two men shadowed him. He stopped in a doorway to make sure they were not his enemies.

"Don't shoot, oldtimer," Prince called to him in a low voice as he approached. He grinned, to let Clay know he had no fear of panic shots from the revolver of his friend.

"I didn't know Frenchy was with you," Sanger said.

"Needing someone to protect me if I got in a jam, I brought him along," Jim said, tongue in cheek.

At the end of the street Clay swung back into the courthouse square. He took pains to avoid dark alleys where he would stand out against the lights. Every minute the tension increased. In front of the New York Emporium, closed for the night, he stood in the entry and searched the shadows around the courthouse with his eyes. Some sixth sense of danger warned him that it would not be long now.

Prince passed, with no sign of hesitation, but out of the corner of his mouth came a whispered warning. "Back of the courthouse pillar."

Sanger's gaze raked the dense gloom opposite and made out a figure close to one of the pillars on the colonial porch. Footsteps sounded on the walk. Yorky drifted past the store, caught sight of the marshal, and said, with unnecessary loudness, "Hello, Blue Blazes, how you doing?"

Clay did not answer. He knew the greeting had been for Holloway's benefit and that if he spoke his own voice would locate him more definitely.

The light ironic words of Prince came to him. "Why, hello, Yorky! Nice to see you up and around again. Too bad I had to puncture you at Hell's Half Acre that night."

The Diamond K cowboy growled an angry response. Apparently he attempted to push past and was being detained.

"What's yore hurry?" Prince inquired, gay and reckless as usual. "Frenchy and I want to know all about yore plans. Is it true you are going to work for a Kansas hoe man?"

"I've taken enough from you!" Yorky cried with an oath.

"You'll take more, if you let Holloway drag you into this trouble," Jim prophesied.

The low hard voice of Holloway cut across the road from the courthouse porch. "I don't need any help on this job. Come out of there where you're hiding, Sanger."

From that instant Clay concentrated on that shadowy bulk against the pillar. Everything else he pushed from his mind.

"I'm here, Rock, if you're looking for me," the marshal called back, and was surprised to find all his nervousness vanish. He had spoken quietly, not raising his voice, each word deliberately spaced.

"I've been lookin' for you a long time, and you've always skulked out. By God, you're trapped now and can't get away. Come asmokin', fellow." The bad man's fury rang out. The indignities he had endured from Sanger swept away his usual cold caution. "We'll find out how much of a hell-popper you are."

Holloway came down from the porch and moved across the grass. He waited at the edge of the road. "Don't hide there in the dark, you four-flusher. Come out an' take yore medicine."

Clay waited, gun in hand, poised on the balls of his feet, body crouched. He neither moved nor answered.

Betrayed by his rage, Holloway flung aside the habit of his life, which was to get an advantage by setting the stage for his killings. He advanced to the dusty road, standing in the middle of it.

"Come out, damn you," he shouted, and before the words had died he flung a bullet at the figure in the doorway.

Wood splintered back of the marshal. Clay fired deliberately. His enemy grunted, staggering forward in the dust, and his second bullet crashed through the window three feet from its mark.

Though Sanger knew his foe was badly hurt, he took no chances. Again his forty-five tore the silence. The force of the shot swung the gunman halfway round. He went down, flinging up a cloud of yellow dust from where his body struck. Arms and legs outstretched, Holloway lay prone.

Clay became aware of another figure on the courthouse porch.

"Come over here with your hands up, Red," Sanger ordered.

Red McClintock did as he was told, but slowly and reluctantly. "I ain't in on this," he said sullenly.

"Take his gun, Frenchy," Clay said harshly.

The deputy did so.

Already a crowd was gathering. Men were spurting out like orange pips from saloons and gambling-houses.

The marshal lost no time in getting the record straight. "Who fired first, Yorky?" he demanded.

Yorky made swift decision not to identify himself further with a lost cause. "Rock did," he answered sulkily.

"You knew he meant to kill me?"

"I knew he had a chip on his shoulder. That's all I knew."

Red too admitted that the first shot had come from Holloway's gun.

"We've known for an hour Rock was trying to get Clay," Prince volunteered. "That's why Frenchy and I stayed close, to prevent him from pulling off an ambush on Clay. Fact is, boys, we ought to give Blue Blazes a medal for tonight's work."

There was a chorus of assents.

When Clay reported to Winters the mayor pronounced it a damn good night's work. Three hours later the marshal handed in his star.

He did not wait for morning to leave town, but rode through the night back to the Circle S. Luck had been with him, unless it was something deeper than luck. Holloway was a better shot than he, but at the last moment his anger had neutralized the advantage. His urge to kill had been too strong for him to wait to get his opponent into the light.

Looking back, Clay could not see that he had done any wrong, though twice he had been forced to kill. But he was sick of violence. He wanted to go to a girl he loved and tell her about it and listen to her words of comfort. He wanted peace and quiet for the rest of his life.

If he could have looked ahead he would have seen a ranch improving under his care, increasing herds, the woman he loved by his side, and many children racing through the house with cheerful shouts. He would have seen his name growing always more respected through the years that were to give him more than his share of happiness.

The employees of THORNDIKE PRESS hope you have enjoyed this Large Print book. All our Large Print titles are designed for easy reading, and all our books are made to last. Other Thorndike Large Print books are available at your library, through selected bookstores, or directly from us. For more information about current and upcoming titles, please call or mail your name and address to:

THORNDIKE PRESS
PO Box 159
Thorndike, Maine 04986
800/223-6121
207/948-2962